The Temptation of Forgiveness

Donna Leon was named by *The Times* as one of the fifty Greatest Crime Writers. She is an award-winning crime novelist, celebrated for the bestselling Brunetti series. Donna has lived in Venice for thirty years and previously lived in Switzerland, Saudi Arabia, Iran and China, where she worked as a teacher. Donna's books have been translated into thirty-five languages.

Her previous novels featuring Commissario Brunetti have all been highly acclaimed; including *Friends in High Places*, which won the CWA Macallan Silver Dagger for Fiction, *Fatal Remedies, Doctored Evidence, A Sea of Troubles* and *Beastly Things*.

Praise for Donna Leon

'Donna Leon goes from strength to strength.'

Observer

'Donna Leon has a wonderful feel for the hidden evils that lie below the façade of the magical city, and Brunetti, sturdy family man and cynic, is an end… the machinations of Italian…

'Leon writes with great literar… about the world's most beauti… mysterious city.'

Spectator

Also by Donna Leon

Death at La Fenice
Death in a Strange Country
The Anonymous Venetian
A Venetian Reckoning
Acqua Alta
The Death of Faith
A Noble Radiance
Fatal Remedies
Friends in High Places
A Sea of Troubles
Wilful Behaviour
Uniform Justice
Doctored Evidence
Blood from a Stone
Through a Glass, Darkly
Suffer the Little Children
The Girl of His Dreams
About Face
A Question of Belief
Drawing Conclusions
Beastly Things
The Jewels of Paradise
The Golden Egg
By Its Cover
Falling in Love
The Waters of Eternal Youth
Earthly Remains

Donna Leon

The Temptation of Forgiveness

arrow books

1 3 5 7 9 10 8 6 4 2

Arrow Books
20 Vauxhall Bridge Road
London SW1V 2SA

William Heinemann is part of the Penguin Random House group
of companies whose addresses can be found at global.
penguinrandomhouse.com.

Penguin
Random House
UK

First published by William Heinemann in 2018
First published in paperback by Arrow Books in 2018

www.penguin.co.uk

A CIP catalogue record for this book is available from
the British Library.

ISBN 9781787461093
ISBN 9781787461109 (Export edition)

Map © Martin Lubikowski, ML Design, London

Typeset in 11/13 pt Palatino
by Integra Software Services Pvt. Ltd, Pondicherry

Printed and bound in Great Britain by Clays Ltd, Elcograf S.p.A.

FSC
www.fsc.org
MIX
Paper from
responsible sources
FSC® C018179

Penguin Random House is committed to a sustainable
future for our business, our readers and our planet.
This book is made from Forest Stewardship Council®
certified paper.

For Ann Hallenberg

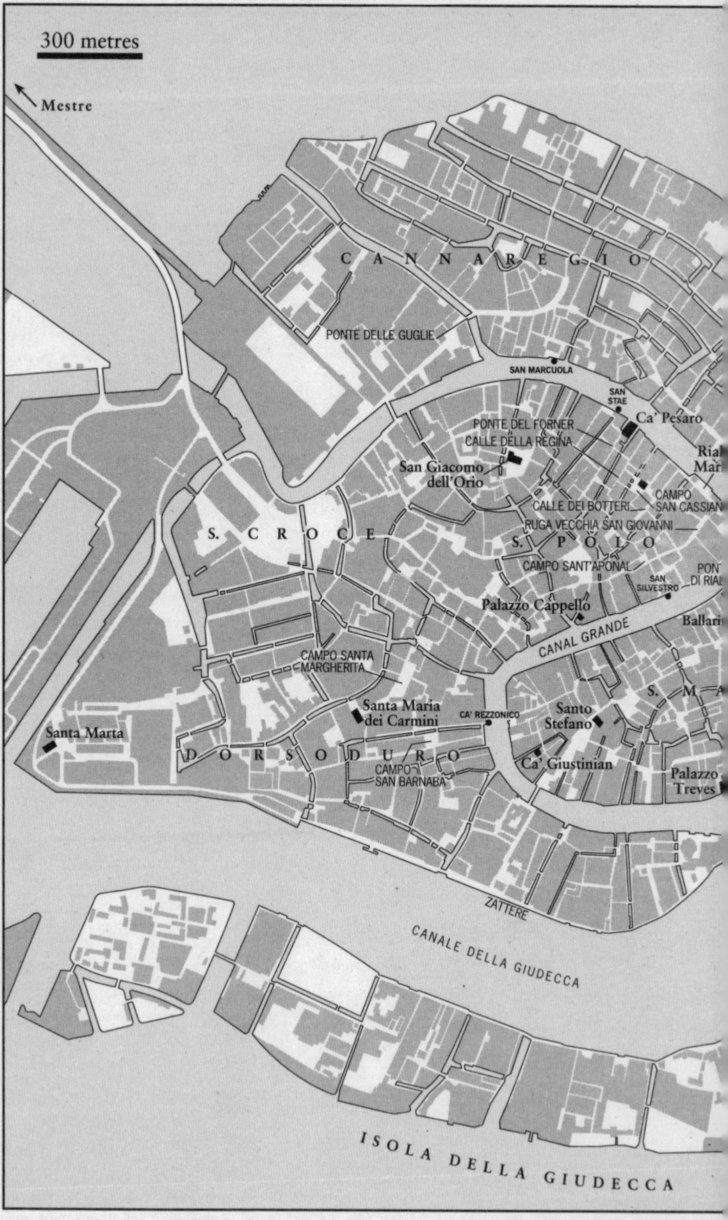
300 metres
Mestre
CANNAREGIO
PONTE DELLE GUGLIE
SAN MARCUOLA
SAN STAE
Ca' Pesaro
PONTE DEL FORNER
CALLE DELLA REGINA
San Giacomo dell'Orio
CAMPO SAN CASSIAN
CALLE DEI BOTTERI
RUGA VECCHIA SAN GIOVANNI
S. CROCE
S. POLO
CAMPO SANT'APONAL
SAN SILVESTRO
Palazzo Cappello
CANAL GRANDE
CAMPO SANTA MARGHERITA
Santa Maria dei Carmini
CA' REZZONICO
Santo Stefano
Ca' Giustinian
Santa Marta
DORSODURO
CAMPO SAN BARNABA
Palazzo Treves
ZATTERE
CANALE DELLA GIUDECCA
ISOLA DELLA GIUDECCA

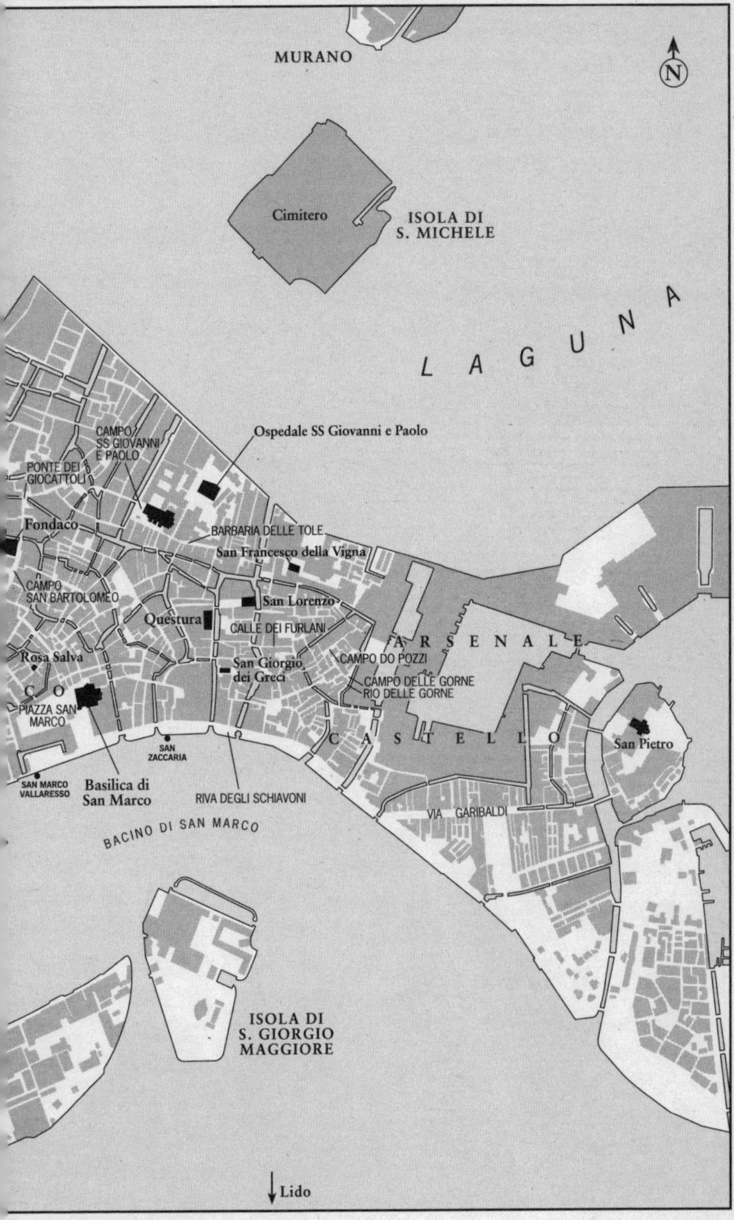

MURANO
N
Cimitero
ISOLA DI
S. MICHELE
L A G U N A
Ospedale SS Giovanni e Paolo
CAMPO
SS GIOVANNI
E PAOLO
PONTE DEI
GIOCATTOLI
Fondaco
BARBARIA DELLE TOLE
San Francesco della Vigna
CAMPO
SAN BARTOLOMEO
San Lorenzo
Questura
CALLE DEI FURLANI
A R S E N A L E
Rosa Salva
San Giorgio
dei Greci
CAMPO DO POZZI
CAMPO DELLE GORNE
RIO DELLE GORNE
C O
PIAZZA SAN
MARCO
C A S T E L L O
San Pietro
SAN
ZACCARIA
SAN MARCO
VALLARESSO
Basilica di
San Marco
RIVA DEGLI SCHIAVONI
VIA GARIBALDI
BACINO DI SAN MARCO
ISOLA DI
S. GIORGIO
MAGGIORE
Lido

The law condemns, but love will spare.

Handel, *Esther*, Act II, Scene 3

1

Having left the apartment smack on time so as to arrive at the Questura on time for a meeting with his superior, Brunetti found himself seated towards the rear of a Number One vaporetto, glancing idly through a copy of that morning's *Gazzettino.* Subconsciously aware that they had just left la Salute, starting to cross to Vallaresso, he heard the boat's motor slip into reverse. A Venetian system of batlike echolocation told him they were still some distance from the left bank of the canal, so the sound of the boat reversing was out of place: perhaps the Captain was trying to avoid something in the water ahead of them.

Brunetti lowered the paper, looked up, and saw nothing. Or, more accurately, he saw no farther than a sober grey wall he recognized instantly as an approaching bank of fog. It was hard to believe his eyes, so clear had the sky been when he'd left his home twenty minutes before. While he had been reading about the latest failure of the MOSE floodgates to function – after more than thirty years of plans and peculation – someone appeared to have draped a thick grey cloth in front of the vaporetto.

It was November; fog was thus to be expected, and the temperature was no warmer than it had been for the past week. Brunetti turned and looked at the man sitting on his right, but saw that he was so rapt by whatever showed on the screen of his phone that he would not have noticed seraphs had they descended and flown in close formation on either side of the boat.

They slowed to a stop a few metres from the grey wall, and the motor slipped into neutral. From behind him, Brunetti heard a woman whisper, *'Oddio'*, her voice filled with mild surprise, not fear. Brunetti looked towards the *riva* on his left and could see the Hotel Europa and Palazzo Treves, but apparently Ca' Giustinian had been devoured by the same dense mist that stretched across the Canal Grande in front of them.

The man beside him finally looked up from his phone and stared straight ahead, then returned his attention to the small screen in his left hand. Brunetti folded his paper and turned to look behind them. Through the back door and windows, he saw boats coming in their direction, others moving away from them towards the Rialto Bridge. A Number Two pulled out from the Accademia stop, starting towards them, but then it slowed and appeared to stop.

He heard the klaxon before he saw the taxi swerve around the stationary Number Two and tear towards them. As it passed the larger boat, Brunetti saw that the pilot was talking to a blonde woman who stood behind him. Just as they passed Brunetti, her mouth opened in what might have been a gasp, or a scream, forcing the driver to turn and face forward. Expressionless, he swung the tiller, swerved around the front of Brunetti's vaporetto and plunged into the curtain of fog.

Brunetti pushed past his neighbour and out on to the deck, listening for a crash from in front of them, but all he heard was the disappearing noise of the taxi. Their own engine throbbed back into life and they began to edge forward. From where he stood, Brunetti could not see if the radar on the roof of the cabin was turning, but surely it had to be or they would not be venturing to move at all.

Then, as easily as if they were aboard a magic boat in a fantasy novel, they slipped through the grey curtain, and sunlight was restored to them. Inside the pilot's cabin, the sailor, completely relaxed, half leaned back against the window, and the Captain looked ahead, hands on the tiller. On the embankment, the *palazzi*, freed of their foggy wrappings, moved calmly to the left as the vaporetto approached the Vallaresso stop.

Behind him, the cabin door slid open and passengers slipped past him and bunched together in front of the railing. The boat docked, the sailor slid back the metal railing, people got off, people got on, the sailor slid the railing closed, and the boat departed. Brunetti looked back in the direction of the Accademia, but there was no sign of fog. Boats approached them and moved away: ahead lay the *bacino*; on the left, the Basilica, the Marciana, and the Palazzo stood quietly in their appointed places while the morning sun continued sweeping up last night's shadows.

Brunetti looked into the cabin, wondering if those inside had seen the same thing he had, but he had no memory of which of them had been aboard when he saw the fog. He would have had to ask them, but anticipation of their looks kept him from doing so.

Brunetti touched the top of the railing, but it was dry, as was the deck. He was wearing a dark blue suit, and he felt the sun warm his right sleeve and shoulder. The sun glowed; the air was fresh and dry; the sky was cloudless.

He got off at San Zaccaria, forgetting his newspaper behind and, as he watched the boat pulling away, leaving behind any hope of verifying what he had seen. He walked slowly down the *riva*, grew tired of pondering the inexplicable, and instead concentrated his thoughts on what he would have to do when he got to the Questura.

The previous afternoon, Brunetti had received an email from his superior, Vice-Questore Giuseppe Patta, requesting that he come and have a word with him the following morning. No explanation had been given, which was normal; the language was polite, which was not.

Most of Vice-Questore Patta's behaviour was predictable for a man who had progressed through government bureaucracy. He seemed busier than he was; he never missed the opportunity to claim for himself any praise given to the organization for which he worked; he had a black belt in shifting blame or responsibility for failure to shoulders other than his own. What was not to be expected in someone who had, with such ease, shimmied up the pole of organizational success was the fact that he had, for decades, remained in the same place. Most men who attained his rank continued to rise, zigzagging from province to province, city to city, until perhaps a late-career promotion took them to Rome, where they tended to remain, like thick clots on the top of yogurt, cutting off light, air, and the possibility for growth from those below them.

Patta, like a Cambrian trilobite, had dug himself into place at the Venice Questura and had become a sort of living fossil. Beside him, petrified in the same layer of silt, was his assistant, Lieutenant Scarpa, another native of Palermo who had come to prefer these pastures new. Commissari came and went, three different Questori had been in charge during Patta's time in Venice; even the computers had been twice replaced. But Patta remained, a limpet attached to his rock, as the waters washed over him and away, leaving him intact and in place, his faithful Lieutenant at his side.

And yet, neither Patta nor Scarpa had ever demonstrated any enthusiasm for the city, nor any special fondness for it. If someone said that Venice was beautiful – perhaps even going so far as to say it was the most beautiful city on earth – Scarpa and Patta would exchange a glance that expressed, but did not state, disagreement. Yes, they both seemed to be thinking, but have you ever seen Palermo?

It was Patta's secretary, Signorina Elettra Zorzi, who greeted Brunetti as he came into the office from where she guarded that of the Vice-Questore. 'Ah, Commissario,' she said. 'The Vice-Questore called a few minutes ago and asked me to tell you he'd be here soon.'

Had Vlad the Impaler apologized for the dullness of the stakes, the message would have been no more astonishing. 'Is there something wrong with him?' Brunetti asked without thinking.

She tilted her head to one side to consider his question, began to smile and then stopped. 'He's been spending a lot of time on the phone with his wife lately,' she said and then added, 'Difficult to tell: he says very little in response to whatever it is she says to him.' She had somehow managed to place a type of listening device – Brunetti did not want to know more – in her superior's office, but he thought it best not to display any knowledge of this.

'When he talks to Scarpa, they go over by the window.' Did that mean the device was on his desk or that Patta suspected something and saw to it that he and his assistant spoke in voices too low to be heard? Or did they just like the view?

'What?' Brunetti asked, eyebrows raised. Her blouse, he noticed, was the colour of beetroot and had white buttons down the front and on the cuffs. It fell with the liquid grace of silk.

She placed the outstretched fingers of one hand over those of the other and made a grille covering part of her desk. 'I've no idea what's troubling him.' Brunetti sensed that this was a question but did not understand how it could be: if anyone knew what Patta was up to, it was Signorina Elettra. She went on, eyes still on her hands. 'He isn't nervous when he talks to his wife. He listens but tells her to do whatever she thinks best.'

'And with Scarpa?'

'With him he does sound nervous.' She stopped, as though to reflect on this and then added, 'It could be that he doesn't like what Scarpa's saying. The Vice-Questore cuts him short. One time he even told him not to bother him with more questions,' she said, forgetting how unlikely it was that she would be able to hear any of this from her office.

'Trouble in paradise,' Brunetti said, straight-faced.

'So it would seem,' she agreed. Then she asked, 'Do you want to wait for him in his office, or should I call you when he comes in?'

'I'll go upstairs. Call me when he gets here.' Then, unable to resist a parting remark, he added, 'I wouldn't want the Vice-Questore to find me rifling through his drawers.'

'Neither would he,' said a deep voice from the doorway.

'Ah, Lieutenant,' Brunetti said easily, directing a happy smile at the man lounging against the jamb of the door to the office. 'Once again, we are two hearts that beat as one in our concern for the best interests of the Vice-Questore.'

'Are you being ironic?' Scarpa asked with a thin smile. 'Or perhaps sarcastic, Commissario?' The Lieutenant paused briefly and then added, by way of explanation, 'Those of us who did not have the advantage of a university education sometimes have trouble telling the difference.'

Brunetti waited a moment to give the question the consideration it warranted, then answered, 'In this case, I'd say it's merely hyperbole, Lieutenant, where the obvious exaggeration is meant to render the entire statement false and unbelievable.' When Scarpa did not respond, Brunetti added, 'It's a rhetorical device used to create humour.' Scarpa said nothing, so Brunetti continued, smiling all the while, 'In philosophy – one of those things we studied at university – it's called the "Argumentum ad Absurdum".' Realizing he had gone quite far enough, Brunetti stopped himself from adding that it was a rhetorical device he found especially suitable to his conversations with the Vice-Questore.

'And it's meant to be funny?' Scarpa finally asked.

'Exactly, Lieutenant. Exactly. It is so clearly absurd to think that I would in any way abuse the Vice-Questore's trust that the mere suggestion is enough to provoke laughter.' Brunetti broadened his mouth as if his dentist had asked him to show his front teeth.

Scarpa propelled himself away from the door jamb with a quick shove of his left shoulder. One instant he'd been lounging casually; the next he was upright and much taller. The speed with which he uncoiled his easy, limp posturing reminded Brunetti of snakes he'd seen in television documentaries: leave them alone and they lie coiled, still as death; make a sound and they become a whiplash unbraiding in the sun, multiplying the range within which they can strike.

Smile intact, even broader than it had been, Brunetti turned to Signorina Elettra and said, 'I'll be in my office, if you'd be kind enough to call me when the Vice-Questore arrives.'

'Certainly, Signor Commissario,' Signorina Elettra agreed and turned to Scarpa to ask, 'What might I do for you, Lieutenant?'

Brunetti started towards the door. Scarpa did not move, still stood effectively blocking the exit. Time stopped. Signorina Elettra looked away.

Finally the Lieutenant stepped towards Signorina Elettra's desk, and Brunetti left the office.

2

On his desk, Brunetti found what he did not want to find, a file that had been accumulating pages ever since its first appearance in the Questura. He had last seen it, perhaps two months ago, when it had spent a week in his in-tray, resting there in the manner of the person a friend brings to dinner, who drinks too much, says nothing during the meal, and then refuses to leave, even after the other guests are long gone. Brunetti had not invited the file, it told him almost nothing, and now he could not think of a way to get rid of it.

The dark green manila folder was used for car-related crimes: reckless driving, leaving the scene of an accident, destruction of speed cameras at the side of the road; driving while drunk or speaking on the *telefonino* or, far more dangerous, texting. In a city with no automobiles, crimes of this sort were seldom brought to the attention of the Venice Questura.

The folder, however, also contained cases involving the illegal acquisition of documents: vehicle registration, insurance, driver's licence, driving test results. Even though these documents had to be registered at the central office in Mestre, any illegal attempt to obtain them, as was common with any crime committed in the joined cities, was reported to the Venice police.

Most of the folder's weight was currently due to an incident on the mainland. After reading the first report, Brunetti had been left with renewed respect for the endless creativity of his fellow man. The crime had originally been detected in the hospital in Mestre, where, over the course of only two days, five men presented themselves to Pronto Soccorso with miniature radio receivers implanted so deep in their ears that they were unable to remove them and had no choice but to go to the hospital. When examined, all of the men were discovered also to have transmitting equipment taped on to their abdomens and miniature cameras attached to their chests, the lenses peeking out through their buttonholes.

Because four of them were Pakistani and none of them spoke much Italian, a translator and then the police were called. All five men, it turned out, had enrolled in the same driving school in Mestre and had previously failed the verbal test, during which they had been asked to explain the meaning of certain road signs. The transmitters, the police later discovered, had been taped to their abdomens by men sent from the driving school, the same men who had inserted the tiny transmitters deep into their ears. During the test, the buttonhole cameras had relayed the signs the men had been asked to identify to distant helpers, who in turn whispered into their ears the meanings of the signs displayed by the examiners.

And thus they passed their exam and were given their driver's licences.

The service cost two or three thousand Euros and had probably, until detected, managed to put hundreds of unqualified drivers behind the wheel, not only of automobiles, but of long-distance trucks and articulated vehicles.

Given that Brunetti could think of no one who had not already seen the file, he decided to keep it on his desk, like a car that could not escape a traffic jam unless its driver had the courage to slip into the emergency lane until it reached the next exit.

He sometimes thought he kept it there to remind himself of how clever people could be, at least in inventing ways to make money.

His phone rang. 'The Vice-Questore has arrived, Commissario,' Signorina Elettra told him in the voice she used when Patta stood near her desk.

'I'll be there immediately,' Brunetti answered and got to his feet.

He found the autumnally tanned Patta in front of Signorina Elettra's desk, speaking with her about his schedule for the afternoon. Today, Patta wore a dark grey suit Brunetti had never seen before; while he waited for them to finish, Brunetti directed his attention to it. He studied the silent caress the jacket gave to Patta's broad shoulders, the gentle fall of the cloth of the single pleat. His glance ran down the sleeves of the jacket and fell upon the buttonholes at the cuffs. Yes, they were hand-sewn, a detail that always won Brunetti's sartorial admiration.

Patta's black shoes, as well, had obviously been made for him, the tiny holes decorating the toes serving only to accent the smoothness of the leather. The laces had tassels. It was difficult for Brunetti to admit how much he admired those shoes.

'Ah, good morning, Commissario,' Patta said amiably. 'Do come into my office.' Over the years, Brunetti had come to believe that Patta adjusted his pronunciation to the importance of the person with whom he spoke. With the Questore, Patta spoke an Italian of impeccable purity, more Tuscan than any Tuscan was capable of. It was the same voice he used with Signorina Elettra. His Palermitano accent thickened in direct proportion to the diminishing importance of the person with whom he spoke. Odd vowel sounds began to appear, 'i' landed on the end of feminine nouns; double 'll's' were transmuted into double 'dd's'; the 'Madonna' became the 'Maronna', and 'bello' became 'beddu'. Sometimes the initial 'i' in words disappeared, only to scamper back into place at the sight of a person of higher station. From the clear Italian of Patta's greeting, Brunetti judged himself to have been promoted a few rungs, a promotion good sense told him would be temporary.

Patta entered the office first and left it to Brunetti to close the door behind them. The Vice-Questore turned towards his desk but then changed direction and sat in one of the chairs in front of it, leaving Brunetti to choose one of the others.

When they were seated, Patta began: 'I'd like to speak to you frankly, Commissario.' Brunetti ignored the chance this remark gave him to ask how Patta had spoken to him in the past and, instead, adopted a pleasant, interested expression. At least Patta had wasted no time with preliminaries.

'It's about a leak,' Patta said.

'Leak?' Brunetti asked, resisting the urge to look at the ceiling.

'From the Questura,' Patta continued.

Ah, that kind of leak, Brunetti told himself and wondered what Patta had in mind. Nothing embarrassing had appeared in either *Il Gazzettino* or *La Nuova di Venezia* for some time, so Brunetti was without advance warning about the information leaking from the Questura.

Uncertain how to respond to Patta's remark, Brunetti returned his glance to his superior's jacket and the hand-stitched buttonholes. Beauty was where you found it, and it was always comforting to see.

'What is it, Commissario?' Patta asked with a return to his normal inquisitorial tone.

Without hesitation, and perhaps for the first time in years, Brunetti answered honestly. 'The buttonholes on your jacket, Signore.'

Startled, Patta pulled his right arm close to himself and stared at the cuff, almost as if he feared Brunetti intended to steal the buttons. After examining them, Patta asked, 'Yes?'

Brunetti's smile was easy and natural. 'I admire them, Vice-Questore.'

'Buttonholes?'

'Yes.'

'You can see the difference?'

'I think it's obvious,' Brunetti said. 'It's such a fine thing to see hand stitching of that quality. Like the foam on a coffee: it's not always there, and to most people it doesn't matter, but when it's there, and you see it, it makes the coffee taste better somehow.'

Patta's expression softened, and Brunetti had the strange sensation that the Vice-Questore was relieved, as at the sudden appearance of a friend in a room where he expected to see only unfamiliar faces.

'I've found a tailor in Mogliano,' Patta revealed. He glanced across to Brunetti and said, 'I can give you his name if you like.'

'That's very kind of you, sir.'

Patta straightened his arm and pulled at the cuff of his shirt, then sat back in the chair.

Brunetti realized this was the first personal conversation they'd ever had – two men speaking as equals – and they were talking about buttonholes.

'These leaks, sir: could you tell me more about them?'

'I wanted to speak to you, Brunetti, because you know people here,' Patta said, reminding Brunetti that this was still the old Patta, for whom any information about the inner workings of the Questura was part of the Delphic Mysteries.

Brunetti waved a hand in the air, to dismiss those hidden truths Patta believed he knew or perhaps to summon them from the vasty deep.

'They talk to you,' Patta insinuated. Hearing Patta's suspicion relaxed Brunetti and told him that, though the subject might be new, the old, adversarial order had been restored. He tossed away his momentary warming towards Patta and returned to his native good sense.

'What is it you think they've been talking about, Vice-Questore?'

Patta cleared his throat with a small noise. 'I've heard rumours that some people are displeased with Lieutenant Scarpa,' Patta said, struggling, it seemed, to keep indignation from his voice. Then, more calmly, as though he considered it of lesser importance, he added, 'It also seems that someone has been talking about a person brought in for questioning.'

Get a grip here, Brunetti told himself, considering the remark about Scarpa. He despised and distrusted the

Lieutenant and made little attempt to hide it, yet Patta seemed oblivious to this, as he was to so much else at the Questura. Best to demonstrate surprise; outrage would be too much. Perhaps with a bit of curiosity? But what about the leaks?

'Are you at liberty to say where you got this information, sir?'

'Both were reported to me by the Lieutenant himself,' Patta replied.

'Did the Lieutenant reveal his source?'

Patta hesitated a moment but then said, 'He told me it was one of his informants.'

Brunetti rubbed at his lower lip with the fingers of his left hand. He allowed a long time to pass before he said, 'I find it strange that an informant would learn something about the Questura that no one here seems to know about.' After a brief pause, he suggested, 'You might ask Signorina Elettra.'

'I wanted to speak to you first,' Patta said without explanation.

Brunetti nodded, as if he understood Patta's reasoning. He probably did: Patta would be hesitant to bother Signorina Elettra with a suspicion that might be groundless. 'Is this informant a reliable source?' Brunetti asked.

'How would I know a thing like that?' Patta demanded. 'It's not my business to deal with informants.' The instinct to institutional survival stilled Brunetti's tongue. He waved his hand and nodded in agreement, then said, 'Someone might have invented this rumour to create friction between the Lieutenant and his colleagues. There's no doubt that the Lieutenant has won a place in the opinion of his fellow workers.' Brunetti paused minimally and then added, while Patta was working out his precise meaning, 'I'd discount the reports, sir. That is, if you're asking my opinion.'

Did Patta stir uneasily in his chair? Brunetti wondered. He waited for what he considered a respectful period of time, then got to his feet. 'If there's nothing else, Vice-Questore, I'll go back to my office.'

3

Brunetti closed the door behind him and turned to Signorina Elettra, hoping she might be able to tell him more. He was surprised to see Vianello standing beside her, leaning down and pointing to something on her computer screen. 'Ah, I see,' the Inspector said in a reverent voice. 'It's so easy.' He nodded in private satisfaction and moved away from the computer. 'I tried to do it twice, but I kept ignoring the obvious.'

Signorina Elettra moved her attention from the screen to Brunetti and raised her eyebrows in silent interrogation. He smiled and shook his head. 'There's always something to be learned from the Vice-Questore.' Then, sure of their attention, he continued. 'Dottor Patta's current suspicion is that information has leaked from the Questura.' He was curious to see how Vianello would respond. When Vianello remained silent, Brunetti added, 'He's probably been watching spy movies, or the Lieutenant has. He's the one who reported the rumour.'

Signorina Elettra, who had turned away when Brunetti spoke, pushed a key and cleared her screen, then keyed in the front page of *Il Gazzettino*, which Brunetti had been reading on the boat. She read a few lines, glanced at Brunetti, but returned her eyes to the screen without comment. Brunetti wondered why the subject didn't interest her: gossip usually did. Perhaps her curiosity did not extend to Lieutenant Scarpa.

Vianello expelled a puff of audible disbelief. 'As if what we do here is a secret.'

Idly, eyes still on the screen, Signorina Elettra asked, 'Did he say what the leaks were about?'

Brunetti glanced at Patta's door and held up both hands, palms towards her. 'Only the suggestion that Lieutenant Scarpa is not the most popular person here.' He didn't bother to mention the other supposed leak, considering it inconsequential.

Scarpa's name had caught Signorina Elettra's attention. Suddenly smiling, she looked at Brunetti and said, 'Impossible to believe.'

Brunetti laughed and replied, 'That's exactly what I told the Vice-Questore.'

'Don't we have anything better to do than worry about the Lieutenant and phantom leaks about him?' Vianello asked.

Brunetti was about to leave, but his curiosity got the better of him and he asked, 'What were you two solving when I came in?'

Vianello and Signorina Elettra exchanged a glance, and the Inspector said, 'Go ahead. Tell him. I can take it. I'm a man.'

'It was one of his son's homework problems,' Signorina Elettra explained.

'Luca's in an advanced class in computer technology,' Vianello explained. 'The teacher gave a problem to the students, and Luca had trouble with it, so I thought I'd work on it because the computers here are much more sophisticated. I thought I might be able to figure it out.'

'And?' Brunetti asked, although he suspected he already knew.

'It was still impossible for me,' Vianello said with a shrug.

Signorina Elettra interrupted him. 'I had to work on it for a long time before I understood what to do.' She turned to Vianello. 'Did Luca find the solution?'

Vianello laughed. 'I asked him at breakfast, and he said it came to him in the night, so he got up and worked on it until he solved it.' He smiled, then sighed.

'Did he get the same answer we did?' she asked. Brunetti noted the kindness of her use of the plural.

'I don't know,' Vianello said. 'He was in a hurry. Said he'd tell me at dinner.'

They were interrupted by Alvise's arrival at the door. 'Oh, there you are, Commissario,' he said and saluted, then leaned against the door jamb, hand on his heart, panting, to show he had run up the stairs. Alvise was the shortest man on the force: were the stairs higher for him?

'There's a woman downstairs who says she wants to talk to you, Commissario,' he said with some effort.

'It might have been easier to phone me, Alvise,' Brunetti suggested.

Alvise's face froze, his hand fell from his heart, and he stopped panting. He stood there, in the spotlight of common sense, for a few seconds before he blurted, 'I know that, Dottore. But I wanted to show her that I knew it was important.'

In the face of that, Brunetti had no choice but to reply, 'Then go and get her and take her to my office if you would.' Alvise, who had resumed panting and could do no more than nod, backed away and disappeared.

None of them said anything until the sound of Alvise's footsteps on the stairs disappeared. 'Why are you always so kind to him, Signore?' Signorina Elettra asked.

Brunetti had to consider this: he had never given conscious thought to how to respond to Alvise. 'Because he needs it,' he said.

'Ah,' was all that Signorina Elettra offered.

'I'll be in my office,' Brunetti said.

Once he reached it, he stood at the window for a while, studying the vine on the wall of the villa on the other side of the canal. Occasionally, a few leaves fell into the canal below. The tide was ebbing, Brunetti noticed. Ah, how poets had loved this as an image of departure, things carried off by the inexorable tide.

He turned towards the sound of footsteps and saw Alvise at the doorway, behind him the top of the head of a woman at least ten centimetres taller than the officer. 'Commissario,' Alvise began, tossing off an impressive salute and stepping aside to reveal the other person, 'this is Signora Crosera. She'd like to speak to you.'

'Thank you, Alvise,' Brunetti said. As he moved towards them, he recognized the woman, although at first he failed to remember where he had seen her. But then it came to him: she taught at the university, and though she was in a different faculty, she was an acquaintance of Paola, who seemed to hold her in high regard. Paola had introduced Brunetti to the woman years before, and then, as happened in Venice, they had bumped into her on the street a number of times; on several occasions she'd been in the company of a tall man with greying hair so straight and thick that Brunetti, conscious of the coin-sized patch of thinning hair at the back of his own head, envied him.

'Ah, Professoressa Crosera,' Brunetti said, taking her hand and hoping to sound as if he had immediately recognized her. She was almost as tall as he, with dark brown hair that fell to her shoulders and dark eyes to match. Her mouth was full: she tried to smile but failed to do more than hoist her lips upwards at the sides.

'Please, come and have a seat,' Brunetti said. He waited until she sat and then decided to go around the desk and sit in his chair, if only to acknowledge that she was consulting him because he was a police officer, not as the husband of a colleague.

She sat on the edge of the chair, knees pressed together, and took quick glances around the office. She wore black trousers and a dark green jacket and looked as though she had not slept well for some time. She bent to place her handbag on the floor beside her chair; when she sat up, she had gained greater control of her expression.

'How can I help you, Professoressa?' Brunetti asked calmly, as though it were quite ordinary for a university professor to sit nervously in front of a *commissario di polizia*.

When Brunetti remained silent, she said, 'I thought it would be easier if I spoke to someone I know.' Immediately she corrected herself: 'Not that I know you personally, Commissario. Paola has never spoken of you, well, not of your profession. Your work, that is. Never. For all she says about what you do, you might as well be a notary or an electrician.'

Brunetti smiled. 'It's probably because she wants to save us both time and trouble.'

'I beg your pardon,' she said, unable to disguise her confusion.

'If she told her colleagues I'm a policeman, they'd be coming to our apartment at all hours to tell us a neighbour was putting in a new bathroom without getting a permit or calling us at three in the morning to report that the students living upstairs were having a wild party.' He smiled, and saw her relax a bit.

'Oh, no, it's nothing like that,' she said and bent down to move her handbag back a few centimetres. 'It's about something serious.' She crossed and then uncrossed her legs, then turned slightly in her chair. The light from the windows fell on the right side of her face, exaggerating the hollow under her temple. She joined her hands together and studied them for a moment. 'I know you and Paola have children,' she said, glancing up momentarily.

'Yes, two.'

'Teenagers, aren't they?'

'Still, but barely,' Brunetti said easily.

Her eyes returned to her hands. 'So do we,' she said. 'Two. A boy and a girl.'

'We, too,' he said. 'A boy and a girl,' he added, although she might know this already. 'And in a few years,' Brunetti continued easily, 'they'll be a man and a woman.' He smiled, as if offering a second handshake with this gift of a personal confidence. 'It's a sobering thought.'

'They're good kids, aren't they?' Professoressa Crosera asked. Brunetti had expected her to say something about her own children, but some people took a long time to relax and accept the fact that they were talking to a policeman of their own volition. They needed the assurance that conversation could be inconsequential, even friendly, before they would be able to loosen themselves sufficiently to start talking about whatever had brought them there.

'I think they are,' Brunetti answered. 'Paola does, too.' He seldom admitted such a thing and so added immediately, driven by something close to superstition, 'But neither of us is a reliable witness, I'm afraid.' It was too early to ask about her children, although they might well be the reason she was there.

'What faculty do you teach in, Professoressa?' Brunetti asked instead, reassuring her again that Paola had not given him any information about her.

'Architecture. I teach part time now because I work as a consultant in urban design. Mostly in Turkey, but in Romania and Hungary, too. I travel a lot.'

Silence fell. Brunetti sat and waited, the tactic he'd learned was most effective. The people who came to see him wanted to talk about something, and sooner or later, if they were left alone and not burdened with questions, they would.

After at least a minute had passed, Professoressa Crosera said, 'My kids are good, too. But my son has . . . has changed.' She leaned forward, and Brunetti thought she was going to reach for her bag and show him a photo of either the still-good daughter or the other child. But she was merely shifting around in her chair and soon grew still again.

'I'm worried . . .' she began, but her voice failed her after this word. She closed her eyes, put her hands to her mouth, and pushed her head up and down against them.

Brunetti turned away and stared out the window, the only decent thing to do. It had started to rain, a patchy, spitting rain that would irritate people and do the farmers no good at all. Though irredeemably urban, Brunetti never failed to think of the farmers when it rained – regardless of the season – wishing them good fortune, enriched soil, good crops. Over the years, the rain had destroyed his shoes, soaked through his raincoats, once ruined his ceiling, but still he welcomed it, approved of it, and took physical pleasure in watching it fall.

The rain grew heavier, and he wondered if Professoressa Crosera had left a coat with the porter downstairs. He had, he knew, two extra umbrellas in his *armadio*: easy enough to give her one when they were finished. But how could they finish when they had not even begun?

'It's about him,' he heard her say. Brunetti saw that her eyes were still closed, although her hands were now folded in her lap.

A splatter against the windows pulled at his attention, and he returned to studying the rain.

'I think I can talk now,' she said in a calmer voice. 'My son,' she said, looking across at Brunetti, who had turned to her and met her glance, 'is fifteen. He's at the Albertini. They both are.' Brunetti, had he not decided that his children should go to state schools, would surely have sent them there. Private, expensive, with a curriculum taught almost entirely in English, the Albertini, housed in a *palazzo* near Campo SS. Giovanni e Paolo, had a good reputation and deserved it: most graduates went on to university, many of them having won scholarships to study abroad.

'It's a very good school,' Brunetti said.

It took some time for her to nod and confirm this.

'How long have your children been there?' Brunetti asked, not wanting to refer specifically to her son.

'Sandro's been there for two years. He's in the second year of *liceo*.'

'And your daughter?' Brunetti inquired mildly, as though this question would naturally follow.

'She's in the fourth year.'

'Are they doing well?' Brunetti asked, as vague a question as he could make it.

'Aurelia is,' she answered instantly, as if responding to a benediction. 'Sandro …' she began, then let her voice trail off. After a moment, she seemed to force herself to finish the sentence. '… isn't. Not any more.'

'Doesn't he study enough?' Brunetti asked from sheer politeness, already considering what the reasons might be for her son's failure to do well.

'He doesn't study,' she said haltingly. 'He did. When he began. But this year …' Her hands sought and found the inflexible arms of the chair. Professoressa Crosera stared at Brunetti's desk, as though reading there school reports about descending grades and deteriorating conduct.

'Hummm,' Brunetti murmured, the sort of concerned noise one made at bad news, any bad news. He wanted her to offer the information, not to have to pull it from her by force of crafty questioning. Brunetti continued to think of possible reasons, and drugs sprang instantly to mind, that first fruit of every parent's nightmare cornucopia.

Recently, Brunetti had found himself unconsciously tightening the muscles of his hips when he walked down the stairs from their apartment. He'd not noticed the strain until he'd one day heard an almost groaning noise escape his lungs as he stepped off the last step and could relax his body. Much the same thing happened when he heard about teenagers veering into the perils of modern life: he tensed his spirit and tightened his mind against the entry of any thought involving his own children and forced himself to remain calm at the news that a teenager was behaving erratically.

'Last year, Sandro was second in his class. But this term – even though it's only been two months – he's had bad reports from his teachers. It's too early for grades, but he doesn't bring books home, and I've never seen him doing any homework. Or reading.'

'Ah,' Brunetti said softly, forced to consider the contrast with his own kids, who brought friends home to study together or went to their homes to prepare for tests; happy with classes, excited at the thought of learning.

She crossed her legs again and then crossed them the other way. 'My husband didn't ...' she began and quickly changed it to, 'Finally I decided I should come here to try to get some information.'

Brunetti, who thought she had come to give information, said nothing. Many people, he knew, considered it a betrayal to reveal anything to the police. How easy would it be for him, Brunetti asked himself, to reveal something about his own children to a stranger? The fact that Professoressa Crosera had come to the police – not to a doctor, the social services, even a priest – was suggestive of the sort of subject she was there to talk about.

'What information is it you'd like to have, Professoressa?'

In a voice somehow shifted to a higher pitch, she asked, 'I know it's a crime to sell drugs, but is it a crime to use them?'

So that was it, he thought with no surprise and was relieved to be able to tell her, 'No. Not to use them. The crime is to sell them, especially near a school or to young people.' He saw the relief this gave her.

'I wanted to make sure,' she finally said. Thoughtful, she continued, 'So if all you do is use them, you won't have any trouble?' At the sound of this absurdity, her face clouded. Hastily, she added, 'With the authorities, I mean.'

'So long as you're not selling them, no,' Brunetti answered, pretending not to have understood the ill-phrased question.

'Do you think that's a good law?' she surprised Brunetti by asking.

Brunetti felt no obligation, and less desire, to comment on the justice of the law and so answered, 'It's not important what either of us thinks about the law.'

'Then what is important?'

'That innocent people be protected. That's what laws are meant to do,' he said. Brunetti, in his heart, didn't believe this: laws, passed by the people in power, were meant to keep them in power. If they also protected innocent people, well and good, but that was nothing more than a welcome side effect.

'I never thought of it that way,' she said.

Brunetti, who never had and did not, permitted himself a shrug. 'I suppose most people don't think much about the purpose of the law.'

'To punish people. That's what I've always thought laws were meant to do.' She reflected a moment and then smiled. 'I think I prefer your interpretation, Commissario.'

Brunetti nodded but did not comment. Allowing his impatience to be heard, he said, 'We were speaking about your son, Professoressa.'

4

The brusqueness in Brunetti's voice startled her. 'Yes, yes. Of course,' she said. She lowered her eyes to Brunetti's desk and appeared to study it. Finally she said, 'I think he's taking drugs.' She stopped, as if she'd done what she'd come to do and could leave now.

Brunetti realized he would have to give things a shove. 'You think or you know?'

'I know,' she said, then immediately added, 'That is, I think I know. The kids at the school talk, and one of them told Aurelia that Sandro was going to be in big trouble because of what he was doing.'

'"Big trouble?"' Brunetti asked. And when she nodded, he continued, 'Did he say it was because of drugs?'

Her surprise was evident. 'What else could it be?' When Brunetti didn't answer, she explained, 'His little sister is in Sandro's class: she's the one who told him.' Voice suddenly growing insistent, she said, 'That's the only thing it could be. Drugs.'

'How long ago did this happen?'

'He told Aurelia about a week ago. She told me two days ago.'

'Why did your daughter wait to tell you?'

'She said she wanted to pay attention to him – Sandro – for a while before she said anything.'

'And did she?'

Her look was sharp. Sounding defensive, she said, 'She tried to talk to him, but he got angry and told her to mind her own business.'

Brunetti thought of his own children and how they occasionally spoke to one another. His scepticism must have been evident in his face, for she said, 'He's never talked to Aurelia like that before. She said he got really angry.'

'What else have *you* noticed, Professoressa?' he asked. 'How has he changed?'

'He's moody, and he doesn't like it if I ask him how he's doing at school. He doesn't come home for dinner sometimes, or he calls and says a friend's invited him to stay and eat.'

'Do you ever doubt that?' Brunetti asked neutrally.

'I'm not a policeman,' she snapped, then looked across at Brunetti and said, 'I'm sorry. I shouldn't have said that.' She stopped there and did not try to explain or excuse herself, and Brunetti liked her for that.

'I've heard far worse,' Brunetti said, then asked, 'Has your husband noticed these changes?'

She nodded a few times, looked away, looked back, and said, 'I told you I travel for work,' and waited for Brunetti to acknowledge this.

He nodded and she went on, 'I'm sometimes away for a few days at a time.'

'And the children? Who takes care of them?' Brunetti had no sooner said it than he realized it was none of his business.

'They go and stay with my sister,' she said.

Because he had already been too invasive with the other question, Brunetti asked nothing about her husband.

His thoughts must have been easy to read because she said, 'My husband works in Verona and sometimes isn't finished before the last train leaves. So he stays with friends, but not often.'

Had this been a normal interview and had Brunetti felt the need to pick at anything that caught his attention, he would have asked, 'Friends?' or, 'How often?' Instead, thinking of the man with the thick grey hair, he asked, 'What does he do?'

'He's an accountant,' she said and stopped. She gave Brunetti a quick glance and looked away, then added, as though it were part of the previous sentence, 'He told me Sandro's too thin and doesn't pay attention to what's said to him.' She stopped and Brunetti was tempted to say that this was the nature of teenagers.

In the face of his silence, she continued, 'If I mention drugs, my husband says it's impossible that Sandro could be taking them.' She pressed her lips together and stared at the floor.

Brunetti decided not to comment on this and asked, instead, 'What else have you noticed, Professoressa?'

She turned to gaze out of the window, where it was now raining heavily. Propping her right elbow on the arm of her chair, she rested her forehead in her right hand then said, 'He doesn't talk much any more. It's as though he were wearing a headset and listening to someone else, or music. I don't know. If I ask him a question, he always asks me to repeat it, and then he takes a long time before he answers.' She looked up at Brunetti and continued. 'I don't think he's sleeping well, and he gets angry easily. He used to be very sweet-tempered.'

As she spoke, Brunetti decided that, although Professoressa Crosera was Paola's colleague, or friend, she was not his, and so he had no obligation to spend much more time on this, a problem that could be better handled by the social services. Unwilling to confront her directly, he said, 'If I'd described my son, three years ago, I would have said most of what you just did, except about the sleeping.'

Her surprise was legible on her face. She folded her hands in her lap, like a student called in to talk to the *preside*, aware that she had done something wrong but not sure just what.

Brunetti let some time pass then said, quite without thinking, 'I'm afraid I still don't understand why you're here, Professoressa.'

This time, without hesitation, she said, 'I thought the police would do something.'

'Could you be clearer about that? What is it you'd like us to do?'

'Find who's selling him these drugs. And arrest them.'

Ah, how wonderful to be able to do that, Brunetti thought. Arrest them and keep them until they went for trial and then have the judges send them to prison, along with the people who worked with them or for them: all the little dealers who sat in the parks, waiting for school kids to come by and sit down next to them, or who met them at a disco or at the cinema or – surprise, surprise – just outside their schools.

Pity it didn't work that way. The reality was quite other: arrest them, take them to the Questura and question them, perhaps threaten them, even though they all knew that was useless; write out a formal notice that they had been arrested. If they were foreign, tell them they had 48 hours to leave the country: and let them go. If they were Italian, say they were going to be investigated, and send them home.

'Well, why don't you do something about it?' she asked in the face of his continuing silence.

Brunetti slid a notebook closer and picked up a pen. He wrote Professoressa Crosera's name at the top, the names of her two children, and the name of their school beneath it, leaving an empty place to fill in her husband's name later. He was tempted to slide it over to her and ask her to show him if anything there gave her an idea of whom to arrest, and on what charge? Instead, holding the pen poised above the notebook, he said, 'If we talk to your daughter's friend, either a lawyer or one of his parents would have to be in the room when we spoke to him. Do you want to give me his name?'

For the first time since she entered the room, perhaps for the first time since this had happened to her son, Professoressa Crosera was faced with the legal consequences of the situation in which she found herself. Once a whirlpool formed, even people sailing on calm and tranquil seas were at risk of being swept towards it and engulfed by it.

'No,' she said, now raising her voice. 'I can't do that to him.' This time, she did not notice her implicit insult to the police.

Brunetti set the pen on the desk and folded his hands in front of him. 'Do you know where your son is getting the drugs you think he's taking, Professoressa Crosera, or what kind of drugs he's using?'

Asked a question she was not prepared for, she evaded Brunetti's glance and stared at her knees.

Brunetti hated what drugs did to people, hated their corroding influence on even the best of spirits, yet he lived with three people who believed that they should all be declared legal. Easy answers, easy answers, why did people always want easy answers?

Drugs changed everything. He'd had women offer themselves to him, men offer him their wives, even their daughters, if only he would not arrest them and put them in a place where they thought they could not find drugs. He'd once seen a woman still wearing her bridal gown dead of an overdose, and once he'd been called to an apartment where a three-year-old boy had died of starvation and neglect during the week-long heroin party his parents had treated themselves to with money stolen from all four of the dead child's grandparents.

'No,' he heard her say. After another long pause and in a much different voice, she added, 'If I asked him, he'd lie to me.' Brunetti watched her accept this, and then she added, explaining it to herself as well as to him, 'I don't know how I know that, but it's true.' She put her hand to her forehead and sat in silence. He was again staring out the window when he heard her say, voice rough and almost inaudible, 'He's my baby, and I don't know what to do.'

He turned back to her; the sight of the woman's tears slipping under her fingers and dripping on to her jacket, where the wool quickly absorbed them, propelled Brunetti to his feet. He went over to the window and stared at the façade of the church. San Lorenzo: a martyr.

Brunetti's father had died a long and terrible death from cancer in a hospital run by people who viewed human suffering as a fine way to pave the way to salvation and who had thus refused to give him painkillers in the last days of his life. Three days before his father's death, Brunetti, by then already a *commissario di polizia*, had stolen a box of ampoules of morphine from the room where the police kept confiscated drugs and weapons and had administered them, at eight-hour intervals, to his dying father. After his father died, in peace and in the arms of his younger son, Brunetti had gone home and broken open the remaining ampoules and flushed all the morphine down the kitchen sink. He believed very little in an absolute sense, but he knew suffering was always wrong.

'Can you do anything?' she asked in her normal voice from the other side of the room.

She was again capable of speech, so Brunetti went back to his desk.

'I can try to find out if drugs are being sold at his school and who's selling them,' Brunetti said. He couldn't remember having heard any rumours about the Albertini, but to find out would at least be a place to begin.

Professoressa Crosera shifted in her chair, suddenly restless, perhaps eager to leave now that someone else was going to take care of things. No, that was not to do her justice. 'Could you give me your phone number?' Brunetti asked.

As she did, Brunetti wrote it in his notebook, then wrote above it, 'Albertini', just in case someone found his book and was curious about whom he had spoken to.

He realized that, as there was so little he could do, there was nothing else to say. One glance at her told him she had little power to tell him anything more, and far less willingness.

Brunetti got to his feet and thanked her for coming to see him. She seemed surprised by this badly disguised dismissal but allowed herself to be accompanied to the door. In an attempt to make up for his sharpness when questioning her, Brunetti smiled and promised to do what he could, not telling her how little that was. After she was gone, he went back to the window to think about the visit and about this woman's sorrow. He was relieved to see that the rain had stopped.

5

After lunch, Brunetti phoned Vianello and asked him to come up. When the Inspector arrived, Brunetti offered him a seat and told him at some length about his meeting with Professoressa Crosera.

Vianello nodded and asked, 'The kids go to the Albertini?'

'Does that make a difference?'

The Inspector crossed his legs and waved one foot in the air. 'It might have, five years ago, but I don't think it does any more: they can find drugs everywhere now.' He uncrossed his legs and set his foot on the floor. Brunetti suddenly noticed how much grey there was in his friend's hair and how his face seemed to have grown thinner. 'It used to be that the kids in the private schools used them less; but that's changing. At least that's what I've been told.'

'By whom?' Brunetti asked, realizing too late that he should not have. Everyone at the Questura kept the name of their sources to themselves.

After a moment, Vianello said mildly, 'By someone who knows. He told me all the schools have the problem now, to one degree or another.'

Brunetti knew this, of course, just as he knew that the air in the city in winter was polluted far beyond the limits which some European scientific agency had established for human safety. But so long as he didn't smell it or feel it in his lungs, Brunetti ignored it, aware that there was nothing he could do to avoid the air except leave the city. So, too, with drugs. So long as it wasn't your own kids ...

'Thank God we were born when we were,' he surprised Vianello by saying.

'What does that mean?'

'That there were fewer drugs around when we were in our teens. Or at least they didn't seem so ... normal, the way they do now. Some of my friends tried them, but I can't remember anyone who used them all the time.' When Vianello nodded in agreement, Brunetti added, 'Besides, I didn't have the money for them.'

'I tried hashish once,' Vianello said, looking at his feet.

'You never told me.'

Vianello laughed at Brunetti's tone and said, 'I try to keep some secrets, Guido.'

'What happened?'

'I was at a party at a friend's house, and I was given some herbal tea,' Vianello explained.

Brunetti found his use of the passive voice interesting. 'You didn't smoke it?'

'No. If I'd gone home smelling of it, my father would have ...'

'Would have what?' Brunetti asked, aware of how seldom Vianello spoke of his father.

'I don't know. Threatened to knock me into next week, probably.'

'Only threatened?' Brunetti asked.

'Yes,' Vianello answered without hesitation or explanation, then asked, 'What did Professoressa Crosera want?'

Putting aside his curiosity to know the rest of Vianello's story, Brunetti sifted through obvious reasons and real reasons and finally answered, 'I think she wanted us to make the problem go away. All we had to do was arrest the people who sell her son drugs.'

Vianello raised his eyebrows at this.

'Even though she offered no concrete information,' Brunetti said. 'She wouldn't tell me who told her daughter that Sandro was in trouble, and she made it clear there was no specific mention of drugs.' He added, his irritation audible, 'I don't know what she thinks we're supposed to do.'

'It's like that Greek thing you've mentioned,' Vianello said, to Brunetti's absolute confusion. The one with the Latin name.'

'*Deus ex machina*?' Brunetti asked, suddenly understanding and smiling at Vianello's reference. 'How helpful that would be: a god flies in, grabs up the problem, and takes it away into the skies with him.'

He gave the god time to fly out of the room before he returned to less fanciful solutions. 'Unless she helps us by talking to her son, there's not much we can do.'

'And so?' Vianello asked.

When Brunetti didn't answer, Vianello got to his feet. 'Let's have a coffee.'

The only interesting thing that happened during the rest of the day was a telephone call from one of Brunetti's informants, who told him that a visit should be made to the fish market – not the one at Rialto but the wholesale one at Tronchetto – the following morning. Brunetti thanked him and said he'd inform the local police and the food fraud branch of the Carabinieri.

'Tell them to look at the clams,' the man said in his usual cheerful manner. 'And perhaps check the tuna. It's travelling without a passport.' He gave a sanctimonious 'tsk tsk tsk' and hung up.

Brunetti had never met this man, although they had spoken on the phone for years. He had first called Brunetti's *telefonino* number six or seven years before, ignoring Brunetti's question of how he'd obtained the number and saying he had some information for him. His call led to the arrest of two men who had robbed a jewellery shop three days before. When he'd called some months later, Brunetti had tried, clothing his question in euphemism and discretion, to ask how he wanted to be paid, which question provoked a burst of laughter. 'I don't want anything,' the man had insisted. 'I just want the fun of doing it.'

Brunetti had demurred at asking what fun it could possibly be and decided to accept the information as the man intended it: a gift. The man called three or four times a year, always with accurate information that led to an arrest but, surprisingly, never about the same crime twice. Fake Parma ham coming in from Hungary; two tonnes of contraband cigarettes landed on a beach near Grado; the man who had stolen an X-ray machine from a dentist's office in Mirano; even the two Romanian con men who had cheated a series of old women into paying what they persuaded them were supplementary electricity bills. Brunetti knew nothing about his caller other than what he had inferred from the familiarity he showed with crime and criminals:

it suggested someone who had, in the past, taken part in crimes such as the ones he reported but who had, for reasons Brunetti could not imagine, turned against his former colleagues. This would explain the accuracy of the information in his calls as well as his complete lack of indignation about the crimes he reported. It might be a private vendetta – thieves falling out – or he could well be a criminal himself, interested only in limiting the competition. Even apart from the value of his calls, Brunetti had grown sufficiently fond of the man to feel concern for his safety and hoped he had given thought to the risk he was running.

After he passed on the informant's message about the fish market, Brunetti decided he had done enough for the day and could leave early. Without telling anyone, he turned right when he left the Questura, then left over the first bridge and away from the centre of the city, letting his feet decide where to take him. He worked his way out to the *bacino,* turned left and headed down farther into Castello, still with no idea of where he wanted to go.

He turned into Via Garibaldi, surprised to find so many people on the street. Had November become a tourist month while he wasn't paying attention? A hundred metres on, he calmed down at the realization that almost everyone around him was Venetian. He didn't need to hear them speaking dialect: their clothing and the unconscious ease with which they walked – not on the alert for something quaint to photograph or a tiny shop where they could find real local handicrafts – told him that they were. His pace slowed, and he went into a bar for a coffee, but changed it to a glass of white wine when he discovered a small bowl with pretzels on the counter. He glanced at the headlines on a copy of the *Gazzettino* and was puzzled by how familiar it all sounded until he glanced at the date and saw that it was yesterday's edition. He closed it, wondering how it was that every issue could contain at least eight pages with headlines that blared news of profound schisms and new formations that would completely change the face of national politics at the same time as nothing changed and nothing happened.

Brunetti fished a Euro out of his pocket and placed it on the bar. 'How is it that we haven't had an elected government for more than five years?' he asked. It wasn't really a question, merely an attempt to voice his perplexity.

The barman put the coin in the till and rang up a receipt for Brunetti. Placing it on the counter next to the empty glass, he said, 'So long as we have football on television, no one much cares if we elect a government or if some ancient politician appoints one.'

Brunetti, who had not been expecting an answer, stood still and considered the man's explanation. '*Ciò*,' he said, thinking that his agreement could best, perhaps only, be expressed in Veneziano. He left the bar and continued down Via Garibaldi and deeper into the rabbit warren of Castello.

He didn't get home until after seven, having walked as far as San Pietro in Castello, where he went in to light a candle for his mother's soul, being of a mind that doing it was probably as good for his own soul as was the glass of wine. The faint odour of cloves greeted him when he got home, luring him into the kitchen to see what Paola was up to. *Spezzatino di manzo* with exotic spices, it seemed, and if he knew anything about vegetables, *Cavolini di bruxelles alla besciamella*.

'If I promise to clean my plate, will you run off to Tahiti with me for a week of wild excess?' he asked as he put his arms around Paola and nuzzled at the back of her neck.

'If you promise to shave before you kiss my neck again, it's a deal,' she said, wriggling away from him and rubbing at his kiss with the palm of her right hand. 'Though I think there's small risk you won't clean your plate.' The smile she gave him as she said this removed any sting from her words.

Having the night before finished reading *The Oresteia* for the first time in twenty years, he went to Paola's study to consult the shelves that contained his books to decide what he would read next. He decided to stay with drama and bent closer to the bookshelves to study the titles. Still not free of the memory of his meeting with Professoressa Crosera and her terrible fear for her son, he was struck by how often the Greeks, too, worried about their children; most of the plays seemed to deal with the devastation children brought upon their parents. Or, he had to admit after a moment, parents upon their children.

He saw the plays of Euripides and recalled a production of *Medea* he'd seen in London, dragged there by Paola, what was it, twenty years ago, more? His eyes remained on the spines of the books, but his memory went to the final scene, she on an elevated platform above the stage, clinging to her two children. And then, instead of carrying them offstage to do the wicked deed, she drew a knife and stabbed and killed them both. Even at the memory of the scene, Brunetti winced and felt a stab to his own stomach.

During his career, Brunetti had watched as a man was murdered in cold blood, and he had seen other people die. The Greeks were right. They knew. We aren't meant to see such things happen: they were meant to horrify, not entertain. No, not *Medea.* He reached forward and pulled out the plays of Sophocles, instead.

Both children were home for dinner, and the sight of them confirmed Brunetti in his decision to avoid reading *Medea.* Without thinking, he reached across the table and put his hand on Raffi's arm. His son looked up, surprised. Brunetti fingered the cloth of Raffi's sweater and said, 'I don't remember seeing this before.'

'*Mamma* brought it back from Rome last winter. Do you like it?'

Brunetti took the opportunity this question offered him to remove his hand and shift back to get a better look at the sweater. 'It's very nice.' He looked across at Paola and said, 'Good choice,' then asked for more *spezzatino.*

I will not ask them about drugs. I will not ask them about drugs. Reciting this mantra, Brunetti ate his *spezzatino,* then asked for another piece. Chiara asked Raffi if he'd take a look at her physics homework and tell her if her answers made any sense. 'I don't understand why I have to study this,' she said. 'I'm never going to have to think about it again, once the class is over.'

'Isn't it supposed to train your mind by showing you the laws that govern the universe?' Brunetti asked.

'Did you take it in school?' Chiara asked him.

'Of course.'

'Did you learn ...' she began but then changed her question to: 'Do you remember anything?'

Unasked, Paola got to her feet and leaned over to spoon two pieces of cauliflower on to his plate, giving Brunetti time to organize an answer.

Deciding to tell the truth, he said, 'I remember some of the laws and that, at the time, I enjoyed being made to think in a different manner about phenomena I'd never understood. It made me look at the world in a new way. I think I found it comforting that there was order in what happened in the universe, even on the grandest scale. And rules.'

'If what our professor tells us is right,' Chiara began, 'then a lot of what you were taught has been – what's the word? – repealed – and I'm being taught new rules or laws of nature. What's to say that my children won't listen to their teachers repeal all the laws I'm being taught now?'

Raffi broke in to say, 'There are Big Rules, and they're not going to change. The universe isn't all some random system that does what it wants and that we'll never understand.'

'The rules also show that the gods can't interfere where they want and do what they want,' Paola added, no doubt happy to have been given the opportunity to take a gratuitous whack at religion in any form.

'But it's a year of my life,' Chiara whined, as though she were tied down and suffering the bastinado.

'Would you rather be taught how to knit and darn socks, the way I was?' Paola demanded, reducing the choices to two.

Brunetti summoned up the image of Paola darning a sock, attempted to stifle his reaction, but quickly lost control of himself and burst into a fit of giggles. He slapped his hand over his mouth, but that proved useless; if anything, the sight of her astonished glance made things worse for him, and he was forced to close his eyes and press his hand harder. All that did was squeeze tears from his eyes until he had to put his napkin to them.

No one at the table spoke; the kids kept their eyes on their plates while Paola studied the top of Brunetti's lowered head. He wiped his eyes and put his napkin back on his lap, then looked across at her.

'I'm tempted to send you to your room without dessert, Guido,' she said amiably, meeting his glance. 'I confess: I was never taught to darn socks, but that's because I refused to take the class in Home Management.' To ward off any accusation of dishonesty the children might launch, she went on, 'I invented the darning as an example of the sort of thing I was forced to do that wasted my time when I was at school. I hope you'll consider it the rhetorical flourish it was.' Her explanation apparently concluded, she gave a gracious wave of her hand to her children, who nodded. Paola smiled, and all the world was gay.

6

As if the departing tourists had decided to take crime with them, little of it was reported to the Questura during the next week. Brunetti called a friend at the Carabinieri to ask about the situation of drugs in the schools and was told that it was already under investigation by a special squad based in Treviso. His conscience salved, Brunetti sought no farther information. He spent some time reading through the files that had accumulated on his desk, five of them containing the CVs of people who were to rotate to the staff of the Questura in February. He found time to go to the firing range in Mestre to fulfil last year's obligation to practise shooting at least once a year. There, he was encouraged to try out new pistols, Signorina Elettra somehow having found sufficient funds to update and upgrade the pistols issued to commissari and higher ranks. After test-firing three of them, then his own service weapon, Brunetti decided that one of the new pistols was lighter and smaller and thus would be less of an encumbrance in those few times he remembered to carry it. The officer in charge was a tall, robust man probably serving his last few years before retirement. He told Brunetti that the pistol he preferred would be available either in May or perhaps not until the end of the summer.

Brunetti slid the pistol across the counter, slipped his own weapon into its holster and put it inside his briefcase. 'Should I call you?' he asked. He snapped his bag closed and prepared to leave.

'No, Commissario. I've been in touch with Signorina Elettra, and I'll call her when they arrive. You can come back then and try it out; see if you still prefer the new model.'

Brunetti thanked him. 'Well, I'll look forward to seeing to seeing you then.' The thought came to Brunetti, and he asked, 'What happens to our old guns?'

'You mean the ones we replace, sir?'

'Yes.'

'They're sent to a foundry and melted down.'

Brunetti nodded, pleased by the answer. 'Better than having them lying around somewhere.'

'Absolutely, sir. Guns are nothing but trouble.'

Brunetti put out his hand. 'I'll remember you told me that,' he said and smiled to suggest he was joking. Brunetti disliked guns, disliked having his, had felt uncomfortable the few times he carried it, and had never in all these years so much as pointed it at a person. It often spent weeks sequestered in a locked metal box at the back of the shelf where he kept his underwear. The bullets lived in a similar locked box, sharing a shelf with the cleaning products in the closet behind the kitchen.

*

Life continued peaceful and dull, until the phone woke Brunetti one night from profound, dreamless sleep. When he finally picked it up, it seemed to have been ringing for ever.

'*Sì?*' he asked, still dull with sleep but aware of what the call would have to be.

'Guido?' a woman's voice asked.

It took him a second to recognize Claudia Griffoni, his colleague and friend. 'Yes, Claudia, what is it?'

'I'm at the hospital,' she said. 'A man may have been attacked.'

'Where?' he asked. He got out of bed and went into the corridor; he reached inside to pull the door closed.

'Near San Stae.'

'Badly?'

'It looks that way.'

'What happened?'

'Someone called the hospital about an hour ago, saying he'd found a man lying at the bottom of a bridge. He thought he'd fallen: there was blood on the pavement.'

'But?' Brunetti asked. Why else would she call him?

'But when they got him here, the doctor at Pronto Soccorso found marks on the inside of his left wrist that might have been made by fingernails. As though someone had grabbed him.' Before Brunetti could ask, she said, 'He took samples. There was a lot of blood on the ground, where he'd hit his head. The doctor says he has a concussion: from the look of it; he says he must have hit the metal railing when he fell. He's trying to find out how bad the damage is.' She drew a breath. 'They called the Questura; I'm on call tonight.'

'Is the bridge sealed off?'

'Yes. Two *vigili urbani* were on patrol at Rialto, so they came: they'll see that no one gets near the bridge. The crime scene crew are on the way.'

'Witnesses?' he asked.

She made a noise.

'You want me there?'

'There or here,' she said.

'Tell me what bridge it is, and I'll go there first, then come to the hospital.'

'Wait a minute. I've got it written down.' He heard fumbling from the other end. 'Ponte del Forner,' she said. 'It's . . .'

'I know where it is,' he cut her short.

'Do you want me to send a boat?'

'Thanks, Claudia, but no. I can get there in fifteen minutes. It's faster.'

'All right. I'll see you here, then. After.'

Brunetti switched off the phone and pushed the bedroom door open. He set the phone back in its stand and walked over to the bed. The top half of Paola's blonde head on her pillow seemed to glow in the light cast by the full moon. He turned on his bedside lamp, saw that it was almost two, and went to the *armadio* and got dressed in front of it. He tossed his pyjamas on his side of the bed and sat to put on his shoes.

He turned off his light, gave his eyes a chance to adjust to the moonlight, then walked around the bed and put his hand on Paola's shoulder. 'Paola. Paola.'

Her breathing changed, and she turned her head sideways to face him. She made an inquisitive noise.

'I have to go out.'

She grunted.

'I'll call.'

She grunted again.

He thought of telling her he loved her, but it was not the sort of declaration he wanted to hear answered with a grunt.

In the hallway, he put on his coat and let himself out quietly.

The night was thick with *caigo*, that peculiar Venetian dampness that fills the lungs, obscures vision, and leaves a viscous, slippery coating on the pavement. He walked towards Rialto, half savouring the sense of being in an abandoned city wrapped in something more than haze but less than fog. He stopped and listened, but there were no footsteps to be heard. He moved off again, towards Campo Sant' Aponal. He was approaching the aftermath of violence and pain and injury, but he felt no distress, only the calm that came of being in his city as it once had been: a sleepy provincial town where very little happened, and the streets were often empty.

As Brunetti entered the *campo*, a man appeared and passed him by, eyes on the ground. In front of the church, he saw another man and a woman walking slowly hand in hand, their heads swivelling from side to side, enchanted. As they grew closer, he heard the thud of their hiking boots, and when they were abreast of him he saw their heavy backpacks. They were blind to him, as well they should be, he thought.

He traversed the *campo*, making his way towards San Cassiano. The near darkness obscured many reference points, but Brunetti had given things over to his feet and the memory they had of these narrow bridges and the even narrower *calli* towards which they led. He passed San Cassiano on his right, over the bridge, down, right, left, another bridge, and fifty metres ahead of him he saw the sudden glare in the fog of a torch pointed in his direction.

'You there, the bridge is closed,' a male voice said at normal volume. 'Go back to Calle della Regina.' He spoke Veneziano as if only a local would be walking in this part of the city at this time of night.

'It's me, Brunetti,' he said and kept walking.

'Ah, good morning, Commissario,' the man said, and the beam of his flashlight lifted for a moment as he raised his hand in salute. For no reason Brunetti could understand, the fog seemed less dense nearer to the bridge. The officer must have realized it, as well, for he turned off the flashlight and reattached it to his belt.

He was one of the *vigili urbani*, Brunetti noticed; not one of his own men. It was then that he heard the noise and the male voices from behind the officer. 'Is that the crime squad?' Brunetti asked.

'Yes, sir.' As the man spoke, the fog cleared on the other side of the bridge, and Brunetti saw the light blooming there.

He walked towards the bridge, the man falling into step beside him. He stopped at the first step and called out, 'This is Brunetti. Can I come up?'

'Yes, sir,' a voice called back, and Brunetti walked to the top of the bridge, noting the thick metal handrail. The *vigile* stayed behind and went back to the beginning of the *calle* to stop people from entering.

From the top, Brunetti saw two of the white-suited technicians following their neat patterns, checking the ground for anything that might have belonged to the victim or his presumed attacker. Ambrosio, one of Bocchese's men, tall and frighteningly thin, even in his puffy white overalls, came up the steps towards Brunetti. 'We're checking to see if anything else fell when he did.'

'The doctor told Griffoni it looked as if someone might have grabbed him and pulled him down the steps,' Brunetti said.

'Yes, sir,' Ambrosio said in the bland voice the tech people used when responding to their colleagues' suppositions. 'She called and told us. We're looking for signs of some other person or what might have happened.' Ambrosio waved down at the area where his colleagues were still at work.

'Any witnesses?' Brunetti asked.

Ambrosio shrugged. 'Since we got here, a couple of people have leaned out of their windows to see what we're doing, but when we ask them if they heard anything, no one has.'

Questioning possible witnesses was not the kind of work the crime squad was supposed to be doing and so he said, 'We'll send some men over tomorrow to go from door to door.' He knew both *Il Gazzettino* and *La Nuova Venezia* would report the incident, and he made a note to have someone call the editorial offices and ask them to insert a request that anyone who had heard or seen a disturbance near San Stae call the Questura. Such requests seldom elicited a response, but that was no reason not to try.

Brunetti called to the men at the bottom of the bridge. 'Can I come down?'

'Yes, sir. We've checked the area.'

'You find anything?' he asked as he started down the steps towards them.

'The usual stuff that's lying around on the street: cigarette butts, a boat ticket, sweet wrapper.'

'Don't forget the dog shit,' said the other as he rose and put his hands on his hips and leaned backwards, as though hoping this would straighten out his back. To Brunetti he added, 'That's the worst part of this job. There's not as much as there used to be, but there's still enough. More than enough.'

Choosing to ignore this, Brunetti asked Ambrosio, who had come to stand beside him, 'That where he hit his head?'

Ambrosio nodded and pointed to a place on the pavement at the bottom of the bridge, where Brunetti saw a wide red stain. 'We found blood on the railing, sir,' he said, indicating the place. 'Looks, to me at least, as if he hit his head there, then scraped it on the wall, and finally landed at the bottom and lay there, bleeding, until the guy saw him and called the hospital.' He accompanied this with a final gesture towards the landing at the bottom of the steps.

Brunetti saw a red smear on the railing and another on the inner wall of the bridge, arguing in favour of the technician's reconstruction.

'You still have much to do?' he asked the other two men.

The taller one, who had been searching at the bottom of the bridge, answered. 'No, sir, not now that we've picked up everything. We've already taken prints from the railing and samples from those three places, so all we have to do is pack and clean up.'

'Clean up how?' Brunetti, wishing he could have resisted the temptation to ask.

'We keep a bucket in the boat, sir. With a rope. We can use the water from the canal to wash away the blood.' He spoke as casually as if he were giving street directions. 'After that, we'll go back to the Questura. If you wait five minutes, we can give you a ride.'

'No, thanks,' Brunetti answered. 'I'm going to the hospital.'

'We can drop you there on the way. No trouble.'

It would be faster, Brunetti knew, just as he knew that in the Pronto Soccorso they had a coffee machine in their staffroom. Brunetti had arrived in the wake of so many emergencies that the staff had come to view him as one of themselves and so let him use it, no matter what time he showed up.

'Thanks,' Brunetti said and moved towards the police launch that was tied to the wall beside the bridge.

The boat got to the ambulance entrance of the hospital a bit after three, the time of bad news. Brunetti thanked the pilot and stepped on to the landing. He made his way to Pronto Soccorso, where eight people sat in chairs against the wall, waiting their turn. The man at the reception desk recognized Brunetti and waved him through.

Brunetti asked about the man who had been admitted with a head injury and was told that he was probably still in Radiologia: there was no bed available for him at the moment. Before Brunetti could ask, the man told him to go and make himself a coffee: he'd probably find his colleague there; she'd come in from Radiologia only a few minutes before.

From force of habit, Brunetti knocked on the door of the staffroom. He heard a chair scrape, feet approach, and then Griffoni opened the door and smiled at him. At three in the morning, drawn and tired; wearing no makeup, washed-out black jeans, brown shoes and falling-down socks, and a man's grey woollen sweater at least three sizes too big for her, she looked good enough for a photo shoot. 'I'm having a coffee,' she said in greeting, then added, 'and saving my life.' She walked back to the table and drank what was left in her cup, then took it over and set it in the sink. 'The machine's still on. Would you like one?'

Brunetti saw no reason why he couldn't make his own coffee and was about to say so when she added, 'I'm not being a subservient woman, Guido. You look more tired than I feel.'

'Then yes,' Brunetti said. 'Please.' He pulled out a chair and waited, silent, until she'd brought the coffee over to him, saying there was sugar in it already. 'Thanks, Claudia. I've been outside for a long time. Had no idea how cold it was.'

'And damp. Don't forget the damp,' she said, giving a very theatrical shiver, then pulling out a chair to sit opposite him. 'Did they find anything?' she asked.

'The usual junk on the ground,' he said and took a sip.

'Horrible, isn't it?' she said when she saw his expression. 'If someone served that in Napoli, he'd be shot.'

Brunetti finished the coffee and took the cup and saucer over to the sink. 'Tasted all right to me, but then, if I were an alcoholic, I'd probably drink aftershave lotion.'

'I think you just did,' she answered.

He smiled and leaned back against the sink. 'Tell me.'

'He's about fifty, and he's got a very bad concussion. The doctor isn't a neurologist, so he can't be more precise than that. He's got bruises and cuts on his head and face, probably from the fall, and the red marks I told you about on the inside of his wrist.' She took a few breaths and went on. 'Since I called you, the doctor's said that the major damage is to the side of his head.' She paused, looking for the right word. 'He said there's a sort of dent in his skull.'

Brunetti's eyes tightened at the word.

'He thinks it could have happened when his head hit the railing as he fell.'

'What's his name?' Brunetti asked, coming closer to the table.

'I don't know. He had a pair of house keys in his pocket, but no identification. And no coat.'

'He probably lives around there,' Brunetti said. 'Can I see him?' he asked.

She shook her head. 'The nurses told me not to go back before five. They're short-staffed as it is, and they don't want anyone on the ward who isn't a doctor or a patient.'

'Did you try to . . .?'

Even before he finished the question, she answered.

'I tried everything short of threats, but they mean it. The one I spoke to tried to be pleasant. It's the only time they have to enter patient information into the computer, and they really don't want anyone around.' Seeing that he was going to speak, Griffoni said, 'Trust me, Guido.' She looked at her watch and said, 'It's just a little more than an hour.' She tried to appear encouraging, but she sounded tired.

He accepted the delay in front of them, and with that, either his adrenalin or his spirit failed him and he was overcome with shaky exhaustion. He had been leaning forward, both hands propped on the back of one of the chairs at the table, but now he had to step around the chair and sit.

He propped his elbows on the table, leaned forward, and put his face in his hands, rubbing at his eyes. Suddenly he wanted nothing more than to wash his face and hands with hot water.

Griffoni got to her feet and said she was going to find a bathroom, but he didn't look at her; indeed, he didn't even open his eyes. He heard the door close and put his arms on the table, his head on his arms.

The next thing he knew, Claudia was saying his name, then he felt her hand on his shoulder. 'Guido, it's after five. We can go up now.'

Silent, tired, the energy of the coffee long since disappeared, he followed Griffoni up to the Radiology department. The nurse at the desk nodded to Griffoni as they came in. 'He's still unconscious.'

'Can we see him?' Griffoni asked.

The nurse looked at Brunetti, who said, 'I'm police, too.'

She nodded, and Griffoni walked past the desk and down the corridor. Towards the end, parked against the left side of the hallway, was a wheeled stretcher on which lay a blanket-covered form. Electrical wires sneaked out from under the blankets and slithered up a metal pole towards a fuse-box-looking thing at the top.

Griffoni pointed with her chin and walked to the side of the bed. Brunetti came up beside her and looked down at the man on the stretcher.

Lying there was the thick-haired man he had seen with Professoressa Crosera.

7

'What is it?' Griffoni asked.

'I know him,' Brunetti answered. 'His wife came to talk to me a week ago.'

'About what?'

'Her son. She's afraid the boy's taking drugs.'

'Is he?' Griffoni had kept her voice low, and as they began to talk about the son, she backed a few steps away from the man on the stretcher. Brunetti followed her.

'It could be. All she could tell me was that the boy was behaving strangely; letting his schoolwork go, not paying attention to what was said to him.'

Griffoni said, quite seriously, 'Only that?'

Brunetti shrugged. 'Pretty much,' he answered, thinking back to what Professoressa Crosera had said to him, and to his own unwillingness to act on it.

'What did you tell her?'

'I tried to explain that there wasn't much we could do. She wouldn't give me any concrete information; I wasn't even sure the behaviour she described was due to drugs.' In response to Griffoni's sceptical expression, he said, 'He's a fifteen-year-old boy and he's become moody and unresponsive.'

Griffoni nodded in understanding and agreement. 'It's strange, but most of the parents I've talked to want to be told it's impossible, that there's no chance their child could …' She finished with a flourish of her hand suggestive of all the things parents did not want to know about their children.

Brunetti glanced at the man; he lay on his back, head slightly tilted away, as though he wanted them to study the bandage that wrapped it in a drunken turban, on this side pulled down across his forehead and ear, on the other at least a hand's breadth above the ear. There was no telling what lay beneath the bandage, nor indeed under which part of it the wounds could be found: a cut sewn closed? A scrape disinfected and covered to keep it clean? A dent? There were rough places and scrapes on his face and a general puffiness around his eyes. He looked to be quietly asleep.

'Let me go and tell them who he is,' Brunetti said. He took out his notebook and paged through it until he found the word 'Albertini'. He glanced at his watch: it was 5.37, a time when a ringing phone presaged only pain. 'I'll call his wife,' he told Griffoni.

She moved to sit on a chair at the foot of the bed so as not to block passage down the corridor. Brunetti went back to the nurses' desk and spoke to the duty nurse. 'I think I know who he is.'

The nurse smiled and said, 'You police people work fast.'

Too tired to joke, Brunetti nodded, as if to acknowledge what she had said as a compliment. 'I've got his wife's number. I'll tell her he's here.' Seeing her confusion, he said, 'I know her, but I've never been introduced to him, so I don't know his name.'

He took out his *telefonino*, checked his notebook, and entered Professoressa Crosera's number. Nothing happened. Turning to the nurse, he said, 'There's no reception here,' and walked back to Griffoni to explain about the phone. 'Let's see if there's anyone at Rosa Salva. I'll call from the *campo*.'

As they emerged into Campo SS. Giovanni e Paolo, where the day was still not in evidence, Brunetti said, 'I wonder if this was because of his son.' His steps slowed as he crossed the *campo*, working out the possibilities and thinking of what he should have asked Professoressa Crosera. He stared up at the face of the statue of Colleoni and envied the man the determination and certainty carved into his features: *he* certainly would have had the truth out of her.

He pressed 'redial', but still there was no reception. With his left hand, he slapped on the glass door of Rosa Salva a few times before anyone came. Recognizing Brunetti, the barman opened the door to allow them to enter, closed and locked it after them.

Inside it was warm, the room rich with the sweetness of fresh-baked pastries. A young woman in a white baker's jacket and hat emerged from the room on the right with a tray of brioche, crossed behind the bar, and slipped the tray into place into the glass vitrine above the counter. Brunetti asked for two coffees.

Smelling the pastries, he gave thanks for coffee and brioche, for sugar and butter and apricot marmalade and a host of other things that were said to be bad for him. Years ago, Paola had scandalized him by saying she'd happily trade her right to vote for a washing machine; he realized he'd be tempted, at least this early in the day, to trade his for coffee and brioche. There was someone in the Old Testament who had traded his inheritance for a dish of something called 'pottage'. The passage had always troubled Brunetti, who surely would have read it with greater understanding if the trade had been for coffee and brioche.

Turning to Griffoni, he asked, pointing to the tray of pastries, 'If the Devil asked you to trade your soul for a coffee and one of those, would you do it?'

The coffees came, along with two brioche on a plate. Taking a napkin, she picked one up, sipped at her coffee, and took a bite. 'First I'd try to get him to settle for three Euros instead,' she said and took another bite, another sip. 'But if he refused, I'd probably agree.'

'Me, too,' Brunetti said and began to eat, happy that fate had sent him such a compatible colleague. When he finished his coffee, he told Griffoni he'd try again to make the call. She pulled out her wallet, placed a note on the counter, and asked for another coffee. Brunetti waved his thanks and went outside.

Feeling the first buzz from the sugar and the caffeine, Brunetti took his phone from his pocket and entered Professoressa Crosera's number. The phone rang once before it was answered by a woman who asked, voice tight with fear or anger, 'Tullio, is that you?'

'Professoressa Crosera?' Brunetti asked.

Wary now, she asked, 'Who is this?'

'Commissario Guido Brunetti, Signora,' he began. 'I'm calling from the hospital. Your husband is here.'

'My husband?' she asked.

'Yes,' he said, keeping his voice even. 'He's here, in Radiologia.'

'What happened?' she asked. When she said no more, Brunetti listened and heard her taking deep breaths.

'It appears he fell on a bridge and hit his head. That's why he's in Radiologia. They've taken some X-rays and are deciding what to do next.' Brunetti did not know if this was true or not, but it might calm her to believe that the hospital had things under control.

'How is he?'

'As I said, Signora, the doctors don't have a clear idea yet,' Brunetti explained, thinking it better not to mention what the admitting doctor had said.

'Have you spoken to him?' she surprised him by asking.

'No, Signora. He hasn't regained consciousness yet.'

Before he could continue, she said, 'I'm coming,' and she was gone. He immediately dialled Vianello's number.

When the Inspector answered, sounding fully awake, Brunetti explained, 'I'm at the hospital. The husband of that woman who came to me about her son last week – Crosera – fell down a bridge last night, perhaps with some help from another person. He's in Radiologia; I'll be here until the neurologist has a look at him.'

'What can I do?' Vianello said without asking for more information.

'Speak to *Il Gazzettino* and *La Nuova*. Tell them a man – no name – was found at the bottom of the steps – Ponte del Forner, over by Ca' Pesaro – and tell them to request that anyone who was in the area around midnight call us if they heard or saw anything.'

'What else?'

'When she gets in, ask Signorina Elettra to take a look at Crosera and her husband, if she can find his name.'

'Usual stuff?' Vianello asked.

'Yes. Any strange friends; any strange anything. Check the son – Alessandro – see if he's ever had any trouble with us.'

'How old is he?'

'Fifteen.'

'Then the information would be sealed because he's a minor.'

'Lorenzo,' Brunetti said in the tone of voice with which one would reproach a child, 'ask Signorina Elettra to do it.'

'Of course.'

Through the silent connection, he could all but hear Vianello putting all of this together. Finally the Inspector said, 'His wife tells you the son is taking drugs, then the father slips and falls on a bridge, and you want us to find out what we can about him and his wife?'

'You're forgetting the son, Lorenzo,' Brunetti said pleasantly.

'Of course. The son.'

'If he didn't slip and fall, then it's related to something he did. So for now, let's have a look.'

'I realize that, Guido,' Vianello said with a brusqueness that suggested he might not yet have had coffee. 'You've excluded a mugging?' he asked, but his heart wasn't in the question.

'What would a mugger do outside at midnight in November, Lorenzo?'

'All right, Guido. I'll take care of this and see you when you get to the Questura.'

'Thanks, Lorenzo.'

'What are you going to do?'

'Go back to Radiology and wait for his wife.'

'Right,' Vianello said and was gone.

The day was growing lighter, and it looked as though the fog had disappeared. Would they see the sun today, that bright, friendly disc that had been so long absent?

Griffoni had been waiting in the *campo* while he was speaking to Vianello. Standing still, she was facing the east. The increasing light coming from behind the Basilica illuminated her face. Brunetti, always a sucker for feminine beauty, liked what he saw, but he also saw the dark signs of tiredness beneath her eyes. 'What time did you go to bed?' he asked, as though it were the most normal question for him to ask.

'Midnight, I think,' she said and turned away from the growing light, thus wiping away the smudges he had seen.

'The call came at one?' he asked, relentless.

'About then. But I'm fine.'

'Why don't you go home for a couple of hours?' Giving her no chance to object he said, 'They'll need some time to check things.' When she still seemed unconvinced, he added, 'Besides, you probably won't be of much use to anyone.'

'In my current state, you mean?'

'If that's what led you to put on brown shoes with black trousers, yes.'

She looked at her feet, as though he'd told her that her shoes were on fire, and said, '*Oddio*, how did that happen?'

'Go home, Claudia,' he said seriously. 'I'll see you later.'

8

When he got to the hospital, Brunetti was told that no ward had yet been found with an empty bed for the injured man, who thus remained in the corridor. He asked a passing nurse if a doctor had been to see the patient yet, but none had. He sat on a chair at the end of the bed and folded his overcoat over his knees. Windows lined one wall of the corridor, allowing Brunetti to look across to the other wing of the ex-monastery. The top fronds of an enormous palm tree were visible on the far side of the courtyard and behind them the windows of a matching corridor. Did similar trouble, equal pain, fill that other place? Brunetti wondered. Did the people there look across and ask the same questions, trick themselves into believing their trouble would be less if it were worse on the other side? And how to measure trouble, how to measure pain?

He turned in the chair to take a quick look up and down the hall. He and the motionless man were the only people there. Brunetti got to his feet and walked to the side of the bed. The man lay still, his hands outside the covers, clear fluid slowly dripping into a needle stuck in the back of his right hand. Brunetti bent his knees and leaned closer to the man, bracing himself on the bed with one hand. Just below the left cuff of the hospital gown, Brunetti saw three small, moonlike indentations on the inside of his wrist. Because the bed was pressed against the wall, Brunetti was prevented from moving around it to see if there was a similar set of marks on his other wrist.

Brunetti went back to the chair and sat. He propped his feet on the low railing at the foot of the bed. He crossed his legs and studied the crucifix on the wall. Did people still think He could help them? Maybe being in the hospital refreshed their belief and made it possible again for them to think that He would. One gentleman to another, Brunetti asked the Man on the cross if He would be kind enough to help the man in the bed. He was lying there, perhaps troubled in spirit, helpless, wounded and hurt, apparently through no fault of his own. It occurred to Brunetti that much the same could be said of the Man he was asking to help; this would perhaps make Him more amenable to the request. As he considered that possibility, Brunetti became aware of a shape at the side of the bed. The woman's sudden presence forced him free of his reverie, and he stood and draped his coat over the railing at the bottom of the bed.

Professoressa Crosera didn't acknowledge him. She walked to the side of the bed, looked at the man, and stood as if paralysed. She raised a hand and touched her husband's upper arm, then removed it and bowed to kiss him on the forehead. The man lay still, unresponsive.

Hesitantly, she touched his cheek, his lips, then pulled her hand back and tightened it into a fist. The man's chest rose and fell, rose and fell, but the ambient noise covered any sound his breathing might have made.

Brunetti crossed his arms but said nothing. She glanced towards the motion and looked at him for no longer than it would take her eyes to photograph him, her face completely free of expression. She turned back to her husband and said, 'Tell me what happened.'

'Your husband was found earlier this morning at the foot of a bridge. He may have fallen, though the doctor who admitted him found marks on his body that suggest he may have been pushed down the bridge.'

'May have been?' she repeated.

'Yes, Signora.'

'You're not sure?'

'There were no witnesses that we know of,' Brunetti explained.

When she did not react, he carried the chair over to the side of the bed. 'Please, Signora,' he said. 'Take this.'

At first it seemed she didn't know what to do, but then she sank into the chair and kept sinking lower in it so quickly that Brunetti feared she would fall off on to the floor.

He acted instinctively, putting his hand on the front of her shoulder and pushing her back in the chair. Her eyes closed for a moment, and when she opened them her astonishment was raw, as though she'd fallen asleep on a bus and been awoken by the unsolicited attentions of a stranger.

'Are you all right, Signora?' Brunetti asked, stepping away from her. 'Should I call the nurse?'

She relaxed at the sincerity of his concern, closed her eyes again and shook her head minimally. 'No, no. I just need a moment.'

Hearing footsteps approaching, Brunetti turned, and a nurse he had not seen before walked past quickly, ignoring them both. She disappeared into a room at the end of the hall. Then, from behind him, he heard the clank of the arriving breakfast cart.

Brunetti stood motionless, waiting for the Professoressa to regain her composure. She was thinner than he remembered her being: he had felt only bone when he'd tried to prop her up. She looked at him, and he saw that, like Griffoni's, her face was drawn and tired, but hers looked as if it had grown that way over a longer period of time. She wore no lipstick and her lips looked so dry he wanted to offer her a glass of water.

She started to speak, gave a small cough, and tried again. 'What have the doctors done?' she asked, then turned her head in the direction of the cart as it slammed into the wall and set dishes and glasses rattling. The noise jolted her to her feet and she shot a quick glance to her husband, who had not moved.

'They took X-rays when he was brought in. But there was no neurologist on call last night. I don't know what they plan for today.'

'You said he fell,' she said.

'Yes. Ponte del Forner, over by …'

'I know where it is,' she said, then, voice growing harsh, she demanded. 'What's wrong with him?'

Brunetti stopped himself from looking at the supine man, silent as these two people discussed what had happened to him as if he were not there.

'I'm sorry, Professoressa, but I know only what the doctor told my colleague this morning, when he was admitted.'

After a long time, she said, 'Our apartment is near the bridge.'

'Is it?' Brunetti asked, seeing no reason to reveal that he had already begun to look into their lives. Instead, he asked, 'Did you know that your husband had gone out?'

She hesitated for some time before she answered this. 'No.'

'Did he seem troubled in any way?' Brunetti asked.

'Troubled?' she asked, as if responding to a word in a foreign language, but finally said 'No', and quickly added, 'Other than about our son.'

Brunetti nodded quite as if he believed her.

'You didn't hear the phone ring or anyone come to the house?' he asked, trying to sound as though he were reciting a list from memory and really had little interest in her answers.

'No. People don't come to your house at midnight, do they?' she asked, suggesting she found it a silly question.

Ignoring her reference to the time when the incident probably took place, Brunetti changed tactics and tone. 'Did you tell him you came to talk to me last week?'

She took even longer to answer this and finally said, 'Yes.' She looked at him, and he saw that her eyes were in fact darker than her hair, the pupil seeming of one colour with the iris.

'What did he say to that?'

'When I told him how little you could do, he told me I'd been wasting my time,' she said, though she seemed embarrassed to say it.

At that moment, the metal breakfast cart, pushed by two white-uniformed attendants, clacked towards them. Brunetti moved to the end of the bed and backed up against the wall. Professoressa Crosera – he realized he hadn't asked her for her husband's name – moved to stand against the wall at the head, both of them doing their best to avoid collision with the cart.

Brunetti waited to see whether the attendants would bang the cart into the wall to spite them for being there for so long while they were trying to work. Instead, they slowed their progress and stopped short of the bed; each slid a metal tray from the cart as quietly as they could and took them into the room on their right. They emerged and, excusing themselves to Professoressa Crosera, delivered breakfast to the next room, and so all the way down to the end of the hallway. When all the trays had been distributed, they pushed the empty cart against the wall and walked back past Brunetti and Professoressa Crosera and out into the waiting area, nodding to both of them as they passed.

Did they speculate, Brunetti asked himself, about the personal configurations clustered around the beds of the patients? Did they hear things said that should not be said, tones that should not be used when speaking to a sick person?

'When will a doctor come?' Professoressa Crosera asked Brunetti just as if she thought he'd know. She touched the corner of her husband's mouth. 'Can he have water?' she asked.

'I think that's taken care of,' Brunetti suggested, pointing to the drip of clear liquid that stood beside the bed, the needle taped to the back of her husband's hand.

Brunetti turned to the sound of footsteps approaching. The older of the two uniformed attendants approached them with a tray holding two plastic cups and two plastic-wrapped brioche. Since they were both still standing, the attendant set it on the chair at the foot of the bed, saying gently, 'You should have something to eat. It will help.'

That broke her: Professoressa Crosera gave a great heaving sob. She covered her mouth with her hand and walked to the far end of the corridor. Brunetti and the attendant could hear her sobs; both turned away to face the door to the waiting area. 'Thank you, Signora,' Brunetti said. 'You're very kind.'

She was a robust woman, stuffed into a uniform she seemed to be outgrowing. One loose strand of greying hair had slipped from under the transparent plastic-shower-cap thing; her hands were red and rough. She smiled. St Augustine was wrong, Brunetti realized: it was not necessary for grace to be arrived at by prayer; it was as natural and abundant as the sunlight.

'Thank you,' he said, smiling back at her.

'I'll be getting on with my work, then,' she said, speaking Veneziano. She left him and went back down the corridor. Brunetti picked up one of the coffees and went to stand in front of the window to drink it. He heard the woman's footsteps as she came back to the bed, heard the rough sound of the sugar envelope being opened. Down in the courtyard, a gardener stood with a hose in one hand, a cigarette in the other, letting water flow into the ground around the trunk of the palm tree.

Brunetti went to the chair and set his empty cup on the tray. The brioche was probably more chemical than flour, but still Brunetti ate it, refusing to let himself taste it. Luckily, the woman had also brought two cups of water, one of which he drank as soon as the brioche was gone.

'Would you like me to go and see if anything is happening?' Brunetti asked.

'Yes, please,' Professoressa Crosera said.

A different nurse was behind the desk now, a woman in her fifties, with very thick greying hair cut short. He showed her his warrant card to let her see his rank, though he had no idea if it would help. Apparently it did, because she looked at him after seeing it and asked, 'How can I help you, Commissario?'

'I'm here because of the man who was brought in this morning, with the head injury. Do you have any idea of when he'll be seen by a neurologist?'

She glanced at her watch. 'Dottor Stampini, the chief neurologist, is always in his office by seven, Signore. The injured man's X-rays are on his desk.' Then she said, in a professionally neutral voice, 'The night nurse told me she took them down to Dottor Stampini's office herself. Will that be all?' she asked.

'Thank you, Signora,' Brunetti answered. 'His wife is here. I'll go and tell her.'

Dottor Stampini arrived at the bedside about fifteen minutes later. He was a surprisingly youthful man with a shock of reddish-blond hair that he occasionally tossed back from above his eyes the way a horse tosses its mane. He shook hands with Professoressa Crosera and then with Brunetti, gave his name but made no attempt to discover who they were and asked them to move away from the bed while he examined his patient.

Brunetti moved a few metres down the corridor; she chose to stand at the nearest window and look out into the courtyard. Brunetti kept his eyes on the doctor.

Dottor Stampini took a small flashlight from the pocket of his white jacket and bent over the man on the bed. He raised the man's right eyelid, shone the light into it, and then did the same with the left. He then moved towards the bottom of the bed, folded back the covers and exposed both legs to the knees. He took a small metal hammer from the same pocket and tapped at the right knee, repeated the blow a number of times, then tried the left knee with the same lack of success.

He replaced the covers and took up the chart that hung from the bottom of the bed. He read the first and second page, then held an X-ray up to the light coming in from the window behind Brunetti. He put it back and wrote on the chart, replaced it, then picked it up again and added something. When he was finished, he came down towards them.

'Are you his wife, Signora?' the doctor asked as he reached them.

'Yes. What's wrong with him?'

'One moment,' the doctor said, turning to Brunetti. 'And you are?'

'Commissario Guido Brunetti. Polizia di Stato.'

The doctor made no attempt to hide his surprise. 'May I ask why you're here, Commissario?'

'My colleague told me that the doctor who admitted the patient to the hospital said he noticed marks on his wrist.'

The doctor turned and went back to the bed. Brunetti watched him examine, first the left wrist, then the right, careful not to disturb the needle in the back of the hand. Then he went to the foot of the bed and wrote on the chart for some time.

'What marks?' Professoressa Crosera asked Brunetti while they watched the doctor. 'What from?'

Brunetti thought she sounded frightened.

'I don't know, Signora. Do you have any idea?'

Her eyes widened at Brunetti's question. As the doctor approached, she shook her head but said nothing.

This time, Dottor Stampini addressed Professoressa Crosera, ignoring Brunetti. 'I've ordered a CAT scan. When I have the results, I'll have a clearer idea of what's going on.'

'Isn't there anything you can tell me, even without the scan?' she asked, managing to keep her voice calm.

The doctor shrugged and flipped his hair off his face again. 'Not really, Signora. I'm sorry, but nothing will be clear until I see the scan.'

'This morning?' she asked, this time failing to keep the fear from her voice.

'Some time today.'

'Thank you, Dottore,' Brunetti said, as if the doctor had been speaking to both of them, then asked, 'You saw them?'

Suddenly impatient, the doctor said, 'The skin is broken. It could be anything.' Brunetti nodded, and the doctor continued, 'If you have no more questions, I'll begin my rounds.'

'Thank you, Dottore,' Brunetti said. Then, as if he'd just thought of it, he said to Professoressa Crosera, 'I have to call the Questura. I'll do it from the waiting room. The connection here is bad.'

The doctor took this opportunity to leave and started down the corridor, Brunetti close behind him, his *telefonino* in his hand.

When they were almost at the stairway, Brunetti put the phone in his pocket and called to the man in front of him, 'Dottor Stampini?'

Stampini stopped and turned. With little patience, he asked, 'What is it?'

Putting on his most amiable voice, Brunetti said, 'I'd like to have a word with you, if you have time.'

Neither of them could ignore how close they were to the nurses at the desk, and so Stampini said, 'All right. We can use my office.'

It was the second on the left and looked much like the office of every other overworked doctor Brunetti had ever seen: books and folders on the desk, open drawers spilling out sample boxes of medicine, back issues of medical journals stacked on the radiators, a disorderly row of cups on the windowsill.

Stampini stopped just inside the door and again asked, 'What is it?'

With no hesitation, Brunetti said, 'His pupils don't dilate, and he's lost the reflexes in his knees. That suggests something serious, doesn't it?'

Stampini's response was similarly direct. 'Are you a doctor in your spare time, Commissario?'

'No, Dottore, I'm not and, believe me, I don't pretend to be. But I've seen a lot of injured people in my career – too many of them, I'm afraid – and the ones with these symptoms are often ...' He broke off and waited for the doctor to say something. When he did not, Brunetti concluded, 'I don't presume to tell you something you know far better and in far greater detail than I do, Dottore.'

Stampini considered Brunetti's conciliatory remark and asked, 'What is it you want to know?'

'If I proceed on the assumption that the marks on his wrist are signs of violence or some sort of attack, I have to organize a criminal investigation and try to find someone who might have seen him before it happened.'

'I see. I see,' the doctor said. Then, in a milder voice, he asked, 'What happened?'

'We aren't sure. He was found lying at the foot of a bridge. When he fell, he hit his head on the metal railing and on the pavement: there was blood in both places.'

'And the marks on his wrist?' Dottor Stampini asked.

'Like you, Dottore,' Brunetti answered with a small smile, 'I see injuries, and I try to draw conclusions. In this case, it could be simple: someone attacked him and pulled him off balance.'

'Was he robbed?' the doctor asked.

'He didn't have his wallet on him. He had the keys to his house in his pocket, and he wasn't wearing a coat; he lives not far from where he was found.'

'The chart says he was X-rayed at three this morning.'

Brunetti nodded. 'He was attacked some time around midnight.'

Stampini stuffed his hands into the pockets of his jacket and stared at the floor. He rocked back and forth on the balls of his feet for a while and then pulled his hands out and shoved his hair back from his forehead. Finally he said, 'He's not going to be able to tell you what happened. Not soon. And perhaps not ever.'

'The X-rays?' Brunetti asked.

Stampini nodded. 'There appears to be a great deal of haemorrhaging. The CAT scan will tell me more, but what I can see from the X-rays doesn't look good.'

'Good in what sense, Dottore? For his full mental recovery?' Brunetti asked. 'Or for his survival?'

Dottor Stampini's expression told Brunetti little. The doctor's right hand rose to his chin and he pushed at the skin of his cheek, as though trying to check whether he'd remembered to shave that morning.

The doctor lowered his hand and looked across at Brunetti. 'Both,' he said, but then he must have thought back over the tangled grammar of Brunetti's question, for he quickly changed it to, 'Neither.'

'I don't understand,' Brunetti admitted.

'Nothing looks good,' Dottor Stampini said, then, 'Don't tell his wife.'

'I don't have to, Dottore. She'll find out soon enough.'

9

Realizing that there was nothing else to say, Brunetti took a step back and prepared to leave the office. The younger man made a hesitant noise, then said, 'Of course, I could be wrong. There have been cases where the blood is reabsorbed and the patient recovers fully.'

Brunetti raised a hand and let it fall back. He could think of nothing at all to say and so left to return to Professoressa Crosera and her husband.

When Brunetti entered the corridor, he saw two male attendants, one at the head and the other at the foot of the injured man's bed, his wife standing nearby. Brunetti remained where he was and waited to see what would happen. The men began to roll the bed towards the door, past him, then out to the elevators. Brunetti and Professoressa Crosera followed them silently into the elevator. No one spoke while it descended.

On the second floor, the men rolled the stretcher into Neurologia. One of them gave some papers to the nurse at the desk, who glanced through them and said something to him, then pushed a button on the wall and the doors to a corridor pulled back, allowing the men to roll the stretcher inside. When Brunetti and Professoressa Crosera attempted to follow, the nurse held up a hand and said, 'You can't go in there.'

'I'm his wife.'

This failed to have any effect on the nurse, who repeated: 'You can't go in there.' Then, relenting a bit, she added, 'Not until they've got him settled in a bed.'

'Is there some place we can sit?' Brunetti asked, eager to get back to the Questura but unwilling to leave the woman until she had seen her husband settled.

He glanced at his watch with no idea what it would tell him. It could still be seven, though it might as easily have been noon: he had been there so long that the numbers no longer separated or marked events. It turned out to be only a little after nine.

'There's a waiting room on the other side of the elevators,' the nurse said and picked up her phone.

The usual red plastic chairs, forged together into lines of five, awaited them. Always this terrible reddish orange; Brunetti could not associate that colour with anything other than suffering.

He stood until Professoressa Crosera took a seat at the end of the row nearest to the door, then, leaving the seat empty where she had placed, not unintentionally, her bag, Brunetti took the next one. 'Could I ask you some questions, Professoressa?'

'You've already asked me some,' she said, eyes on the door.

'I know that, and I apologize for troubling you. But if the signs that your husband was attacked are confirmed, then a crime was committed, and it's my job to find the person responsible. The only way I can do that is to have a closer look at your husband's recent behaviour to learn if anything unusual happened to him or if anything he said or did might lead to the person who did this to him.'

She listened in silence.

'Were there any unexplained phone calls, subjects he seemed reluctant to discuss, people he didn't want to talk to, maybe because of the trouble with your son?'

In the face of her continuing silence, Brunetti went on, 'You said you were worried about your son; your husband must have been, as well.'

'Wouldn't you be?' she asked angrily.

'Any father would be, Signora,' Brunetti answered mildly and then added, 'And any mother.' He realized he had unconsciously stopped using her title and addressed her as he would any woman.

She turned away from him and pushed back in her chair, looking at the open doorway.

'As I told you, I have two children, both teenagers. I'm never free of worrying about them and what might happen to them.'

Not bothering to look at him, she asked, in a polite, social voice, 'Is this something they teach you in police school, Commissario? How to earn the trust of the people you're questioning?'

Her question insulted him, but it did not offend him; he couldn't, however, resist the luxury of laughter, which surprised her. 'No, Signora,' he said when he stopped. 'We were taught to try to bond with the men we questioned by talking about football. When I entered the police, no one thought we'd ever have to question a woman. I suspect our teachers believed they'd all be at home, taking care of the kids.' He straightened his face and said, 'I want to find the person who did this to their father, and I'm asking for your help.'

She turned back to him to ask, 'Even if what I say might endanger my son?'

'Your son is too young to be in any legal danger. The worst that could happen to him is that he'd be sent to speak to a social worker or psychologist, but only if the judge declared him sufficiently dependent on drugs to need professional help.'

She turned away again and studied the door. 'But what if what I told you put my son in greater danger?' she asked.

Brunetti examined her words. 'Greater danger.' Greater than the danger his father had been put in? Greater danger than he was in now, presumably because the dealer had somehow found out that his mother had gone to the police? Had her husband decided to confront him, and was it the dealer who had met him on the bridge?

'Are you afraid of the person who's selling him the drugs?' Brunetti asked.

She turned to face him. 'Only if the police fail to do anything about him, Commissario.' Before Brunetti could protest that she was exaggerating, she went on. 'No matter what you do, the dealers will be free to do what they want.'

'Did your husband speak to Sandro?' Brunetti asked, unwilling to discuss what the police could and could not do.

His question surprised her, and he watched as she tried to think of how to answer it.

'I can't tell you that,' she finally answered, and again Brunetti was left with two ways to interpret what she said.

'Nothing we do to the dealer will put your son in jeopardy,' Brunetti insisted.

'If he attacked my husband, and you arrest him the day after?'

'Not if he's arrested for selling drugs. I'm sure your son isn't the only person he sells them to.'

She laced her fingers together. 'I need time to think,' she said, 'I have to ask my husband.'

Brunetti kept his face neutral and said only, 'He might not remember what happened.' That was certainly true of head injuries, Brunetti knew.

'No,' she said in a voice grown solid with decision. 'I want to ask him.'

Brunetti recognized that it was futile to insist, just as it was futile for her to think of asking her husband anything. He got to his feet and said, not without embarrassment, 'I'm sorry, but I don't know your husband's name.'

She looked at him, startled, then cast a look of such yearning tenderness towards the ward where her husband had been taken that Brunetti turned his eyes away from her face.

'How strange,' she said slowly; Brunetti returned his attention to her.

'Excuse me?' he asked. 'I'm afraid I don't understand.'

She smiled her first real smile: it wiped years from her face. 'It's usually the woman who is the nameless appendage to her husband.' Her face suddenly tightened, and she drew her lips together; Brunetti feared she would begin to cry again.

Instead, she took a breath and said, 'Tullio Gasparini.'

He thanked her and left, wondering, as he often did, if he would ever understand the secrets of the heart.

10

On his way to the Questura, Brunetti thought the first thing they had to do was find the man who was selling drugs to the students of the Albertini, Sandro Gasparini among them. For the moment, he was the most likely suspect in the attack. The simplest way to find him was to talk to the boy, but that would require the consent of the mother, who would surely insist that a lawyer be present. If she absolutely refused, they could have the boy followed, but where would he find the manpower for that? Or a magistrate to authorize it?

Why would a man be out on the street around midnight, coatless, with only his keys? Could he have left his home with no one noticing? Brunetti stopped in his tracks: where had the boy been last night and this morning? He thought back over his conversation with Professoressa Crosera and could not remember asking her that. She had been at home when Brunetti called: if her son had been missing, surely that would have been the first thing she'd ask any policeman. When she went to the hospital before dawn, would she leave her home without explaining to the children where she was going? Had they both been there to tell?

He pulled out the new phone Signorina Elettra had procured for him, went online not without difficulty and found the number of the Albertini, and keyed it in. The phone rang four times before a woman answered. 'Good morning. This is the Albertini School. How may I help you?'

'Good morning, Signora. This is Commissario Guido Brunetti. I'm calling about one of your students.'

After some moments, she asked, 'Commissario of Police?' as if other kinds of commissari were in the habit of phoning.

'Yes. May I speak to the Director?

This silence was longer, the result either of confusion or of reluctance. 'One moment, please,' she finally said. 'I'll pass you to Signora Direttrice Rallo.'

The Director answered on the second ring. 'Bianca Rallo,' she said.

'Signora Direttrice,' Brunetti began, 'this is Commissario Guido Brunetti. I've called to ask about one of your students.'

'I don't mean to be impertinent,' she began in a well-educated voice, 'but what assurance can you give me that you are who you say you are?' She was distant, polite, almost ironic.

'Signora Direttrice,' Brunetti answered with equal politeness, 'May I suggest a way around your doubts? If I might?'

'By all means.'

'Allow me to ask my question, and then call the Questura and ask to speak to Commissario Griffoni. You can give the answer to her.' He allowed her to digest this, then added, 'I'll need a few minutes to call them and tell them to put you through to her immediately.' After a shorter pause he asked, 'Would this be acceptable, Signora Direttrice?'

'It depends on what your question is,' she answered in a pleasant voice.

'We believe the father of two of your students, Tullio Gasparini, may have been attacked on the street last night. I'd like to know if Sandro came to school this morning.'

'That's all?'

'Yes.'

Her silence drifted out from the *telefonino*. Brunetti looked at the water in the canal beside him and saw how high it was.

'All right,' she answered. 'I'll call them in five minutes.'

Wasting no time, Brunetti ended their call, dialled the central number of the Questura, and asked if Griffoni had come in yet. When he heard that she had, he told the operator that there'd soon be a call for her from a Signora Rallo. The operator was to phone Commissario Griffoni immediately and tell her to expect the call.

He put his phone back in his pocket and continued towards the Questura. When he got there ten minutes later, he asked for Vianello but was told that the Inspector had come in but had been sent to Marghera to sit in on the questioning of a suspect in a case of domestic violence and wasn't expected to be back that day. Brunetti went to Griffoni's office. He noticed that she now wore a black skirt and jacket and had changed the telltale brown shoes.

'What happened?' she asked when he came in.

Rather than answer her question, Brunetti asked his own. 'Did she call?'

'Who?'

'The *preside* of the Albertini, to tell you whether the son was at school today.'

'No.'

When all Brunetti did was nod, Griffoni stood to reach over her desk to pull the second chair closer. 'Sit down, for heaven's sake, Guido, and tell me what happened.'

Brunetti obeyed and told her about his conversation with Professoressa Crosera and what had happened in the hospital after Griffoni left. Her office was so small that their knees were close to touching under her desk, even though he was half sitting in the doorway. 'She was stunned by it. She collapsed when she saw him.'

'Real collapse or false collapse?' she asked.

'Real, I think.'

'Did she know he had gone out?'

'She said she didn't, but I don't believe her.'

Griffoni, no stranger to lies, merely nodded. 'What about the son? Was he there when you called her?'

'I don't know.' With some embarrassment, Brunetti added, 'I didn't think to ask her.'

Griffoni smiled. 'Hence the phone call from the *preside*.' After a brief pause she added, 'Good for her. You could have been anyone. A kidnapper.'

'Claudia,' Brunetti said, reaching across to tap the back of her hand with his index finger. 'We are in Venice. We are not in ...' His voice trailed off. He thought for a moment and said, 'Imagine that. I can't name a city where there's been a kidnapping in the last few years.'

She looked at him and quickly looked away. After time for reflection she said, her surprise audible, 'I can't, either. It's as if it's gone out of fashion.'

Brunetti had reservations about that. 'It's more likely that people don't report it any more. Just pay and hope it works.'

'But we'd hear, wouldn't we, sooner or later?' she asked.

'I suppose so,' Brunetti admitted and, taken aback by his own savagery, added, 'I hate it. More than any other crime. And I hate them.'

'More than murderers?' she asked.

'In a way.'

'Why?'

'Because it replaces life with money or because they trade life for money.' He failed to control the severity of his voice.

'I've never heard you like this,' she said.

'I know. It's worse than anything. I'd put them all in jail for ever: the kidnappers. Anyone who helped them, too. If they knew what they were going to do, and still helped them; even if it was only to give them a postage stamp so they could mail the ransom note, I'd put them in jail for the rest of their lives.' By an act of great force of will, Brunetti stopped himself from saying more.

'You worked on a case?' Griffoni asked.

'Yes, one of my first, more than twenty years ago.'

'Bad?'

'They took the daughter of a family from Naples.'

'Where did it happen?'

'Sardinia. It was when I was stationed in Naples: three of us were sent.'

'Did you find them?'

'Yes,' Brunetti said gruffly.

'How?'

Brunetti waved this away with one hand. 'They were stupid.'

'But?' she asked in response to something unspoken.

'But the girl died.'

'Did they kill her before they got the ransom?'

'I sometimes wish they had,' he answered. Griffoni did not prod him, but Brunetti still explained. 'They buried her in a box. When the police arrested them – there were four of them – they told them where the box was. But by the time they dug it up, she was dead.'

Griffoni said nothing.

'Can we talk about something else, Claudia?'

Before she could answer, her phone rang.

'Griffoni,' she said. She raised a hand to Brunetti, nodding as she did. 'Yes, he told me, Signora.' Then, after a pause, 'No, we're more or less equal, only he's been here longer than I have. Yes, he is, originally from Castello, I think.'

She looked at Brunetti, put her head back and closed her eyes, using her right hand to make rolling waves in the air as she listened. 'Yes, he's told me about the incident. He was in the hospital with the man this morning.'

Griffoni covered her eyes with one hand, something she did when impatient. 'Of course, I understand, Signora Direttrice.' Then Griffoni was silent for a long time. She moved her hand to the top of her head without opening her eyes, as if she wanted to keep the lid on, and continued to listen, letting loose an occasional murmur of agreement.

Finally she removed her hand, saying, 'He's there?' She opened her eyes and glanced at Brunetti, let out a neutral 'Hummmm', and said, 'Thank you, Signora Direttrice.' Then, slipping into that particular descending cadence used to end a conversation, she said, 'I'm sure my colleague will be very grateful to learn this.'

A few more polite noises, and then she hung up the phone. 'As you heard, he's there. The school policy is to contact the parents immediately if a student fails to arrive for classes.' In a different, more curious, voice, she said, 'What do you know about the boy?'

'Only what I've told you: fifteen, second year of *liceo*. Troubled, not doing well in school.'

'And using drugs,' Griffoni supplied.

'His mother was convinced enough to come and see me.'

Griffoni, whose office did not have a window, went and stood with her back against the wall, arms folded. 'Do you think the attack was the result?' she asked, and Brunetti realized he was relieved that she did not question that it had been an attack.

'The two things are related in time,' Brunetti said. 'What I want to do is find something that leads from one to the other.'

Griffoni, following the path between the two events, said, 'If Gasparini already knew who the dealer was but didn't want to involve us, he could have approached him or threatened him somehow ...'

Brunetti nodded: he'd already been down that path.

'We know who some of the dealers are, the ones at the schools,' he said. 'I know the names of at least two.'

Griffoni nodded to show that she perhaps knew other names.

'One of them owes me a favour,' Brunetti began. 'It's time to call it in now.'

Griffoni remained as she was, giving no sign of impatience or curiosity. She looked across at Brunetti as if it were quite normal for a man to sit in a chair in the middle of her doorway, its two back legs in the hallway, while she stood with her back against the wall and looked at him.

Brunetti heard someone walk by in the corridor behind him but did not turn around. When the footsteps disappeared, he finally said, 'I'll ask him who's in charge at the

Albertini.' He was struck by how casual he had made it sound, as if a dealer had a licence to sell drugs to the students at the school.

'Will he tell you?' Griffoni asked.

Brunetti nodded. 'A long time ago, my brother wrote a letter of recommendation for his son, who was applying for medical school in England.'

'Medical school?' she asked.

'Radiology. My brother's chief technician at the hospital in Mestre. The boy worked with him for two years: he said he was the best assistant he ever had. Why shouldn't he write him a reference?'

'Indeed,' Griffoni agreed. 'What happened?'

'He's Assistant Chief Radiologist in a hospital in Birmingham.'

'And the father pushes drugs?' Griffoni asked in bewilderment.

'And the father pushes drugs.'

'Evviva l'Italia,' Griffoni said.

11

They remained like that, in easy companionship, for a while until Brunetti got to his feet and moved the chair back to its usual place against the wall, where, instead of blocking the door, it now blocked any attempt Griffoni might make to reach her desk from the right.

He paused at the door, but before he could speak, Griffoni asked, 'And when your informant gives you his name?'

'I'll have a word with him.'

'When you do, would you like me to come along?' she asked.

He had thought of taking Vianello. Griffoni was certainly very good at playing the role of good cop: she could suggest with a glance that she disagreed with Brunetti, could ask him a question in such a way as to show solidarity with the person who was being questioned, and could, upon occasion, oppose Brunetti's decisions or conclusions in such a way as to show the suspect that she was completely persuaded by the story he or she was telling. But she was a woman, and a man who dealt drugs would better be visited by a man.

'Thanks for offering, Claudia,' he said. 'It's always a joy to work with a person as cold-blooded as you can be, but in these circumstances, I think it would be better if I went alone.'

She smiled. 'To be called cold-blooded is a compliment any woman would be pleased to have, Guido.'

He went back to his own office, again amazed that she tolerated the shoebox which Lieutenant Scarpa had somehow persuaded Vice-Questore Patta to assign her. In Patta's defence, Brunetti imagined only that the Vice-Questore had never considered it sufficiently important to climb the steps to take a look at her office and thus had no idea what six square metres looked like or what remained after a desk and two chairs were placed into that space. He had no doubt that Griffoni would somehow make the Lieutenant regret his actions. She was Neapolitan, so it would happen. It would take some time, but it would happen. Brunetti smiled at the thought.

He closed the door when he entered his office and took out his *telefonino*. From memory – he had never written it down – he dialled the number of his dealer friend, who answered with his name.

'Good morning, Manrico,' Brunetti said with the affection he could not help feeling for this man; at least for part of him. He was reluctant to let that part of him dominate the conversation, so he kept his voice cool and asked, pointedly, 'How's Bruno?'

'Ah, Dottore,' Manrico said, recognizing the voice after all this time. 'Tragedy has struck my family.' The words wept, but the tone of voice chirped.

'I hope it's a happy tragedy,' Brunetti replied.

'The happiest. Bruno's getting married. In July.'

'And the girl's father's a policeman?' Brunetti asked.

'Oh, far worse than that,' Manrico answered in sombre tones.

'Tell me.'

'She's Scottish.'

'No,' Brunetti allowed himself to gasp. 'And Protestant?'

'Oh, that doesn't matter any more, Commissario. But there's more.'

'What?'

'She's a doctor.'

'Your son's marrying a professional woman who's Scottish?' Brunetti made a long, deep humming noise. 'I can understand your pain, Manrico.'

'Thank you, Dottore; I knew you would.' Then, as if to prove that he was not really a clown, Manrico said, 'Since you began by mentioning Bruno, I suppose you want to remind me that I owe you a favour.'

'I've never done it before, Manrico,' Brunetti said, as though he felt obliged to defend his reputation. 'Not in six years.'

'Seven. What is it?'

'I'd like to know who's in charge of the Albertini.'

'I assume you're not speaking of the *preside*.' Manrico's voice had lost all sense of fun or raillery.

'No, I'm not,' Brunetti answered.

Silence. Brunetti clutched his phone tighter and commanded himself not to speak. He walked to the window and looked down at the dock, where Foa stood, wiping the railings of the police launch.

'This your official phone?' Manrico asked.

'Yes.'

'Then I'm afraid you'll have to wait until you get home tonight,' the dealer said in such a serious voice that Brunetti was prepared for him to hang up without explaining.

But then Manrico's usual cheerfulness returned and he said, 'One more thing, Commissario.'

'Yes?'

'The wedding's the fifteenth. If I send you an invitation, will you come?' Even his long pause sounded happy.

'Will it be here?' Brunetti asked, hoping the answer would be no because then he could legitimately refuse.

'No. It's at her father's church.'

'Does that mean what I think it does, Manrico? That things are really that bad?'

'That's right, Commissario; only it's worse. Her father's a bishop.'

Brunetti congratulated Manrico again, wished him many grandchildren, and hung up. He couldn't wait to tell Griffoni. But first he went to see Signorina Elettra and found her standing at the window. After Griffoni's tiny cubicle, Signorina Elettra's office seemed enormous, especially because of the three windows on one wall. Much of the room was taken up by her desk, on which stood a computer, and a table, which he had never known to hold anything save a large bouquet of flowers, as was the case today, and the current copy of *Vogue*, also there.

She turned towards him when he came in. What light the day was willing to offer came from behind her, so he could not see her expression, but her posture – what he sometimes thought of as her aura – seemed tired and heavy-burdened. '*Bon dì*,' Brunetti said. 'I came down to see if you've had time to take a look at Gasparini.'

With a brief nod, Signorina Elettra returned to her desk. She sat and hit a few keys, summoned up a page and glanced at it, saying, 'There isn't very much about him. He's an auditor for a chemical company; works in Verona. His residence is listed in Santa Croce, near San Stae; name and number are in the phone book. His name doesn't appear in any police record in the Veneto, and I can't find any trace of him on social media.' She looked at Brunetti and added, 'It's strange the way a person seems non-existent if he's not on any social media, isn't it?'

Brunetti, who was not on any of them, just as Paola was not, answered, 'I suppose so.'

'There was no mention of a wife,' she confessed.

'Professoressa Crosera. I don't know her first name,' Brunetti said automatically. 'She teaches architecture at the university and is a consultant in urban design – whatever that is – in Turkey and somewhere else.'

Her eyes widened, as though she had to see more of him in order to believe that he could manage to find something she had failed to find. 'How did you learn that?'

'I asked her,' Brunetti said laconically, then smiled and inquired, 'Is that cheating?'

'Probably not,' Signorina Elettra had the honesty to answer. 'It's just that it seems such an old-fashioned way to get information.'

'But you checked the phone book for "Gasparini", didn't you?' Brunetti countered.

'Yes,' she admitted. 'Online, though.'

Disappointment made him ask, 'That's all you found?'

'That's all I found for the moment.'

'If you have time, could you take a look at the wife, as well?' he asked, trying to make it sound as though there were some sense in doing it. Changing his tone, he said,

'I asked Vianello to call the papers and ask them to put the usual appeal for witnesses in their stories. It might have some effect.'

Her right hand was halfway to the keyboard of her computer, but she paused and waved it vaguely in the air, then said, 'You know people don't like to get involved with us.' For a moment she looked beyond him, as though checking something written on the wall, and added, 'Not just us: the state in any way.' She went on, her voice tentative, as though she had to speak this through before she'd understand what it was she wanted to say, 'The contract's been broken, between us and the state, or been dissolved, but no one wants to make the news public. We know there's no contract any more, and they know we know. They don't care what we want or have any real interest in what happens to us or in what we want.' She turned to him and shrugged, then smiled. 'And there's nothing we can do.'

Brunetti was astonished to hear spoken what he had so often thought himself. Without pausing to think, he said, 'It can't be as bad as that.'

She turned away from him and looked at the screen, as though she'd lost interest in what he had to say or didn't agree with him but didn't think it worth the trouble to talk about it. He went back to his office, musing on the fact that both he and Signorina Elettra worked for this unresponsive, negligent state.

Because he'd been awake since two, Brunetti decided to treat himself well and walked down to Al Covo for lunch. On the way back, he gave thanks, as he always did, that the restaurant was only ten minutes from the Questura and never failed to send him back a new and happier man.

Unfortunately, this new man was confronted with old problems: he called Professoressa Crosera's *telefonino* but was told to leave a message; he called the hospital and received no information about Gasparini. He called Gasparini's home number every hour, but the phone rang unanswered. Finally, at about five, he decided he had no choice but to pass by the hospital on his way home, and called Griffoni to tell her where he was going.

He might as well have saved himself the effort: Professoressa Crosera was in her husband's room, but when he went in and said good evening, she held her finger to her lips and pointed to her husband, lying now in a proper hospital bed. Brunetti indicated the door and the corridor beyond, but she shook her head and did not speak. Brunetti knew there was no likelihood that their conversation would disturb her husband, but it was not his right to tell her that.

He stepped up to the bed and looked at Gasparini. The pale liquid still dripped into the back of his hand.

Brunetti nodded to the woman and went out to the nurses' desk and asked for Dottor Stampini, hoping that the doctor had learned something from the CAT scan. They told him the doctor had already left. Choosing to believe this, Brunetti decided to go home, too.

12

He entered a silent apartment, but years of experience told him it was not empty. The scent of pine forests filled the hallway, which meant that Raffi had used Brunetti's shampoo again, and in the living room, Chiara's red wool scarf trailed down the back of the sofa. Guido Brunetti, super-detective, he complimented himself as he went down the hall to Paola's study.

He stuck his head inside the door and found her lolling in complete abandon on the sofa, a book propped on her chest, a pencil in one hand.

'Hard at work, I see,' he said, coming into the room. He walked over and bent to kiss her forehead.

'Just like you: so busy you couldn't call and tell me about the man who was found,' she said in fake umbrage.

He sat at the other end of the sofa and pulled her feet on to his lap. 'How did you find out about that?'

'I wondered why you'd left so early, so I looked at *Il Gazzettino* online and found the story this afternoon.' She let the book fall open on her chest. 'That could mean only one thing.' Her tone lightened as she went on. 'I also wondered if you'd take time for lunch and whether you were dressed warmly enough – those silly things wives think about.'

He took her left foot and began to push her toes back and forth. 'I didn't want to wake you.'

She smiled and admitted, 'It's not easy, I know.' She closed the book and leaned aside to place it on the table. 'Tell me,' she said.

'Remember I told you about the woman who came to talk to me a week ago, afraid that her son was using drugs?' He had not told her who it was, only the inconclusive story of a woman who lacked the courage to trust the police and left without giving any detailed information.

She nodded.

'It was a colleague of yours: Professoressa Crosera. The man in the hospital is her husband. It looks as though he was attacked on the street.'

Paola pulled her foot free from him and sat up in the sofa, facing him, legs pulled beneath her. 'Elisa's husband? I can't believe it. He's an accountant, for God's sake.'

She paused for a moment as if suddenly conscious of what she'd just said, and added, 'I mean, he's such an ordinary man: no one would want to harm him.'

A reason could always be found to want to harm some other person, Brunetti knew. 'There are signs that someone grabbed his arm and shoved him down the steps of the bridge. What did *Il Gazzettino* say?'

'Only that a man was found unconscious on the street,' Paola answered. 'There was no mention of an attack, only that people were asked to call the police if they saw anything that might be related to the incident, which they said took place near Ca' Pesaro. They didn't even give his initials, the way they do when they don't want to provide a name.'

Brunetti did not understand the ways of *Il Gazzettino* and thus remained silent.

'Is Elisa with him?' Paola asked.

'Yes. I recognized him and called her this morning. She's still there, I think.'

'Ah, the poor woman,' Paola said. 'First the son, and now this.'

'Did you know about the son?' Brunetti asked, careful to keep his voice neutral.

Paola looked at him sharply. 'Of course not. She'd never tell me something like that. I simply assumed it because she was worried enough to go and talk to you. That means she knew something.'

'But she said she didn't,' Brunetti insisted.

'Of course she'd deny it. You're the police.' Paola might as well have been reading the multiplication table, so certain was she of her conclusion.

Brunetti decided to leave that remark alone and said, instead, 'She said she wanted to talk to her husband before telling me anything else.'

'When will she be able to?' Paola asked.

Brunetti looked at the back of his hands, then at her, wondering how to tell her. 'Maybe never,' he finally said. When he saw Paola's reaction to this, he temporized. 'That's what the neurologist said after he'd seen the X-rays. He said he needed a CAT scan to be certain. They did that today.'

'The results?' she asked.

'I don't know. When I went back to the hospital, the doctor had already left. I can call him tomorrow.' He allowed her to assimilate this, then added, 'He said there was a chance he might be wrong.'

Paola nodded. She turned and put her head back on the pillow, extended her legs and prodded at his thigh with her feet. 'Poor woman,' she said again. Then, after some time, 'Poor everyone.'

She closed her eyes, opened them for a time to study the ceiling, and then closed them again. Brunetti rested his right hand, quiet, on her feet and closed his own eyes. Soon he felt his reality begin to loosen and drift off from him. He remained seated, but he was somewhere else, and there were people passing by. He felt something move in his hand and he jerked up, suddenly awake but uncertain where he was.

'What's wrong?' Paola asked.

'Nothing. I must have fallen asleep. It's been a long day.' He closed his eyes and leaned his head against the back of the sofa.

'I've been thinking,' Paola said.

Brunetti was awake enough to say, 'Always dangerous.'

Together, their voices finished this family mantra … 'especially in a woman.'

That done, he asked, 'Thinking what?'

'Legal things. But you've probably already thought about them.'

'Tell me,' Brunetti said, aware that he had not given much legal thought to Gasparini's situation.

'If he doesn't die, but just lies there for the rest of his life, what can the attacker ever be charged with?' Before Brunetti could begin to answer, she added, 'I know, I know, you have to find him first. But when you do, what crime has he committed?'

Brunetti gave this some thought, testing the idea of assault. 'That will depend on what happened on the bridge.'

'And in the absence of witnesses, how will *that* be decided?' He heard scepticism in her voice.

Eyes still closed, Brunetti nodded. 'You're right, of course. If we get a match for the DNA, that person could very well say he was attacked by Gasparini.' He considered this and then added, 'We have to find him first.'

'He'd have to explain why he didn't report it to the police,' Paola added. 'If he knew Gasparini was injured, he'd have to report it, wouldn't he?'

'Yes, but some people probably wouldn't. At least if it's a minor thing, even if they're the victim. Imagine someone coming to us after attacking another person, even in self-defence: the idea's ridiculous.' He thought about this, then said, voice rich in the surprise with which one announces a discovery, 'No one trusts us.'

'Then you must place your hopes in *Il Gazzettino* and *La Nuova*,' Paola said, forcing a note of religious piety into her voice.

The thought of it drove Brunetti to ask, 'Would you like a glass of wine?'

With the wine, Brunetti brought his copy of Sophocles, decided on *Antigone*, and settled in at Paola's feet to read the time away until dinner. He read half of the Introduction, written by a professor of psychology at the University of Cagliari. In it, the author presented a Jungian interpretation of the play, with Antigone as an archetype of the Mother and Creon of the Trickster. One's darker side, The Shadow, Brunetti learned, could be exterior or interior: it could be your enemy or it could be yourself. Brunetti cheated and looked to see how many more pages of the Introduction remained to him. Fourteen. He set the book face-down on the table in front of the sofa and took a sip of wine – a very nice Collavini Ribolla Gialla he'd been saving for a special book – and sighed at the different sensations life could offer.

Fortified, he picked up the book and flipped past the rest of the Introduction and began reading the play. He recalled the opening scene, Antigone explaining to her sister Ismene that the King, Creon, had forbidden that funeral rites be performed for their brother, Polyneices, whom Creon had declared a traitor to Thebes. His putrefying body lies outside the city walls, subject to the appetites of vultures and jackals.

Antigone has decided that he must be buried, and that she will do it. She asks her sister if she will help her, and Ismene – poor, cautious Ismene – will have none of it. 'The law is strong. We must submit to the law in this, and even in things that are worse.'

'I don't think so,' Brunetti said aloud.

Paola prodded his thigh with her left foot. 'What?'

'A Jungian psychologist has informed me that one's Dark Shadow can be either interior or exterior, and now Ismene is telling me we must submit to the law.'

'I hope there are other options,' she said, not bothering to look up from her own book.

'No. And now Ismene tells me that "We are mere women, and we cannot fight against men."'

This time, Paola lowered her book and looked at him. Smiling, she said, 'So I've always believed,' and raised the book again. But then, before he could continue reading, Paola said from behind the book, 'If memory serves, Ismene is about to protest, "I have no strength to break laws that are made for the public good."'

Brunetti took one hand off his book and patted her ankle. 'That's why they're classics, dear.'

She did not choose to dignify his remark with a response.

He read on and soon came to that fatal declaration from Antigone: 'I am doing only what I must do.'

It might as well have been Professoressa Crosera speaking, doing what she had to do, choosing to obey the law she accepted, that gave mothers the right to do anything to protect their children. Seek information from the police and solace from the fact that her son could not be arrested, and to hell with anyone else's child.

Antigone was obeying her own law. He turned the page and found her words: 'But I will bury him. And if I must die because of it, I say that this crime is sacred.' His hands sank to his lap and he sat, book abandoned, and tried to think of what it would be so to value your sense of what is right, or whatever you chose to call it, as to perform a ritual you believed to be necessary, knowing that your death was the inescapable result of doing so. Brunetti believed he would die for a person: his children, his wife. But for an ideal, a rule?

His thoughts turned to Gasparini, that other father. What might he have been capable of doing in order to protect his son? Brunetti considered that possibility for a time. Could it be that he'd got it backwards, and Gasparini had been the aggressor on the bridge? Brunetti chided himself: only now did he consider the possibility, as if the man's injuries made him necessarily a victim or because, having spoken to his wife, Brunetti would not think it gentlemanly to suspect him.

'Oh, by the way,' Paola interrupted him. 'There was a note for you in the mailbox.'

'Where is it?'

'On the kitchen counter. I thought you'd see it there.'

'No, I didn't,' Brunetti said, getting to his feet. In the kitchen he found an envelope with his name printed on it in block letters – no stamp. It stood braced against the pepper mill. He slipped his thumb under the tab and opened it. Inside, written in the same hand, he read,

'Gianluca Fornari, Castello 2712.'

13

The next morning, Brunetti arrived at the Questura at nine. When he was told that Commissario Griffoni had not yet arrived, he went to her office and left a note on her desk, asking her to call him when she could.

On the steps he met Alvise, who told him that Vianello had come in briefly but had had to return to Marghera again because the wife in the domestic violence case was now volunteering information about her husband's activities in Venice.

Brunetti was disappointed that his friend and sounding board would be gone again, taking with him the experience and good sense with which he listened to Brunetti's descriptions of events. There was no need, however, for Alvise to know this, especially when the officer was trying to be helpful. 'Good you told me, Alvise,' Brunetti said.

'He told me you'd say that, sir,' Alvise answered with a smile, pleased to be the bearer of what he thought was important information. 'He asked me to tell you he went back because it's related to the break-in at Signor Bordoni's.'

'Thank you, Alvise,' Brunetti said in a warmer voice, recognizing the name but not sure why. He climbed the stairs, sounding out the rhythm of the syllables with his steps: Bor-DON-i, Bor-DON-i. On the third sounding of the name, it clicked into place and Brunetti remembered the robbery, three years before, when thieves had opened the *porta blindata* to the Bordonis' apartment by spraying liquid nitrogen on the hinges and bolts and shattering them, then lowering the metal-framed door to the ground, a job that suggested the participation of at least two people. The family was on holiday in Sardegna at the time, the live-in maid out for the evening to play *burraco* with her friends, as she did – Brunetti recalled – every Tuesday.

The maid had come home at eleven and, finding the door lying on the floor in front of the apartment, had dialled 113 and gone downstairs to seek refuge with the neighbours until the police arrived.

When the officers entered the apartment, they found the place in complete order: nothing damaged, nothing thrown carelessly to the floor, the lights on, just as the maid had left them. Everything seemed fine, and the police had begun to wonder why the door had been removed to no purpose – Brunetti remembered reading this in their report – until they entered the study of Dottor Bordoni. Three paintings – which the maid, who had memorized them from years of dusting, described as a fat woman with no clothes on; another woman in a black dress with a black servant holding a red umbrella for her; and a third female, this one perhaps a girl but not looking like a real human being – were gone. It was only on the family's return the following day that Brunetti – who had been given the case by Patta because he 'knew about paintings' – learned that the female portraits were by Renoir, Van Dyck, and Picasso.

Everything else was correctly in place. The three paintings were gone, evaporated from among the other paintings in whose company they had lived for years. No attempt was made by their thieves to contact the owner, nor were the paintings ever mentioned by those who occasionally sold information to the Art Fraud Police.

And now Vianello, called to assist with an interrogation in a case of domestic abuse, might have caught a glimpse of them. Or so Brunetti hoped.

He stopped at Signorina Elettra's office, but as he entered he remembered it was Tuesday, which meant she would have had one of the pilots take her on a police launch to the Rialto market to buy flowers. He wrote Fornari's name and address on a piece of paper, added a question mark, sealed it inside an envelope, and laid it on the keys of her computer.

When he reached his office, he dialled Professoressa Crosera's home phone and let it ring until he was told to leave a message and he'd be called in good course. He told her his name and gave his number and said that he would like to ... but before he could finish speaking, the line suddenly clicked open. He hoped it would be the Professoressa answering and waited expectantly for her voice, but the line went dead.

He dialled the central number for the hospital and asked to speak to Dottor Stampini in Neurologia and, when asked, gave his name and said it was police business, volunteering nothing more than that.

Dottor Stampini was soon on the line. 'Good morning, Commissario,' he said and then went on without the formality of an introduction, 'I'd like to be able to give you better news than I can, but the CAT scan is fairly clear.' He paused and, in a far less impersonal voice, asked, 'Do you understand the jargon?'

'To some degree,' Brunetti answered.

'The major damage is to the parietal bone, which was fractured during his fall, perhaps when he hit the railing, perhaps when he hit the pavement. This created a subdural haematoma, and until the brain absorbs the blood, his condition won't change.'

Brunetti didn't know whether the doctor expected him to question this; he decided not to. 'Have you spoken to his wife?' he asked, instead.

'Yes, I have.'

'And?'

'She hears the words and understands the phrases, but she doesn't want to understand the significance, or the possible consequences, of what I've told her.' When Brunetti did not comment, the doctor said, 'I suppose you're familiar with this kind of response, Commissario.'

'Yes. Unfortunately.'

Stampini's voice slowed and grew warmer. 'Have you spoken to her?'

'No, Dottore. I've left a message. I hope she's gone home.'

Stampini said instantly, 'I think she's still here. She told me this morning that she'd spoken with her sister and sent the children to stay with her.'

When it seemed the doctor had finished, Brunetti asked, 'Has anyone come to the hospital to see her?'

'Not that I know of.'

'What do you suggest, Dottore?'

'I think it would help if someone would come and take her home. She has to get some rest, or go somewhere where she can be with people she knows. There's no sense in her staying here.' Before Brunetti could speak, the doctor went on, 'The only thing she's told me is that you were very kind to her.'

This surprised Brunetti, who had no memory of being anything but firm. 'Is there some message you're giving me, Dottore?'

Stampini laughed or sighed: Brunetti couldn't tell. 'Yes, I suppose I am. I think you might be able to persuade her to go home for a while. He's not going to wake up,' the doctor said but quickly added, 'not for a long time. She should go home, or go to her sister and be with her children. Something. But get away from here.'

Brunetti thought about what he might do. Finally, he said, 'Will you be there much longer?'

'All morning, at least until noon,' the doctor said, trying to sound professional, but then he added, 'She's a good woman, Commissario.'

'I'll be there soon,' Brunetti said and hung up.

He dialled Griffoni's *telefonino* and, not bothering to ask where she was, told her he was at the Questura but going back to the hospital. For a moment, he thought of asking her to meet him there. Woman to woman, it might be easier, somehow, to persuade Professoressa Crosera to leave the hospital. As he gave more thought to what he had seen of her, however, he decided she would not like the intrusion of another person. Thus he limited himself to telling Griffoni that he'd been given the name of the man who worked in front of the Albertini and had passed it to Signorina Elettra. He added that he'd be back at the Questura as soon as he could, broke the connection, and left to return to the hospital.

*

Brunetti went directly to Neurologia, where he found a different nurse, who told him that visiting hours did not begin until three. When he said he was a police official, coming to talk to Signor Gasparini's wife, her demeanour changed, although not by much. Almost grudgingly, she said he could enter the ward.

He went down the corridor and knocked lightly on the door to Gasparini's room. There was no response, so he opened it and put his head inside. Gasparini was exactly as he had left him. From the door, Brunetti saw his wife's back and head, the top half of her body lying on the bed perpendicular to her husband, the rest seated in the chair where Brunetti had last seen her.

Her right hand held her husband's left, and she was asleep, the top of her head just touching his left hip. Brunetti stepped back into the corridor, closed the door, and knocked far more loudly, waited, knocked again.

Within moments, the door was pulled open and she was there, looking startled and angry and not bothering to hide either. She pushed past him and out into the corridor, pulling the door closed. 'What's wrong with you?' she demanded, voice ragged with exhaustion. 'Do you want to wake him up?'

Brunetti took another step backwards but said nothing, wanting her question to reverberate in her mind. Finally, when her face told him she understood what she had just said, he answered, 'That would be a good thing, Signora.' He spoke in an entirely normal voice, making it clear that he meant what he said.

This was enough to wipe all expression from her face. As though she'd taken a step backwards, only to find nothing under her foot, she banged against the door, making far more noise than Brunetti had by knocking.

'I've come to take you home, Signora.' Before she could protest, he said, 'Dottor Stampini told me your children are with your sister. Let me take you home; have something to eat, and have your children come home, too. And then you can think about what to do.'

'There's nothing I can do,' she blurted out, trying to make her voice steely but failing on the last word. Her face grew flaccid with despair and then tightened in fear.

Brunetti, knowing there was no comfort he could give her, said, 'You can cook something for your children to show them you're all right and life is normal.' Before she could protest about the word, Brunetti said, 'That's what they need, Signora. Their father is sick and in the hospital, but they need things to continue as close to how they were as you can make them.' When he saw her prepare to speak, he kept talking. 'They might be teenagers, but they're still children.'

He stopped after that and watched as she considered his advice. She raised one hand but let it fall again, then gave a dispirited shrug and said, 'Perhaps.' She turned and went into the room, leaving the door open for him.

Gasparini was the same, save that the circles under his eyes were darker today, especially on the left side.

Professoressa Crosera walked to the side of the bed, leaned over her husband, and pulled the covers up, although the room was hot enough to make Brunetti uncomfortable. She placed her hand lightly on her husband's cheek, as though it was morning at home and she was going to let him sleep a bit more while she made them some coffee or went out to get the morning paper so he could read it in bed, the way he liked to.

She picked up her coat and bag and walked over to Brunetti. 'Quick, before I change my mind,' she said and walked out the door and down the corridor.

Outside, Brunetti discovered that the sun had decided to flirt with them: there were patches of light on the pavement of the *campo*, and he reached automatically to unbutton his coat.

Brunetti turned right and started over the bridge. 'Where do you live?' he asked.

'Near San Stae,' she said, then, 'I'd like to walk.'

She was looking ahead, so she didn't see him nod. It didn't matter; there was only one way to go. At the Ponte dei Giocattoli, she said, 'Remember the toy store?'

Indeed Brunetti did: his children discovered it early on and never walked past it without insisting that they go in, 'just to have a look'. Gone now, like the rest of the toy stores. Tourist junk, instead; useless toys for bigger children, all made in China, masquerading as Venetian. 'My kids loved it,' Brunetti said.

'Mine, too.'

At the newly-transformed Ballarin, he didn't bother to ask her but went in and up to the bar. 'What would you like?' he asked.

'A macchiatone and a brioche, please,' she answered. Then, as if coming out of a dream, she added, 'And a glass of water.'

He ordered, and their coffee and the brioche were soon on the bar, along with a glass of water, which she drank first, and thirstily. She sipped at her coffee but ate the brioche quickly, hungrily. Brunetti paid and they left.

During the brief time they had been in the bar, the *calle* had filled up until it was as crowded as it once was only at Christmas. The crowds shoved them together until Brunetti jutted out his elbow, clearing enough space to allow him to move away from her. Up the bridge, down, and now along the front of the Fondaco, where the lines of Chinese tourists had started their daily ritual visit to their new god, a twenty-first-century shopping mall.

Brunetti drew his spirit tight and turned towards the Grand Canal, then left along the *riva*, not having to lead her. The Rialto Bridge stood to their right, and they went over it like people on an escalator, locked in by those moving in front of and behind them, unable to stop, unable to move faster than the slowest person near them, unable to pause lest they be trampled by the people behind.

At the bottom, she grabbed at his arm and pulled him to the right. 'Get me out of this, please,' she said. Brunetti took ten fast steps straight ahead and then cut right and into the *campo* in front of the church of San Giacomo.

He stopped, facing the bit of the Canal they could see through the break in the buildings. She started to walk towards the water, and he came along beside her. She walked all the way to the waterside and looked across at the rear façade of what had once been the Post Office. She stopped two metres from the Grand Canal.

'I can't help looking at it as a Venetian and not an architect,' she said.

'Do you like what they did?' Brunetti asked. He'd been inside and seen the shops, had gone up to the terrace and viewed the city as he had seldom seen it before; a circle of beauty, all of it excessive, all of it perfect.

'I don't like the result,' she said, 'but some of the restoration is very well done.'

'What don't you like?' Brunetti asked, using his question as a means to bring her back to normality but also interested in what she had to say.

'Because it's just an expensive variant of the places near San Marco that sell the cheap masks and glass made in China.'

Brunetti remained silent. He agreed with her, but he was curious about her reasons. 'What do you see that's the same?'

'There's nothing for Venetians to buy in either place. Olive oil that costs fifteen Euros a half litre? Seven-hundred-Euro boots? A coffee that costs twice what most bars charge?' Before Brunetti could comment, she went on. 'And as far as the other places go, what Venetian wants a glass elephant or a plastic mask?'

He heard her using the arguments he'd heard so many times, given so many times and remarked, 'Paola often asks, "'Where can I buy a zip?'"'

She turned her head to him quickly, something close to shock on her face. 'Does Paola *sew*?'

Brunetti smiled at the question. 'Good heavens, no. She uses it as a metonym for what residents need and buy, rather than what tourists buy. Zips, underwear, potato peelers.' He stopped and, like a car giving one last backfire, added, 'Thread.'

She took a step back from him and studied his face.

'What's wrong?' Brunetti asked, hoping he hadn't somehow offended her.

'A policeman who uses the word "metonym",' she said, shaking her head. 'No wonder Paola married you.' She turned and started walking towards the market. Because it was the weekend, they managed to pass through it with relative ease. Brunetti noticed many empty places where formerly had stood fruit and vegetable stalls; half the fishmongers were gone.

Out of the market and along the water, then into Calle dei Botteri and two more bridges, and then she pulled her keys out of her bag and opened the street door. She closed it after Brunetti, started up the steps and stopped on the top floor, the fourth. Professoressa Crosera opened the door to the apartment, and he followed her inside. She led him through a small vestibule into a large living room with two comfortable sofas and a view back towards the market and, far off, the campanile of San Francesco della Vigna. She removed her coat and tossed it over the back of the sofa, then went around and sat at the far end. He saw four black-and-white photographs on the wall behind the larger sofa, each showing what appeared to be hundreds, perhaps thousands, of small circular blobs arranged in parallel straight lines.

Curious, he stepped closer and saw that they were, as he'd thought, part of the Salgado series of photos of gold mines, he forgot where, perhaps South America somewhere. He stepped back from them and looked at Professoressa Crosera. She had locked her hands between her knees and was leaning forward and staring at the floor. She pushed herself upright and against the back of the sofa and looked in his direction.

Suddenly nervous and uncomfortable, Brunetti went and got her bag, which she had set down beside the door, and placed it beside her. 'Perhaps it would help if you called your sister, Signora, and let her know you've come home,' he said and walked over to the farthest window, studying the buildings and towers in the distance. Behind him, he heard her begin to talk. Even though she kept her voice low, he could still understand what she said.

Brunetti noticed that the window to his right was really a door to a small terrace. He opened it and stepped outside, pulling the door closed. Her voice disappeared. To his right, he could see the Campanile di San Marco, squashed between two clouds that some trick of perspective made look like two large pillows offering to prop it up. He swept his eyes farther to the right and began playing one of his oldest games: 'Which Church Is That?' Because he was alone, he couldn't verify his guesses, but the tilted tower was easy to recognize as Santo Stefano's.

Brunetti turned just as she put her phone back in her bag and looked in his direction. He went inside and approached her. Somehow, her sister had managed to calm her: that was evident from her face. 'Signora, sooner or later, we'll begin a formal investigation of what happened to your husband.'

'What will that achieve?' she asked.

'For your husband, very little, I'm afraid,' he said, unwilling to be an ally to her self-deception. Then, more firmly, 'I'd like to be able to find the person who did this.'

'I'm not sure that will help anything,' she said. 'Or anyone.'

'It might stop the person from doing it again,' Brunetti offered.

'Would I sound cruel if I said that's not of much importance to my husband? Nor to me.' She smiled, one of the saddest things Brunetti had seen in his life.

'Not cruel, Signora, not by any means. But I'm asking you to make the decision, not your husband.'

'What decision?' she asked, honestly surprised.

'To let us ask you questions and ask questions of your friends,' he said, not daring to mention her son. 'Is there anything you, or they, think might be related to what was done to your husband?'

'I told you about the trouble with my son,' she said.

'Yes,' Brunetti agreed. 'Was there anything else that was troubling your husband?'

She thought about this for what seemed to Brunetti a long time and finally answered, 'Growing old. Whether his company could survive the economic crisis. Global warming, his paunch, what our daughter and her boyfriend did together.'

He smiled, and she asked, 'Did I say something funny?'

'It was like looking in a mirror and seeing what I worry about all the time,' he answered. 'And I'd add having a boss who dislikes me at times,' Brunetti said.

'Anything else?' she asked dispassionately, rejecting his offer of a more relaxed atmosphere.

'About what I'd like to do as part of the investigation?'

'Yes.'

'I'd like to take a look through his belongings; his study, if he has one,' he said, continuing to avoid reference to her son.

She nodded at this, but Brunetti didn't know if it meant her husband had a study or she would agree to let him look through it. Or perhaps she was merely acknowledging that she understood his request. Hoping that it was the second, he said, 'I'd like to do it now.' Sensing her reluctance, he thought it might be time to play the trump card of her son's safety: few mothers could resist the power of that appeal.

She looked at her watch, but before she could speak, they heard the front door open and then a heavy thud as it was pushed back against the wall. Surprise catapulted her from her chair, and Brunetti wheeled around to face whatever was coming.

Two teenagers came quickly into the room, a boy and girl of almost the same height, though the boy's face showed that he was younger than his sister. He wore jeans that hung loosely on his hips, a brown leather jacket, and a pair of almost-new Stan Smiths. The bottom part of his head had been shaved to the height of his eyebrows, the rest left long to create a strange two-tiered effect. He had his mother's dark eyes and, although his body was very thin, his face was still rounded by the puppy fat of childhood; his jaw had yet to take on the angularity of adolescence.

He stopped short when he saw Brunetti; his eyes shot to his mother, back to Brunetti, back to his mother, showing that this was an uncommon configuration. 'Who's he?' he demanded. His face was tight and his lips pulled back from his teeth in a primal declaration of menace.

The girl turned to him in surprise, disapproval written on a face that was a younger version of her mother's. 'Sandro,' she said, voice tight and filled with reproach.

The boy looked at her, obviously unable to decide between outrage or contrition. 'All I did was ask who he was,' he said to his sister, his voice wilting in the echo of her reprimand.

Brunetti smiled at them and said, 'I'm Guido Brunetti. Your mother asked me to accompany her back from the hospital.' He turned to the Professoressa and said in casual farewell, 'If there's anything else I can do, call Paola, please.'

Then, speaking to both children, he added, 'That's my wife. She and your mother are colleagues at the university.' He took a few steps towards the door and, when abreast of them, paused and said, 'Your mother's been at the hospital with your father all this time and hasn't had anything to eat. I think it would be good if you'd take care of her. Perhaps you could help her make lunch?'

'What's wrong with him?' the boy asked in a strained voice.

Instead of answering, Brunetti turned back to the boy's mother, who told them, 'The doctors said you can both visit

Papà tomorrow. Until then, I'm the only person they'll let see him.'

The boy started to speak, but his voice failed to find words and turned into a light moan. It lasted a few seconds, and then he asked, 'Is he going to die?'

That brought his mother to her feet and to his side. Wrapping her arms around him, she said in a voice Brunetti could hear struggling to remain calm and hoped the boy could not, 'Don't be silly, Sandro. He's got two nurses and the best doctor in the hospital. You and Aurelia can come and see him tomorrow.' She turned to Brunetti for confirmation. 'Isn't that right?'

'If Dottor Stampini says it's all right, I'm sure they can.' Brunetti nodded to the woman and took the opportunity to leave. As he reached the door, he heard three sharp, barking sobs, but a sense of decency stopped him from turning to see which one of them it was.

14

As he let himself out of the building, Brunetti felt that the day had decided not to throw in its lot with winter quite yet and had returned to early autumn: by the time he reached Campo San Cassiano, he was sweating under his jacket. He thought about taking off his coat, but when he recalled the route he'd have to take to get home for lunch, all in the shade, he merely unbuttoned it and pulled it open for a moment. He turned to face the sun, feeling rather like a late-season sunflower trying to beat the odds.

Had the sun been an old friend, packing and preparing for a three-month vacation, Brunetti would have told him he'd miss him and wish him a good time, down there in Argentina and New Zealand, spending the winter months – wisely – by the sea and staying warm. When he turned into Ruga Vecchia San Giovanni, he was proven right and rebuttoned his coat for the rest of the walk home.

Brunetti couldn't shake himself free of the thought of Gianluca Fornari. He pulled out his phone and dialled Signorina Elettra's number while climbing the first flight of stairs.

'Good morning, Commissario,' she said pleasantly, as though a call from him was what she'd been waiting for since she arrived in the office. Before he could ask, she said, 'Signor Fornari has been known to us for some time. Since he was eighteen, as a matter of fact.' Brunetti was about to say he was surprised that a man well known to them would have restrained himself until he was an adult, when she continued, saying, 'He has a file with the Juvenile Office, but I didn't want to go looking around in there so soon after making inquiries about Alessandro Gasparini.'

Ah, she was calling it 'making inquiries' now, was she? Brunetti threw that thought to the ground and pinned it there with his foot while he asked, 'And the file he has with us?'

'He's spent eleven of the last twenty years as a guest of the state,' she answered, gave a little grunt, as though stretching to retrieve something just at the end of arm's reach, then said, 'Ah, yes, here it is. Five years for a series of robberies in Mestre and Marghera – he was in prison from when he was twenty until he was twenty-five – and then three more – from when he was twenty-nine until he was thirty two – for selling drugs to minors in Padova.'

Brunetti heard a page turning. 'He was thirty-four when he went in again. Same crime, selling drugs. But he was released a year and a half ago.'

'And since then?'

'I can't find any record of employment. There's no sign that he's paid taxes in those years.' As was common with most people today, the way she said this suggested approval, though with Signorina Elettra, Brunetti was never certain what her sentiments were.

He reflected on what she must have done in order to get that information, and he marvelled: she could get in, even there. 'Has he been in any trouble with us since then?' he asked calmly.

'Nothing. I called the Vigili Urbani to ask if they'd had any contact with him. A few of them remembered him from years ago, but no one could recall having had anything to do with him, even seeing him, for a long time.' After a moment, she added, 'One of them said he's married and said the wife is a good woman. No children.'

'And now he's selling drugs to the kids at the Albertini?' It did not occur to Brunetti to question the information Manrico had given him.

'I've no idea, Dottore,' she said. 'I'll see what else I can find.' He was about to end the call, when she added, 'I checked their phone records, and there were no calls between him and Gasparini.'

Arrived at the landing in front of the door to his apartment, he thanked her for the information she'd found. 'I'll be in about three,' he added, said goodbye, and broke the connection.

He put the phone in one pocket, took his keys from another, and let himself in. He did a human radar scan of the house and concluded that no one was home. It was then that he remembered: the chairman of Paola's department had requested her – 'begged' was the word she'd used when telling him why she wouldn't be home – to sit in on an interview with one of the people who had applied for a teaching position; Raffi was playing basketball, and Chiara's Art History class was being shown the Restoration

Laboratory at the Accademia Museum. Paola would no doubt be invited to an expensive lunch in return for her time, the kids would have fun, while he had no choice but to search for leftovers in the refrigerator and eat alone, with only the newspaper for company, unless Paola had taken that with her to read during the interview. 'Oh, you do whine, don't you, just?' he asked himself aloud.

He went into the kitchen and opened the refrigerator, where he found a saucepan and, on the shelf below, a dish covered with aluminium foil. He pulled them out, placed them on the counter, and took the lid from the pan. Cream of celery root soup. The other had a note on top: 'You don't have to heat them.' Peeling back the foil, he saw what looked like veal meatballs wrapped in speck.

Turning on the oven, he stuck the plate inside, then put the pan on the stove and turned the flame to medium. He pulled down a bowl and took a glass from the cabinet. Leaving the soup to heat, he went back to the bedroom and picked up his copy of *Antigone*, which he had left face-down last night.

Back in the kitchen, he pinned it flat with a serving spoon and a small plate from the drying rack. He found another spoon and stirred the soup, then licked the spoon to test how hot it was.

He sliced some bread, looked in the refrigerator again and quelled his disappointment at not finding a salad. He stirred the soup, filled a glass from the tap, not because of Chiara's sensibilities but because he was too lazy to open a bottle of mineral water, and sat at the table.

He found his place and looked for the scene where he had left off the previous night. His eye fell on something he had underlined decades ago, when he read the play at school. As he recalled, it was something Ismene had said:

Ismene, ever wise, ever cautious, ever subservient. There it was, with his own, decades-old fading, faint underlining: 'I must obey the ones in power.' He glanced away, trying to imagine what he, an eighteen-year-old boy, had understood of power and its uses.

He smelled something burning and ignored it, thinking that his imagination had caught the scent of the funeral pyre on which the body of Eteocles, the loyal brother, had been burned with full honours, his traitorous brother's body abandoned to scavengers.

That smell again. He turned aside and saw the steam rising from the saucepan. *'Oddio,'* he muttered, jumped to his feet and grabbed at the handle. He pulled the pan off the flame and set it on the marble counter, hoping it was not burned irredeemably.

He found a soup bowl and poured it out, then tipped the pan a bit to the side, the better to see down to the bottom. It looked all right, so he stirred the rest around a few times, added it to his bowl and carried it to his place. He took a sip of water and set the glass to the right of the bowl and went back to his reading while he waited for the soup to cool.

Creon now, prating away in that voice so favoured by powerful men: how they loved to hear themselves use it, and they probably loved to hear it in those they judged to be their equals. Simple thoughts, simple ideas, simple commands. 'See that you never side with the people who disobey my orders,' the King commands, and the leader of the Chorus falls over himself in his haste to agree: 'Never. Only a fool would be so much in love with death.'

After the sentry reports the crude attempt at burial, Creon unleashes the ultimate weapon of the bully: sarcasm. 'When were the gods last seen helping traitors?'

Brunetti took a receipt from Rosa Salva from his pocket and slipped it into the page and closed the book. Knowing that to continue to read would cause him to pay no attention to his lunch, he pushed the book to the other side of the table and began to eat. He wished only that Paola had left him that day's *Gazzettino*, for its ham-fisted, factual accounts of death and misery could in no way trouble him to the degree that Sophocles' world of invention and fancy did.

When he returned to the Questura, he asked about Vianello, but there had been neither sight nor sound of the Inspector. Griffoni had come in at one but had gone out for lunch and was not yet back. As he went up the stairs to his office, he tried to think of what he would do if he wanted to sell drugs to students but did not want to risk arrest.

He did his best thinking at the window, so he went and studied the façade of the church of San Lorenzo and considered the possibilities. Fornari could have one of the students do the selling for him, but this would not change his legal liability, might even worsen it, should the student be apprehended. And he'd have to share the profit, hardly a wise decision. The important thing would be to limit or, better, eliminate direct contact between himself and his customers. So long as he did not actually put the drugs into the hands of a minor, there was no serious crime involved. Therefore, he'd have to find a place to leave the drugs and a reliable person who would see to the sale.

Once the students knew where the drugs were available, they had only to go there, hand over their money, and get them. Not entirely whimsically, Brunetti asked himself if, in ten years, drugs would be delivered by drone.

He remembered a friend of his mother, insatiably curious about the doings of her neighbours and a gossip of majestic proportions. Whenever his mother saw her go by, she would tell her son that the woman was on her way to *'curiosare'*, one of his mother's uses of language. If only she'd had the advantage of schooling beyond the fourth grade, what might she have done? He'd never told anyone, not even Paola, how much he missed her still.

He had no clear idea of the situation or arrangement that might make the sale of drugs invisible, thus there was nothing for it other than to go over to the Albertini and *'curiosare'*.

He heard someone knock at his door and called out, *'Avanti.'* Vianello came in and closed the door after him. The grin on his face remained there as he approached Brunetti's desk and took one of the chairs in front of it.

Brunetti walked back to his desk and sat. Vianello said nothing. 'All right, Lorenzo,' Brunetti finally declared, 'you can stop grinning now and tell me what happened.'

The Inspector slumped down in the chair and stretched his legs out in front of him. He crossed his ankles and observed the tops of his shoes.

'Are you going to sit there and preen, or are you going to tell me?' Brunetti asked in false exasperation.

Vianello's grin disappeared. 'I got there before they were ready to begin the interrogation this morning. Pastore, the man I was working with, said he wanted to show me some of the things they found in the thief's apartment when he was arrested.'

Brunetti shifted in his chair and folded his arms across his chest.

'All right, all right,' Vianello said quite amiably. He took an envelope from his inside pocket and placed it on the desk in front of Brunetti. 'Have a look.' He pointed to the envelope with conscious melodrama.

Brunetti lifted the flap and saw some sheets of paper. He pulled them out, unfolded all three, and spread them flat in a row on the desk in front of him. He saw colour photocopies of what looked like photos of three paintings, all portraits of women. In the first, a black servant held a red umbrella above the subject's head; in the second, the woman had eyes of different sizes; and the third showed a very robust naked woman bending forward to wipe her feet with a towel.

'Bordoni,' Brunetti said, recognizing them instantly. 'The guy they were questioning had these? In his apartment?'

'Yes.'

Brunetti rapped the back of his fingers against the three sheets of paper in turn and asked, 'Did he have these photocopies of the paintings or the paintings themselves?'

'Only the photocopies,' Vianello answered.

'And the paintings?'

Vianello shook his head. 'There were a lot of things in his apartment, but no paintings.'

'What did they find?'

'There were photos of other paintings. He also had a number of watches, jewellery, some Renaissance brasses, a small Roman statue of a goddess, an Iznik tile, and about twelve thousand dollars. In dollars.'

'Any of this reported missing?'

'They've found the owners of the tile and four of the watches. They're looking through their records to see if any of the other things have been reported stolen.'

Brunetti considered what his friend had told him. 'So he's a professional.'

'It would seem so.'

'The fact that he has photocopies of these paintings means either that he photographed and then copied them after he stole them …'

'So he could show them to prospective clients,' Vianello finished for him.

'Or that he was given the photocopies by someone else to show him exactly which paintings to take,' Brunetti finished, and this time Vianello nodded.

They sat silent for a while, considering possibilities.

'What has his wife said?'

'Nothing. She said she thought her husband sold fire insurance,' Vianello said with a straight face.

'Fire insurance?' Brunetti asked. 'How did she explain the things in their house?'

'She didn't. She said her husband had always had good taste.'

'Who called to report the domestic violence?'

'The people in the apartment across from them,' Vianello answered.

'How does he explain the objects in the apartment?' Brunetti asked.

Straight-faced, Vianello said, 'Some of them were in a briefcase he found on a train.'

'But didn't report finding?'

'He said he didn't think there was any law that said he had to.'

Brunetti ignored this and asked, 'Does he have a history with us?'

'He's been arrested for burglary seven times. Six years in jail, total.'

'Did anyone ask him about the photocopies?'

'Yes. He said he didn't want to throw them away because, if he ever found the owner of the briefcase, he'd probably want to get everything back.'

It took Brunetti some time to answer, and when he did, all he could think of to say was, 'I see.' Then he asked, 'Will you talk to him about these?' tapping a finger on the girl with different-sized eyes.

'Tomorrow. Pastore said I can have a half-hour with him while they're on their coffee break.'

'Long break,' Brunetti observed.

'Yes, it is, isn't it?' Vianello agreed. 'I figured it could take some time to persuade him that it might be wise to agree to a trade. He tells me where he got the photocopies, and I tell my friends he's been cooperative with us.'

Brunetti picked up the photocopies one by one and studied them. The frame on the portrait of the woman under the umbrella was simple black, undecorated. The woman wiping her feet was surrounded by a golden frame, ornamented with tiny carved wooden rosettes. The photocopy of the painting of the woman with the strange eyes showed it had been unframed. He went back and looked at the naked woman and noticed that, on the far right, at a small distance from the tiny rosettes of her frame, a thin black vertical bar bled to the side of the photocopy and seemed to extend both above and below the painting. The woman with the odd eyes had the same black bar a bit to the left of the unframed edge of her portrait. As with the other painting, the black bar extended above and below the edge of the portrait.

Brunetti stared at the three paintings for a long time. Then he picked up the photocopy of the woman under the umbrella and folded the sheet of paper vertically so that the black frame of the painting was at the edge of the photocopy, as well. He took the other two photos and folded their sides vertically so that the black frame of the centre painting became the black vertical bars that ran so close to the sides of the other paintings.

He set them in a horizontal row and they became a sort of female triptych, the black frame of the central portrait now equidistant from and longer than the other two paintings.

Brunetti looked at Vianello. 'Is this the way they were hanging in the Bordonis' apartment?

The Inspector nodded and smiled. 'You're very clever, Guido. It took me much longer, and I had to call Bocchese to look at the photo Dottor Bordoni gave us of how the paintings were originally hung.'

'So the original photo was taken in their home? Before the robbery?'

'Presumably.'

Brunetti studied the three photocopies again. In a house as filled with art and paintings as the Bordonis', a thief would have far less trouble if he had a road map with easily understandable signs.

'This is what you want to trade?' Brunetti asked.

'Exactly what I told you, Guido: he gives me the name of the person who took the photo, and in return I speak a few words to my friends.'

'Will your friends agree?' Brunetti asked.

Startled by the question, Vianello sat up straight. 'They already have. They'll speak to the magistrate and explain that he's been a very helpful witness.'

Brunetti smiled and said, 'I'm surprised you didn't ask them to tell the magistrate he probably did find the bag on a train.'

'I thought about it,' Vianello said in a voice filled with regret. 'But with the record he has, my friends weren't willing to go that far.'

15

Brunetti looked at his watch and asked Vianello, 'You doing anything now?'

'No.'

'Good. You want to come over to the Albertini with me?'

Vianello got to his feet.

'I'd like to see what happens when the kids get out of school,' Brunetti said. 'Chiara gets out at five, so maybe they do, too.'

'All right. Let me get my coat. I'll meet you downstairs,' the Inspector said and started towards the door.

Minutes later, they left the Questura and turned automatically in the direction of the school, in Barbaria delle Tole, not far from the hospital. Brunetti remembered playing soccer – badly – in the *campo* as a student but could no longer remember the friends with whom he had played.

They crossed the bridge in front of Palazzo Cappello and kept on straight until they turned to head up to the school.

'What are we looking for?' Vianello asked. 'I'm not sure what someone selling drugs would look like.'

Brunetti shrugged. 'Neither am I. There's been no mention of Fornari since he was released from jail a year and a half ago, yet he's supposed to be in charge of drugs at the school.' He slowed and turned to look at his friend. 'What do you think that means?'

Vianello stopped in front of a shop on the right and looked at a squat brown vase in the window. 'The older I get, the more I like Japanese objects,' he said, to Brunetti's considerable surprise.

'Why?'

Vianello rubbed at his bottom lip as he thought about this. 'They're so uncomplicated, so simple.'

'Perhaps not to the Japanese,' Brunetti said.

'But to Venetian policemen, I think they are,' Vianello said. 'Look at that,' he added, pointing down at the vase. 'It looks like it's glowing, doesn't it? As if there were something burning inside.' When Brunetti did not answer, Vianello stuffed his hands in the pockets of his trousers and turned away from the window to resume walking.

'It could mean he's franchised the work to someone else,' Vianello continued, as if he had not stopped to look into the window. 'It could be he's tired of being in jail.'

'He should be,' Brunetti agreed, 'after all those years.' In the information Signorina Elettra had provided on Fornari, there had not been much to his life when he had not been in prison.

They passed the gates of the school, open to the *calle*. No students were to be seen in the large courtyard; the only sign of life was a border collie sitting alert in the far left corner, as though it had parked its flock and was waiting for the time on the meter to run out.

There were benches in the *campo*. They'd be less conspicuous if they were sitting there, reading the papers, so Brunetti stopped at the kiosk and saw that there were no newspapers left. He bought a second copy of the *Espresso* they already had at home and a two-month-old *Giornale dell'Arte*, which he passed to Vianello. They sat on a bench that faced down the *calle* that led to the school and began to read. Minutes passed; they flipped through the pages, occasionally glancing towards the school to see if any students had appeared. After another ten minutes, Brunetti found himself involved in an article about the former Director of the MOSE project, now living in Central America and claiming to be too infirm to return to Italy for trial.

Over the years, Brunetti had read reports of the total spent on the project that varied from five to seven billion Euros, and now this one suggested quite calmly the possibility that the *'progetto faraonico'* would never function. Just like that: millennium-old tidal patterns destroyed, vast areas of land and sea covered with cement, an unknown quantity spent, and now they blithely announce it might never work. He turned the page.

A low noise, reminiscent of the sound of surf, made them look up at the same time, and they saw, and heard, Exodus: the Chosen Ones of an expensive private school were heading towards the *campo* in a wide wave of Moncler and North Face. Grey, dark grey, black, dark blue, and almost all of them wearing jeans so dilapidated and shredded that they would have outraged their families' cleaning women, for surely the families of these boys and girls would have cleaning women.

The boys were tall and lanky, most of them, the girls apparently easy in their company. Some walked side by side, either as friends or as couples. Brunetti knew the difference but didn't know why he knew it: perhaps it was what the boy touched when he put his arm around the girl. A general murmur, interspersed with the sharp crash of laughter, preceded them.

The wave approached. In the midst of it, one centimetre from the heels of a tall dark-haired girl and looking like a bit of flotsam, quick-stepped the border collie. Tongue lolling in adoration, the dog occasionally glanced up at her before shifting minimally in response to some signal from the flock.

As they entered the *campo*, a few of the students broke free and went into the tobacco shop to emerge with small packs of cigarettes, which they opened to offer their classmates. Others drifted towards the kiosk where Brunetti had bought the magazines. They paid, and took the magazines the Asian man inside the kiosk gave them. When was it, Brunetti wondered, that kiosks had ceased to sell primarily newspapers and magazines, and now sold compact discs, trinkets, key chains, and T-shirts? And when had the men inside ceased to be Italian?

The wave washed past them and splashed out into the *campo*: some went into the bars for a coffee or a Coke; others continued across to climb the bridge and disappear down the other side.

As he studied them, Brunetti watched to see if an adult approached any of them or if, in fact, any of the adults in the *campo* paid attention to them. It seemed not.

A boy with gleaming black hair that came down to his shirt collar pushed open the door of Rosa Salva and moved towards the bridge. He'd taken only a few steps when a girl shoved open the door and started after him, shouting,

'Gianpaolo, wait for me.' He turned, but did not smile, and she began to run in his direction. Brunetti looked away.

'She'll learn,' Vianello said. Then, after a moment, he added, 'Or else she won't.'

Brunetti set the magazine on the bench beside him, folded his arms over his chest, and turned his attention to the last building in the row that started with Rosa Salva. From the windows of the fourth floor, a person could easily see the mountains as well as the façades of the hospital and the basilica that lay there as visual gifts: for decades, he had envied the people who lived in the apartment. He studied the windows and thought about what the kids had done when they entered the *campo*.

Turning his head to Vianello, Brunetti asked, 'You ever know boys to read scandal magazines?'

'Read what?'

'Those magazines that have pictures of actors and actresses and six-page spreads of George Clooney's wedding.'

'Oh, sweet Jesus; don't remind me of that,' Vianello, who had worked double shifts for four days during the festivities some years before, implored him. He gave a little shake of horror to dismiss the memory. 'Why do you ask?'

'Because four boys just bought magazines like that. And they paid twenty Euros for each of them.'

'How do you know?'

'Because I watched. They each paid with a twenty-Euro note, took the magazines, and didn't bother to wait for change.'

'Very interesting,' Vianello said.

Brunetti, whose feet had grown cold while they sat, stamped them on the ground a few times. 'All they'd have to do is agree on names and amounts. A certain magazine means a particular drug, and a certain number of copies means the amount of the drug the buyer wants. At the end of the day, the man in the kiosk sends an order in an SMS, and the requested magazines get delivered the next day.' After a moment's reflection, Brunetti added, 'It's safer than keeping stock there permanently.' And finally, he said, 'It's like DHL: delivery within 24 hours.'

Vianello considered this and then asked, 'How is it that you sit here for five minutes and you see a system that might work, while people who've worked here or lived here for years haven't noticed anything?'

Brunetti thought about this, before answering, 'They probably do know, Lorenzo, but they're not going to come and tell us. We're lepers. Well, sort of lepers: no one wants to be seen with us or talking to us because they'll end up having trouble. They live around here, remember.'

'That's a bit exaggerated, wouldn't you say?'

'Of course it's exaggerated, but it's still what they think. After all, why should they bother? They know the same people will be doing the same thing in a few days, or a week, or a month. If they come in to report a crime, we'll take their name, and then someone might find out they talked to us.' Before Vianello could object, Brunetti said, 'I know that doesn't happen, but I'm talking about what people believe.

'And if they call, then we have their phone number and we can find out who they are and come to ask them questions.' He turned and looked directly at Vianello. 'If you were an ordinary person – not a policeman – would you report a crime?'

Vianello ignored the question and asked, 'How's Fornari involved in this?'

Brunetti, suddenly aware of the cold sinking into him, got to his feet. 'I wish I knew.' He looked at his watch and saw that it was a bit before six, one of those awkward times when it was too early to go home but too late to bother to go back to the Questura.

'There's nothing else for us to do here,' Brunetti said. 'We might as well go home.'

'Are you calculating double-time for the time we sat in the cold?' Vianello asked.

Brunetti laughed and clapped his friend on the shoulder.

16

Brunetti's good spirits stayed with him all the way home and came up the stairs with him. Raffi was in the kitchen, eating a prosciutto sandwich the same size as the Greek-Italian dictionary he held in his other hand. When he saw his father, he said, mouth full, 'This is to sustain life until dinner.'

A silent Brunetti passed in front of him and pulled out the bottle of Ribolla Gialla they had not finished the evening before. 'So is this,' he said as he plunked it down on the counter and found a glass. Then, with the cunning of the snake, Brunetti took another glass and tipped it towards Raffi. 'Want some?'

Mouth full with another bite, Raffi could only shake his head. He swallowed and said, holding up the sandwich, 'Not with this. I'd rather have water.'

Aha! Brunetti's mental detective exclaimed. *No interest in alcohol, so perhaps none in drugs.* He opened the refrigerator and, while Raffi continued eating, took a bottle of mineral water and poured his son a glass.

Raffi stuffed the last piece of sandwich into his mouth and spoke around it. 'Thanks, *Papà*.'

'Escaping text analysis?' Brunetti asked, nodding at the dictionary.

Raffi put his head back and rolled his eyes. Then he raised one finger in the air in a very professorial gesture and said, 'ἀδύνατον τὸν μηδὲν πράττοντα πράττειν εὖ.'

That said, he drank the water and set the empty glass in the sink with the sort of decisive click his mother made when turning a gesture into a statement, and went back towards his room.

I would have recognized that, years ago, Brunetti told himself, digging away at the Greek but failing to uncover the meaning.

Dinner was spent trying to decide whether to accept an invitation from Paola's parents to go to their house near Dobbiaco for the week between Christmas and New Year.

Brunetti sat quietly, trying to enjoy his cod with spinach, while amusing himself by anticipating the three responses. Paola said she hated Dobbiaco, hated the cold, and no longer enjoyed skiing. Raffi said he'd love to go but would have to check with Sara. Chiara, never one to disappoint, lamented the fact that the family had so many houses that they kept empty for much of the year, dismissing her mother's assertion that keeping staff year-round both ensured that the houses would be kept safe and saw that people had work, an argument Paola had perfected, years ago, to stifle Raffi's socialistic pronouncements about the ownership of property.

'That's not the point,' Chiara went on, shifting gears in the high dudgeon she employed to move from reason to reason. 'It's an act of environmental vandalism to keep these places open and use up all the resources it takes to maintain them.'

'Oh, don't be silly, Chiara,' her mother said. 'You know your grandfather covered the roof with solar panels.'

Raffi chimed in, sounding pleased. 'He sells the extra energy to the electric company.' Brunetti remembered once having a son who was a declared enemy of capitalism, who longed to see the entire wicked system destroyed. How could he, the boy's father – and a policeman, to boot – have failed to notice when the kidnappers from the European Central Bank came in and replaced his own son with a replicant?

'Does that mean you don't want to go, angel?' Brunetti asked Chiara.

His question brought down the temperature of her fervour. 'I didn't say that, *Papà*,' Chiara insisted. 'I'd like to go. To get away from the pollution here.' There is an ecological justification for everything, Brunetti thought but did not say.

'What about you, *Papà*?' Raffi asked, perhaps mindful of his father's kindness in giving him a glass of water.

'I'd enjoy going, too.'

'But you hate skiing,' Chiara said instantly.

'But I love the mountains,' Brunetti answered with a smile.

The subject drifted away after that, to be postponed until another time. Paola restored harmony, or rather, her fresh chestnut and hazelnut cake restored harmony.

It wasn't until later, as he lay in bed with *Antigone* in his hands and his wife at his side, that Brunetti recognized Raffi's quotation. 'Aristotle,' he said aloud. '"It is impossible for the man who does nothing to be happy."'

*

The next morning, he girded his loins when he got to his office and called down to his superior to ask if the Vice-Questore had time to see him. Sighing heavily, Patta told him he could come now, if he hurried.

When Brunetti entered, having lingered in Dottor Patta's anteroom only long enough to ask Signorina Elettra if she could have a look at Fornari's private life, he found the Dottore deeply engrossed in an open file. Hearing Brunetti come in, the Vice-Questore, in the manner of Saint Augustine in his study, when interrupted in his labours by the spirit voice of Saint Jerome at the window, glanced first at the light coming from his left and then at Brunetti, and then at the floor, as though in search of the little white dog who had so recently been sitting at his feet. After a moment he allowed his gaze to clear and return to the things of this world. 'What is it, Brunetti?' he inquired.

'It's about Signor Gasparini, Vice-Questore,' Brunetti said in a voice he kept low.

'Gasparini?' asked Patta. 'You'll have to refresh my memory, Brunetti.'

'Of course, Signore,' Brunetti answered.

'Take a seat,' Patta said with easy command.

Brunetti crossed to the chair he usually sat in when speaking to the Vice-Questore. 'The man who was found at the bottom of the bridge two nights ago.'

'Mugging, wasn't it?'

'It seemed that way, Signore,' Brunetti said.

'What do you mean, Brunetti?' demanded an instantly suspicious Patta.

'The attack might have been planned, Dottore.'

'By whom?'

'His wife came to see me a week ago; she told me she was worried that their son was using drugs.'

'Are you saying you think the son did it?'

'No, Signore,' Brunetti said with no sign of the exasperation he felt. 'Signor Gasparini might somehow have learned the name of the man who's selling drugs to the students in his son's school.' Brunetti was reluctant to explain that he had received the information from one of his informers. He paused to await Patta's comment or query.

'And you think this led to the attack?'

'It's a possibility, Dottore,' Brunetti answered mildly. He made no comment on the lack of street crime in Venice, not wanting the Vice-Questore to see it as a hidden criticism of his native city, Palermo.

Patta sat back in his chair and folded his hands, fingers intertwined, across his stomach. Even the weight of his hands seemed unable to wrinkle the smoothness of his shirt.

'What do you want me to do?'

'Nothing, sir. I wanted to alert you to the possible connection: I'd like to find the man said to be selling drugs to the students.'

'You have children,' Patta said. 'Are you worried for them?'

'Less here than I would be in another city,' Brunetti said and then hastened to add, 'Milano, for example.'

Patta nodded, leaned forward and said, 'I understand. All right. See what you can find out.'

'Thank you, sir,' Brunetti said and got to his feet. If he managed to tiptoe to the door and let himself out without another word, he might well be able to add this conversation to the short list of peaceful interchanges he'd had with Patta.

Just as Brunetti reached the threshold, Patta said from behind, 'Good luck, Brunetti,' shocking him so that his hand almost slipped from the handle.

'Thank you, sir,' Brunetti said again and left.

Outside, he leaned back against the door and closed his eyes. He took two deep breaths, unable to believe what had just happened.

'What is it, Signore?' Signorina Elettra asked in a nervous voice.

Brunetti opened his eyes and saw her at her desk, one hand on the edge, as if she were about to push herself to her feet and come to his aid. 'Are you all right?'

'Yes,' he said in a whisper, holding up his hand. 'The Vice-Questore just wished me good luck in finding a suspect.'

She sat down, and Brunetti added, making his way towards her, 'During the entire time I was there, he was pleasant and attentive to me.'

'There must be something wrong with him,' Signorina Elettra offered.

'Or he wants something from me,' Brunetti reasoned out loud.

'You'd never tell him anything important, would you, Signore?' she asked.

Brunetti held up the back of his right hand to her and pointed at the tips of his fingers with the index finger of the other. 'Not without bamboo shoots being driven under my nails,' he said.

She looked relieved. 'I wonder what he's after.' Signorina Elettra took a piece of paper from her desk and extended it towards Brunetti.

He saw that she had written the name of Fornari's wife, followed by a date and two sums in Euros. 'Since he's been out, he's been receiving a disability payment, and she's being paid to take care of him.'

'And the disability?' he asked, wondering what sort of scam Fornari and his wife were using now.

'His prison records state that he was released for medical reasons,' she said.

'Meaning?'

'The records state that he has health problems that can be more easily treated if he's at home with his family and able to get to the hospital for treatment.'

'Any mention of what the problem is?'

'It could be a serious illness,' she said, sounding not the least bit convinced. 'My experience working here, however, suggests the possibility that he's figured out a way to have the social services pay both him and his wife a salary while he contracts out his drug business to the highest bidder.'

'Can you get into ...' Brunetti began but quickly corrected himself. 'That is, can you check his hospital records to see if they give a reason?'

'I'd just started that, Signore,' she said. 'If you go upstairs, I'll tell you when I find something.'

Signorina Elettra called a half-hour later. 'I found his hospital file. It's not good, and I was wrong.'

'What is it?'

'Lung cancer. The bad one. Well,' she temporized, 'one of the bad ones. It's why they released him.'

'Do the records give you an idea of what shape he's in?'

'No. They name the type of chemotherapy he's being given and how many cycles he's had, and that's all.'

'How long has it gone on?'

After a short delay, she said, 'Since he was released. He had two long cycles of chemo, and then radiation. And now he's been back in chemotherapy for the last three months. Once every three weeks.' After a pause, she added, 'His doctors decided he's too weak to get there by himself, so he's taken there by Sanitrans.'

'When was he last in the hospital?'

He heard papers being turned, accompanied by a light humming sound. After some time, she was back, saying, 'He had *chemio* last week, and he's scheduled for another cycle in two weeks.'

'And he's kept all of his appointments?'

More paper noise, then, 'Yes.'

'Good,' Brunetti said. His response had come unsummoned: Fornari was a drug dealer and an ex-convict, but he was also a man with cancer.

After a long hesitation, she asked, 'Had you thought of one possibility, Commissario?'

'Such as?'

'If he's been in this business for a long time, then he has connections among his ... colleagues. He could run the business from his *telefonino*. All he'd need is a reliable courier.'

'It's an interesting idea, Signorina, and I thank you for it,' Brunetti said. Then he asked her to call him if she learned anything else, and replaced his phone.

He pulled open his bottom drawer, rested his heels on it, and leaned back as far as his chair would permit and studied the ceiling. For the first time, he noticed a beige blot about the size of a compact disc, though with tentacles, descending from the place where the wall above the window on the left met the ceiling. Above his office was the mansard where, centuries before, the servants had lived. Up there, the rooms on this side of the building served as a general deposit for old furniture and filing cabinets and were seldom visited. Low-ceilinged and wooden-floored, the rooms had few windows, and those very small. He had been there years before and had noted the state of the window frames, but his office was then on the other side of the building, so he had not seen a problem.

In Fornari, however, he did see a problem. A man going through the chemotherapy prescribed for a particularly vicious kind of tumour was hardly likely to be delivering drugs to another part of the city, nor standing in front of a school, in the cold, selling drugs. He was even more unlikely to find sufficient strength to accost, assault, and hurl a man down the steps of a bridge.

Brunetti reconsidered the spot on the wall. He was reluctant to see Fornari as a dead end, no matter how parlous his state of health. The wife. Colleagues. A telephone. How easy it would be for Fornari to send someone else.

He went over everything he had discovered about Gasparini, another man with a nice wife. At times it seemed to him as though Italy were a country filled with men who had nice wives. For heaven's sake, *he* was a man with a nice wife.

He got to his feet, deciding in that instant to go and *curiosare* down at the far end of Castello. It would be better to go alone so that he and Fornari could have a quiet little talk, drug dealer to drug dealer.

17

He found the address in *Calli, Campielli e Canali*; near the wall of the Arsenale that ran along the Rio delle Gorne. He couldn't remember the last time he had been in that neighbourhood, though he did remember that there was a large tree in Campo delle Gorne, and a friend of his had once tried to sell him a half-share in a boat that had a docking space along that wall.

He'd refused the offer, knowing then, with Raffi just born, that the concerns of life could not include a boat. Boats belonged to the frivolity and freedom of youth or to the endless, sometimes empty, hours of age. Most men had more than enough to occupy them with families and work. A boat was a girlfriend and not a wife.

As he studied the map in *Calli, Campielli e Canali,* he hoped it would reanimate his feet's memory and take him there easily. He got lost only twice, and one time really didn't count: at the end of Calle dei Furlani, he started to turn right but caught himself in time and turned left. A few minutes later, entering Campo Do Pozzi, he continued straight across and walked to a dead end before he admitted defeat and turned back to the *campo* and then to the left, down and out into Campo delle Gorne.

A tall, attractive blonde woman stood by the edge of the canal, looking down at something in the water, a robust white dog sitting side-saddle at her feet. Brunetti approached and said, not knowing how he knew she was English but so certain that she was that he addressed her in that language, 'Is something wrong, Signora?'

'It's Martino's tennis ball,' she said. She smiled and added, 'Nothing to be done, I'm afraid.'

Brunetti looked into the canal and saw the furry yellow ball, floating off to the left. 'If I were thirty years younger, Signora, I'd dive in and get it for you,' he said impulsively. If she had a dog, then she lived in the city: all the more reason for a bit of Italian *galanteria*.

She laughed aloud and years scattered from her. She turned to study his face. 'If I were thirty years younger, I'd want you to,' she said. Then, looking down at the dog, she said, 'Come along, Martino: we can't have everything we'd like.'

She gave Brunetti another smile and turned back towards the church of San Martino Vescovo.

Cheered by the encounter, Brunetti continued along the water and turned left into a narrow *calle* into which no light shone. The door was on his right, so low and broad as to seem almost square. He looked for a bell and, finding none, knocked a few times. He waited a moment, knocked again, and when there was still no response, made a fist and pounded out five sharp blows.

He heard a voice, then footsteps, and then the door was pulled back by a woman of about his own age, tall and too thin, who stepped out into the *calle*. 'Are you here to see Gianluca?' she asked in a voice that expressed hope. She had red hair that had gone white at the roots three centimetres ago. The skin around her nose and mouth repeated the same colours, with small flecks peeling off irritated, reddened skin. Her eyes were lapis blue, so blue that for an instant Brunetti thought she must be wearing contact lenses, but she was not the sort of woman to bother with such things.

'Yes, I am,' Brunetti answered, without a smile.

She seemed not to expect one and stepped back inside, holding the door open. 'Come in. He's upstairs.'

Brunetti passed in front of her, careful not to say anything, and found himself in a damp corridor, a wooden staircase on one side. This might well have been one of the houses built for the workers in the Arsenale at the turn of the last century: many of them had been transformed into bijoux bed and breakfasts; this one had not. He climbed the stairs, heard her coming up behind him.

When he reached the first-floor landing, she said from behind, 'To the right.' He turned and saw another door, this one a proper rectangle, standing slightly ajar, light and heat emerging from it.

'Go in,' she said and moved up behind him, forcing Brunetti towards the door. He pushed it open without asking permission and entered a low room with a beamed ceiling, though not beamed in the way he was accustomed to seeing. These beams were worm-eaten and encrusted with dark remnants of the smoke that must have poured from the sort of coal-burning stove he remembered his grandparents had used. There were two windows, close together, but whatever stood on the other side of the glass was obscured by the humidity that covered and trickled down the surface.

The condensation made Brunetti all the more conscious of the heat that seemed to pour from the walls as well as from the two electric heaters that stood in front of the sofa on which half lay, half sat a pale-faced man with long, lank hair. It was almost noon, yet no light came through the windows: Brunetti didn't know if it was due to the narrowness of the *calle* or the height of the surrounding buildings. He knew only that he was in a trap, or a cave, or a prison cell.

The man looked across at him. 'Who are you?'

'My name's Guido.'

'Did they send you?'

'Yes,' Brunetti answered, putting as much impatience as he could into the monosyllable.

'What do they want?' The man's voice was a smoker's voice, slimy and unpleasant.

Brunetti smiled, pulled over a chair, and sat without being asked. 'What do you think they want, Signor Fornari?'

Brunetti turned to look over his shoulder and saw the woman standing at the door. 'Does she have to be here?' he asked roughly.

'No,' Fornari said. 'Get out.'

The woman obeyed and surprised Brunetti by closing the door quietly.

When Brunetti glanced back at the other man, it looked as though he had fallen asleep. His face was flushed, either by the heat or by whatever drugs he was being given. Or perhaps by the illness itself.

Fornari might once have been handsome. His nose was thin and fine, the arch of his brows strangely elegant. Well-defined full lips contradicted the cadaverous cheeks above them.

He opened his eyes, grey and faintly cloudy, and asked, 'Will they wait?'

'You should know better than to ask that, Signor Fornari,' Brunetti said with exaggerated politeness.

'I've always paid them on time. I've been a good client,' he insisted.

The wetness of the voice, as though some soggy thing were trapped in his throat, set Brunetti's teeth on edge. 'That was then,' Brunetti said impassively. 'This is now.'

When he had drifted away, Fornari's head had tipped to his right side, and now he had to struggle to push himself upright. Brunetti saw his hands, little more than claws, push at the seat of the sofa, drag a pillow from behind his back. He thought of the man's voice and quelled the impulse to move close enough to help him.

'My wife took the money last night. You got it, didn't you?'

Brunetti confined himself to nodding.

'So why did they tell her they're getting a new supplier?'

'For the Albertini, you mean?' Brunetti asked.

Fornari flashed him a surprised look. He was weak, but he was no fool. He nodded, but his expression was wary.

Brunetti put on a shrewd face and said, 'We've got someone who can take care of both. The Albertini and Marco Polo. Besides, look at you. How much longer do you think you can run things?' Then he added, not bothering to disguise his contempt, 'You think no one's noticed your wife? You think she's able to do this?' Then, raising his voice and taking it closer to anger, Brunetti asked,

'You think we'd take the chance of using her? Might as well hire a circus clown.' He forced out a small, deprecating laugh, as though Fornari had told him a joke that wasn't very funny.

'Is that why there was no delivery today?' Fornari asked, all suspicion vanished.

'What do you think?' Brunetti demanded.

'Then what happens to us?' Fornari asked, voice wobbling towards panic. He was interrupted by an enormous cough that pulled him forward to the edge of the sofa. There followed another and another and then an extended series of long, choking noises that made Brunetti want to flee the room.

The door opened and the woman was there, a clean white towel in her hands. She bent over the choking man and turned him towards the back of the sofa and on to his side. She wedged the towel between his face and the sofa, then lifted his legs and put them on the seat.

The coughing continued, wet and horrible and filled with the approach of death. Nothing, no one, could survive the power of that cough; lungs could not remain in place with that savage force filling the room. Brunetti got to his feet and went out into the corridor. He closed the door and stood there for what seemed a long time, listening to a life being coughed away.

Finally, with gasps and pauses and long moments of silence, the coughing slowed to a stop. Brunetti unclasped his fists and pulled his hands from his pockets. After another few minutes, the woman emerged from the room. She looked at Brunetti, making no attempt to veil her contempt for his weakness. 'He's asleep. You can go.'

He started down the steps, the woman close behind him as though she wanted to be sure she saw the last of him. When they got to the bottom, he waited for her. She walked past without looking at him and opened the door.

'What did they tell you when you took the money last night?' he asked.

'That they didn't want me. They've got someone new to do the deliveries. I'm fired.' Her face screwed up, as though she were going to cry, but then she breathed a long sigh, almost of relief.

Anger or impatience coloured her voice. 'I told you, I'm fired.' Then, with the same suspiciousness as the man, she asked, 'Didn't they tell you?'

He shrugged, as though it was the sort of thing that happened in all big companies: failure of information transfer from one division to another; no prompt updating of human resources policy; delayed termination notice.

He walked in front of her, again without excusing himself, and left the apartment. She didn't bother to slam the door.

18

As he started back towards the Questura, Brunetti thought over his conversation with Patta. Luckily, he had told the Vice-Questore only that there was a possibility of a connection between Gasparini and the drug dealer. The coughing shadow he had just spoken to was not the person who had accosted Gasparini on the bridge, nor did his wife seem to be a person capable of such a thing. Fornari lacked the strength to make a phone call: he could never have organised the attack on Gasparini.

So here it was: the one obvious connection between victim and suspect coughed away. He needed to go back to the beginning, start from there, looking at things he might have dismissed while considering Professoressa Crosera's son's possible involvement in drugs.

He took his phone and dialled Griffoni's number.

'*Sì*,' she answered.

'I'll be there in ten minutes.'

She was at her desk, which he saw had been moved and now faced the wall. Though this forced her to look at the cracks and peeling paint from a distance of little more than half a metre, it allowed her visitor the luxury of not having to sit in the open doorway. By serpenting past the back of her chair, another person could now sit in the other chair, as small as a stool, and talk to her with the door closed. Yet departure had to be negotiated by the two people sharing the office to decide who was to move first.

Brunetti stopped at the open door and swivelled his head to study the tiny space. 'Putting the desk there gives the room a sense of grandeur,' he said and slipped past her to sit in the guest chair.

Smiling, she closed the door and turned to him. 'What is it?' she asked. When he hesitated, she added, 'You sounded stressed on the phone.'

He had decided to tell her without preliminaries. 'I went to see Fornari. He's dying of lung cancer in a pit of a house in Castello and could no more attack anyone than he could rise up on angel wings and fly to the hospital for chemotherapy.'

'So where does that leave us?'

'With evidence that Gasparini was attacked but no one to suspect for it.'

'You're excluding a random attack?' she asked.

'Absolutely,' he said and resisted the impulse to add, *This is Venice, after all.*

She moved forward in her chair, as though preparing to stand, but abandoned the attempt and turned to face him more fully. He noticed that she was wearing a black T-shirt and a black woollen jacket. The single strand of pearls looked real; he knew the blonde of her hair was.

'That's good,' she said. 'That you don't think it was random.'

'Why?'

'Because then there's a motive. And once there's a motive, there will be evidence leading back to it.'

Brunetti believed the same thing. 'There's knowing and then there's finding,' he said.

She leaned against the back of her chair and picked up a notebook and pen. 'Tell me everything you've learned.'

It took him a long time to tell her: what Professoressa Crosera had told him, this time in greater detail; her refusal to allow him to speak to their son and his chance meeting with the boy, and the boy's aggressive behaviour. He finished with his visit to Fornari and his wife and the misery of the place, though it had been, he realized only now, clean and tidy. There had been no mess or clutter, and Fornari had worn freshly ironed pyjamas. It was the cough, Brunetti admitted, but only to himself, that had dirtied the place.

When he was finished, Griffoni closed the notebook and placed it to the side of her desk. 'Nothing in there,' she began, waving towards the notebook, 'would lead me anywhere.' She paused, considered, and then corrected herself. 'Except back to Professoressa Crosera. I think it's worth talking to her again.'

Brunetti was in complete agreement with this: he knew how adept Griffoni could be at playing good cop, especially with female witnesses. 'All right. I'll see if she'll talk to us. Maybe we can ...'

Griffoni broke in to say, 'If she's at the hospital, it shouldn't be there. That would be too much for her.'

Brunetti pulled out his *telefonino* and held it up. Griffoni nodded, and he found and keyed in the number.

It rang nine times, ten, and on the eleventh she picked it up and said her name.

'Signora, it's Commissario Brunetti. How is your husband?'

'As you saw him the last time. He's still here; there's been no change.'

'Ah,' Brunetti sighed. 'I'm very sorry for your trouble, Signora, but I'm afraid I have to add to it.'

'Did you find the person you think attacked him?' she asked in a far more neutral voice than Brunetti would have expected. But then it occurred to him: what difference was there between knowing and not knowing, really?

'No, we haven't. That's why I'd like to come and talk with you again.'

'Here?' she asked, sounding alarmed.

'No. At your home. If you would permit that.'

'What good would it do?'

He realized that finding the guilty person would do no one any good at all and never would. It would do bad to the person who had committed the crime and to their family; it could do bad to the family of the victim, too, for all they'd have was the temptation of vengeance, and Brunetti had seen how quickly vengeance corrupted all who went near it.

'It's not my job to do good, Signora,' he admitted. 'Only to find the guilty person and see that they are arrested.'

'What will that change?' she asked. Her voice was very low: he had to struggle to hear it. He thought he could hear rattling noises in the background, but he wasn't sure.

'When would you like to come?' she suddenly asked, surprising him.

'After lunch, perhaps? Would three o'clock be convenient for you?'

'Yes,' she said and hung up.

'She agreed,' Brunetti told Griffoni.

'Good,' Griffoni said. It will be better in her home, I think.'

'Better because she'll be more relaxed?' Brunetti asked.

'Yes,' Griffoni answered and got to her feet. 'And because we can take a look around.'

They had lunch together. Brunetti had called Paola to tell her he had to talk to someone, and she'd been completely accepting of his news, explaining that the children would be content with what she gave them, so long as there was a lot of it.

'Work?' he asked, wondering if she had a paper to prepare or exams to correct.

'Reading,' she said and left it at that.

At lunch, he and Griffoni talked about a case that was filling the local papers, concerning a doctor from Egypt who was accused of having killed his sixteen-year-old daughter, having found what he considered flirtatious messages on her Facebook account sent by a boy in her class, an Italian boy. One of the messages that had driven the man to murder was, 'Your answer in history class today was very good.' Another time the boy wrote, 'Do you have time for a coffee after class?' Because the father was no adept at following the order of messages on Facebook, he did not notice that she had not responded to the first and had said, 'No' to the second.

The father had stabbed her while she was asleep, later telling the police that he could not have done it if she had been awake and looking at him: he loved her too much.

Brunetti and Griffoni spoke of the incident with the despair that comes at the realization of human prejudice and stupidity. 'She was sixteen years old, and he killed her because a boy asked if she wanted to have a coffee, for the love of God,' Griffoni said. 'If I think of what I was doing when I was sixteen ...' she began and covered her eyes with her right hand.

'You aren't Egyptian,' Brunetti said.

'Neither was she,' Griffoni shot back. 'She came here when she was three years old. Is she supposed to behave as if she'd been raised in a tent in the desert?'

'The father says he wants to die, wants us to kill him.'

'Oh, Guido, give it a rest, would you?' she shot back, hiding neither her surprise nor her anger.

'What does that mean?' he asked, startled by her vehemence.

At the approach of the waiter with their pasta, both stopped talking. As soon as he was out of hearing, Brunetti repeated, 'Tell me what that means.'

Griffoni sprinkled cheese on her pasta, speared some peas one by one, then a final piece of yellow pepper, before twirling her fork full of *tagliolini*. The pasta remained suspended on the end of her fork while she looked at him. 'It means it's all nonsense. He doesn't want to die. He wants to suck up to Westerners and make them believe his heart is broken because he murdered his daughter.'

She set her fork down and put her face in her hands but continued speaking. 'He isn't content with having murdered her: now he wants sympathy because he's a victim trapped between two cultures.' She removed her hands and picked up her fork. 'It makes me want to scream: it's all so orchestrated and fake.'

'You really think that? You don't believe him?'

This time, her fork slammed against her plate. 'No, I don't believe him. And I don't believe those old men who say they had to kill their poor, suffering wives because they just couldn't stand to see the woman they loved become another person because of Alzheimer's.' She made a fist and set it on the table. 'Tell me when you've ever read about a woman giving the same excuse for murdering her husband.'

Brunetti noticed that the people at the next table were looking at them nervously, probably afraid they were a husband and wife having an argument.

'What about the girl's mother? Surely you believe her.'

'Because she's a woman, you mean?' Griffoni demanded with soft-voiced sarcasm. Before he could answer, she said, 'No, as a matter of fact, I don't: I think she probably handed him the knife.'

Brunetti was so surprised that it was his turn to set his fork on his plate and stare across the table at her. Where had all of this been hiding for so long?

'That's a bit severe, don't you think, Claudia?' he asked, keeping his voice calm and conversational.

'You read the papers, didn't you? She said she went in to wake her daughter up for school, and when she saw the blood, she screamed and ran out of the house. She'd slept beside her husband and woke up to find her daughter murdered in her bed.'

Brunetti nodded. This, indeed, was the story that the papers had printed and were still printing.

'You think he'd come back into the bedroom and slip into bed quietly, Guido? He'd just stabbed his only child seven times, and he goes back to bed, and his wife doesn't even wake up, and off he goes to sleep?'

Brunetti looked at his pasta, no longer wanting it.

'They found blood all over his pyjamas, Guido. Or better, *we* found blood all over his pyjamas. And in their bed. And we found his wife's fingerprints on the handle of the knife.'

'She said it was on the floor, and she picked it up without thinking.'

'And washed the blood off and put it back in the kitchen drawer? How'd it get into the drawer, Guido? And who washed the blood off?'

The waiter approached their table, but Griffoni waved him away. She opened her mouth, closed it and then took five or six very deep breaths.

She reached across the table and put her right hand on his arm. 'I'm sorry, Guido, but I get crazy when I have to listen to this.'

'To what?'

'To men explaining their violence towards women and expecting people to believe they really didn't have a choice. I'm sick to death of it and sick of people being taken in by it. He murdered her because he was losing control of her. It's as simple as that. Anything else is just smoke in our eyes and an appeal to our desire to feel good about ourselves because we're so tolerant of other cultures. And it's fake, fake, fake.'

She stopped and stared at him for a long time, weighing something Brunetti couldn't identify. 'And, if I might add, only men are stupid enough to believe it because they feel the same desire to control women and – if truth must be told – secretly sympathize with it.'

She beckoned the waiter and, when he came, told him he could take the plates away and bring them two coffees. They were very quiet when he picked up the plates.

19

Both of them preferred to walk. Not bothering to try to exchange idle conversation, they reached Gasparini's home just past three. Brunetti rang the bell, and soon they were seated in the living room where he had spoken to her – had it been only yesterday? Professoressa Crosera had turned strangely pale. Her hair was the same rich brown, but that only made the other change more obvious. Her skin had faded and resembled parchment. The curves of her cheekbones had been replaced by angles. Two days had done this to her, Brunetti thought.

'Professoressa Crosera,' Brunetti said, after refusing what had been a pro forma offer of coffee, 'we'd like you to talk about your husband.'

She looked at Brunetti, then at Griffoni, then back to Brunetti, as though waiting for him to translate what he'd said into a language she could understand. 'What do you mean?' she finally asked. Even her voice was grey, with the flat inertia of lack of sleep and constant fear.

'I found the man who was selling drugs at the school,' Brunetti said.

Her eyes leapt back to his face, and she asked, 'Did he do it?'

Brunetti shook his head. 'It would be impossible for him; he's very sick.'

'Is he in the hospital?' she asked, and Brunetti wondered if she would try to find him there and do him harm.

'He was: he's having chemotherapy.' Wanting to test her, he added, 'But it doesn't look like there's any chance it's going to be of any help to him.'

'Good,' she said savagely.

Brunetti was at a loss how to respond. As if she had not spoken, he went on, 'He isn't capable of having attacked your husband. I'm sure of that.'

'So?'

'It has to have been someone else.'

Professoressa Crosera turned her attention from him and asked Griffoni, 'Did I surprise you with what I just said about him?' Brunetti realized she wanted to know what another woman's reaction would be.

'Not at all,' Griffoni answered.

'Even if I want him dead?'

'If he was selling drugs to your son, it's an entirely natural reaction.' Griffoni's voice was filled with Delphic calm.

'Would you think the same?'

Griffoni clasped her hands and rested them in her lap. Looking at them, she said, 'I don't have children, so I can't feel what you do.' Then, before the other woman could speak, she went on, head still lowered. 'But I think it's what

I'd want, too.' That said, Griffoni raised her head and looked at the other woman, face expressionless.

Professoressa Crosera nodded but said nothing.

Brunetti saw that his only choice was to pretend that the conversation had been proceeding in linear form since he'd said he wanted her to talk about her husband. He was conscious he'd thought of Fornari as the assailant: now he had nothing. 'We'd like you to tell us about anything unusual your husband did or said in the last few weeks or anything strange that he might have mentioned or talked about.'

'Even something in the newspaper he commented on,' Griffoni offered. 'Or a subject that angered or excited him.'

Professoressa Crosera closed her eyes and raised her right hand to rub at her forehead. She pushed at the skin, as though trying to smooth it up to her hairline. 'Tullio's a calm person: it's seldom that he gets angry. He's patient, doesn't yell at the kids. He works hard.'

'What sort of things do you talk about together?' Griffoni risked asking.

She had to think about this for a while, as though the man lying in the hospital bed was an obstacle to her memory of the other one, the man she had married. 'Our work, both his and mine. The children. Films we've seen. Our families. Where we want to go on vacation.' Her voice had slowed with each subject, and now it stopped. She raised her right hand in a helpless wave. 'We talk about what everyone talks about.'

Brunetti tried again. 'Has he mentioned any trouble at work?'

Her glance was sudden, almost fearful: Brunetti interpreted it as meaning she had never thought that her husband might have been in danger.

Reading her expression, he realized how improbable it all sounded. Gasparini worked in Verona, for heaven's sake: how likely was it that some jealous colleague or angry client would come to Venice and roam around the city until he conveniently met his unsuspecting victim on a bridge?

'Or someone here in the city with whom he's had trouble of any sort?' Griffoni asked.

Professoressa Crosera, who had lowered her head after Brunetti's question about her husband's work, raised it to meet Griffoni's glance. 'No, nothing. At least nothing I know about.'

Brunetti took the opportunity to say, 'Yesterday, I asked if I might look through his belongings.' He waited to let her acknowledge his having asked. 'Would you let us look through them?' Her face tightened in resistance, but before she could speak, Brunetti remembered her voice when she'd said the word, 'Good', and he added, 'It might help find the person who did this to him.'

'You believe that?' she asked.

'I don't know what will help, Signora,' he admitted, surprised at his own frankness. 'That's why I'd like Commissario Griffoni to have a look, as well. She might notice something I don't.'

Professoressa Crosera put her fingers back on her forehead and made the same upward pushing motion. 'Go ahead, then. It's the second door on the left.'

They found the room in order: the bed was made; there was no discarded clothing. Brunetti walked over to what must be the door to the bathroom and poked his head inside. Here the same order prevailed, save for a shelf above the sink that held cosmetics and lotions.

The wardrobe was a modern, white thing, enormous, set in the middle of the far wall of the room. Brunetti pulled open the two doors; one squeaked terribly. They stepped back to get a better view. A row of men's shoes were lined up on the right side. Above them, the waistbands of trousers peeked from below matching jackets, and to the right of those hung a few jackets and at least twenty shirts, all white.

The left side held dresses, skirts, slacks, shirts, and two long gowns all mixed together with no attempt at order. At least a dozen pairs of shoes stood below, some of them next to their partners. Griffoni moved back and stood with her arms folded, as if to get an impression of the two people who shared the space from the state in which they left their respective sections. Three shelves stood to each side of the hanging clothing; three drawers below the shelves.

Men's winter hats and gloves sat on the top shelf, beneath them heavy sweaters, and beneath those lighter sweaters and sweatshirts; the feminine side repeated the same contents on the same shelves, though there was considerably less order in their arrangement.

'He's a neat man, wouldn't you say?' Griffoni asked, pointing with her chin to the piles of folded clothing.

'It looks that way,' Brunetti answered, thinking of what must be the dull routine of an accountant's work. 'And his wife?' he asked.

Instead of answering, Griffoni stepped closer to the left side of the wardrobe and touched the material of one of the gowns and two of the dresses. 'She knows what suits her.'

'I don't understand,' Brunetti said. Griffoni reached up with palms pressed together and slipped them between the two dresses to separate them. 'Look at these,' she said. 'They're perfect for her: cut, material, the way they'd fall from the shoulder.' She removed her hands, and the dresses went back to caressing one another. 'She knows what looks good on her.'

'And those?' Brunetti said, pointing to the shoes below, lying around in drunken disorder.

'They all have wooden shoe trees, Guido. Did you notice that?'

No, he hadn't: he had been too busy seeing that some were not standing neatly next to their mates. 'And at least five pairs are hand made,' she added.

'And him?' Brunetti asked, wondering if he'd be asking her to interpret their handwriting next.

'Orderly, perhaps annoyingly so at times; very conventional and fixed in his ideas.'

'You read all that from the way his suits are lined up?' Brunetti asked.

She smiled. 'He has three grey suits, Guido,' she said, pointing to his side of the wardrobe. She started at the top drawer on the right side and worked her way down, opening, putting a hand inside to move things around, and closing them one after the other. Underwear, socks, and handkerchiefs. She pulled open the third one and looked inside. Instead of reaching in, she put her hands behind her back and said, 'Just look at what we see.'

'Meaning?' Brunetti asked with more than a hint of impatience.

'Meaning that, in the midst of all that order, here we have the secret centre of the man.'

'Oh, come on, Claudia,' Brunetti said, 'that's nonsense.'

'Just look,' she said, pulling the drawer out farther and stepping away from it.

Brunetti bent over the open drawer and then knelt on the other side to take a better look. It held all manner of things that appeared to have been dropped in helter-skelter. There were bunched-up banknotes with Arabic script and portraits of men in headdresses. There was an envelope he found, which, when he opened it, held boarding passes for flights to and from Dubai four months before. There were two key rings with keys that, when they examined them, appeared to be for different locks. There was a small malachite hippopotamus, a receipt for thirty Euros spent to charge up his imob travel card, two separately wrapped cough drops, and a well-worn leather wallet. Brunetti opened it and slipped his finger into the various slots; all were empty, as was the larger slot in the back, where bills were usually kept.

Under a few ten-pound notes, he found more receipts; two for restaurants and one for the purchase of three printer cartridges at Testolini; one of those cartridges – black – had somehow got itself into the drawer. Brunetti flipped through some papers held together with a paper clip and found that they were not receipts but coupons for cosmetics, each for 154 Euros, all made out to 'Gasparini'. There were four AAA batteries in an unopened package, a flashlight that didn't work, more receipts, and three more coupons. He stood and slipped the drawer closed with the toe of his right foot.

'Not so fast, Guido,' she said and bent to pull the drawer open again. 'There's no order here; the things have nothing in common, unlike all his other things.' She picked up the envelope and pulled out the stiff pieces of cardboard. 'Why did he keep only these two boarding passes? These are people who travel. Didn't you tell me his wife travels a lot for work? '

Brunetti nodded, but he still had no idea what she was talking about.

Griffoni pulled the drawer out and set it on the table between the room's two windows. One by one, she removed its contents. She placed all of the objects in a long line, running from the drawer to the end of the table and then back again in a second row.

The line began with the boarding passes and, next to them, the currency printed with the portraits of the men in headdresses. Next she put down the leather wallet, and next to that the malachite hippopotamus. The AAA batteries lay beside the printer cartridge; then came the stack of coupons, the flashlight, the cough drops, the key rings, receipts, currency. More receipts and a few objects not seen before appeared, all in a line that swung around and back to the empty drawer.

Griffoni examined the boarding passes. 'People say Emirates is the best airline,' she said, and put them back into their envelope. She set it down and picked up the flashlight, which still didn't work. She went through everything, picking up each piece, reading and trying to decipher any text she saw.

While she was busy studying a hotel bill from Milano, Brunetti picked up the coupons held together by a paper clip. He studied the first one again and then turned them over one by one, examining each. Finally he looked at Griffoni and asked, 'Why would a man have nine hundred Euros in coupons for cosmetics?'

For some reason, he thought of the boys accepting the scandal magazines at the kiosk. Boys didn't read them. Men didn't use cosmetics, at least not nine hundred Euros' worth of them.

'It doesn't make any sense, does it?' Brunetti walked over to Griffoni and handed her the papers.

She did as he had, examining them again one by one. 'Nine hundred and twenty-four, to be exact,' she said, handing them back to Brunetti.

'Let's ask her,' Brunetti said. He slipped the coupons into the pocket of his jacket, and together they put everything back into the drawer.

Failing to find Professoressa Crosera where they had left her, Brunetti and Griffoni walked towards the kitchen. They had not heard the boy enter the apartment and so were surprised to find him sitting at the table, an enormous sandwich in one hand. His mother sat opposite him, a cup of what might have been tea in front of her.

'Oh, excuse me,' Brunetti said, stopping abruptly in the open doorway. Griffoni bumped into him with a muffled 'Uh'.

Professoressa Crosera half rose from her seat. The boy set his sandwich on the plate in front of him and started to get to his feet. Brunetti smiled, and Sandro tried to do the same. He had more colour in his face today and seemed calmer. He managed a polite, *'Buongiorno, signori,'* and looked at his mother, uncertain what to do.

'Please. Don't disturb yourself, Signora,' Brunetti said. 'We have only a few more questions. We'll wait for you in the living room.'

Before Professoressa Crosera could say anything, the boy asked, 'Have you found the man who hurt my father?' He tried to make his voice sound very grown-up, but he failed to cover the note of fear in his question.

'Not yet,' Brunetti answered. 'That's why we'd like to speak to your mother again.'

'About what?' she asked, sounding curious, not offended.

'Some of the things we found, Signora,' Brunetti said, giving no farther explanation. 'We'll wait for you in the *salotto,*' he told her and turned away from the doorway. He led Griffoni down the corridor and back into the living room; they sat where they had been and waited for her to return.

Professoressa Crosera arrived a few minutes later and closed the door behind her as she came in. Brunetti got to his feet. 'What is it?' she asked, standing in front of the door.

'We've looked through your husband's belongings, and there's one thing we don't understand,' he said, pulling the coupons from his pocket.

She looked at them and, puzzled, asked, 'What are they?'

'Coupons for cosmetics: we don't understand how he could have such a large credit for cosmetics.' Then, remembering what he'd seen, Brunetti added, 'His name is on them.' He passed them to her. She looked through them briefly, then handed them back.

She walked over and sat on the sofa, and Brunetti resumed his seat next to Griffoni. She glanced at her watch, as if uncertain that she'd have enough time to explain. She looked as though she were trying to smile and said, 'That's his aunt.' She spoke the noun in a manner that led him to believe she had a great deal more to say about this aunt.

Neither of them spoke.

'Zia Matilde,' she said with studied neutrality. 'Matilde Gasparini. She's the Gasparini on the coupons. For some reason, my husband brought them home the last time he saw her and said he had to talk to someone about them. She's eighty-five, so only God knows what she's doing spending so much money on cosmetics.' Professoressa Crosera sounded displeased at the thought.

Brunetti could hardly say anything about the foolishness of women, could he? Nor about the desire not to let go of youth; not to a woman with a husband struggling not to let go of life and certainly not with Griffoni sitting next to him. All he could think of to say was, 'Did he tell you anything about them?'

Surprised, she answered, 'Only that he didn't understand what she told him about where they came from.' Then she added, 'He went to see her when she came home from the hospital, and that's when he found out about them. She told him that wasn't the moment to trouble her by asking about them.' She smiled and shook her head in memory of what she probably considered her husband's aunt's folly.

'The hospital here?' Brunetti asked, to keep the conversation going. When she nodded, he asked, 'Why was she there?'

'Her *badante* couldn't wake her up one morning, so she called an ambulance. We were away, so she didn't reach us for a few days and was very upset.'

Brunetti confined himself to an inquisitive tilt of the head, and she continued. 'When Tullio went to the hospital, he found her doctor before he found her. He said she'd apparently mixed up her medicines and taken too many sleeping pills. He said it often happens to old people.'

Both Brunetti and Griffoni nodded. Griffoni added a sympathetic noise, as if she, too, had stories to tell about old people.

'Tullio told the doctor that he was her nephew, not her son, and didn't know much about her health because she'd always been healthy and never spoke about it. He never even learned the name of her doctor.

'This doctor told him his aunt wasn't as healthy as he seemed to believe and that her records showed she'd been diagnosed with Parkinson's and was taking medicine for it. There was also a prescription for something against early-onset Alzheimer's.'

She raised her eyebrows and closed her eyes for a moment, then went on, 'When Tullio finally saw her, he was shocked by the change. He told me she was suddenly an old woman and very confused. She kept telling him to go to her house and get those coupons because she was afraid Beata, the *badante*, would steal them. She wouldn't rest until he promised to go that same day.'

'And did he?' Brunetti asked.

She nodded, 'She made him give his word, so he had no choice but to go and get them.'

She shook her head at this and said, 'Beata's been with her for ten years; she's like a daughter to her. It's crazy to think she'd steal anything. Besides, she's had ten years to do it.' The more she spoke of the aunt, the more exasperated Professoressa Crosera sounded.

'She was sent home the next day – this was about two weeks ago – and he went to see her there. Twice. She asked him about the coupons again, told him to keep them safe, and he had to promise her that he would.'

'Have you seen her?'

'Not since she was taken home,' she said. 'Only my husband goes. Went.'

'Has anyone told her about your husband?'

She shook her head three or four times. 'I called Beata and told her. She hadn't heard anything. I asked her to try to keep the news from his aunt if she could; she said it would be easy because no one comes to visit any more.'

'Why is that?' Griffoni broke in to ask.

'The people who knew her are all dead or in nursing homes,' Professoressa Crosera answered with the brusque finality of a closing door.

A breathy 'Ah' escaped Griffoni, who turned to Brunetti for a clue as to what he wanted to do.

He took out his notebook, saying, 'Could you tell us her address, Signora?'

'You aren't going to talk to her, are you?'

Brunetti had learned, early on, that witnesses would tolerate anything except sarcasm, so he rejected the idea of telling Professoressa Crosera that her husband's aunt would perhaps be more help to them than the malachite hippopotamus. He smiled and said, 'The coupons are the only things we've found among your husband's belongings that seem out of place, Signora, so I'd like to find out about them. If only to exclude a possibility.' He paused, considering, then asked, 'Would you allow me to take them with me?'

'You won't upset her, will you?' she asked.

Griffoni interrupted to say, 'No. I give my word.'

Professoressa Crosera looked at Griffoni for a few seconds, then gave a quick nod. 'And if you don't find out anything?' she asked.

'Then we'll have to try to find something else,' he said, wishing he had something better to offer her.

'She lives opposite the Carmini,' Professoressa Crosera said, 'the building just in front of the bridge. I'm sorry, but I don't know the number. If you walk down the middle of the bridge, it's the door you'd walk into. Fourth floor: her name's on the bell.'

Brunetti got to his feet; both women stood. She led them to the door, where all three stopped. It was only then that Brunetti remembered he had not asked how her husband was, but the thought had no sooner come to him than Griffoni said, 'I wish you strength in this, Signora.' She turned to leave. Brunetti followed her out, saying nothing.

20

As they walked down the steps, Brunetti reflected on the grace of what Griffoni had said. Only a southerner could display deep emotion with such a conventional wish, so simply stated. It was directed at the person in need, aimed at helping her, not at the unconscious victim, who, however much he might be in need of help willed or bestowed, would never hear or understand it, nor be helped by it in any real way. Not for the first time, Brunetti was aware of the dissonance between his impulse towards suspicion of southerners and his frequent wonder at their instinctive grace of spirit.

Outside the door, Brunetti paused in what another Venetian would recognize as a brief consultation with the GPS implanted in him at birth. There was no greater sign than the quivering needle of a compass makes before finding sharp north or declining west.

Path clear, he set out, and Griffoni fell into step beside him. He led them towards Campo Santa Margherita and then through it the long way and down alongside the church of the Carmini until they were in front of the bridge. They stopped to study the building made conspicuous by two central bricked-up windows on the second floor. 'Why'd they do that?' Griffoni asked.

'Structural problems, I'd say. The *palazzo* is directly on a canal, and they tend to shift around a bit.'

'You make it sound so ordinary,' she said, smiling.

'I suppose it is.'

'But why brick up the windows?'

'They probably realized only after the windows were there that they weakened the wall.'

'Ummm,' she agreed and started up the bridge. In front of the door, she found the bell for 'Gasparini', waited for Brunetti to come up and stand beside her, and rang it.

After some time, a woman's voice asked through the speaker phone, *'Chi è?'*

Brunetti tapped Griffoni's shoulder lightly, and when she looked at him, he pointed at her face: a woman's voice would be far better received than a man's.

'Professoressa Elisa has asked us to stop by and see Signora Gasparini,' Griffoni answered in a voice she made sound friendly and warm.

'Signor Tullio's wife?'

'Yes.'

'Are you from the hospital?'

'No,' Griffoni answered. 'The Professoressa asked us to pass by and see how Signor Tullio's aunt is.'

'Is Signor Tullio all right?' the woman asked.

Griffoni looked at Brunetti, who nodded. 'Yes,' then added, 'Thanks be to God.'

'Ah, yes,' the woman answered. 'I pray for him every day.'

'May we come up and speak with her for a moment?' Griffoni asked.

'Of course, if Professoressa Elisa has sent you.' After a second, the buzzer sounded and the door opened. They entered an enormous, high-ceilinged atrium with the usual white and red chequerboard paving. At the back, large glass doors led to a garden that ran at least a normal city block to a high brick wall. Fruit trees slumbered in damp misery, hunkered down until springtime. The steps in the double flight to the first floor were broad and low, worn away in the centre by centuries of feet going up and down. The doors of two separate apartments faced them on the first landing and then again on each successive landing up to the fourth, where there was only one door. Seeing it when they reached the top, Griffoni asked, 'Does that mean the whole floor is hers?'

'Probably,' Brunetti answered, thinking of what the combined size would be. He rang the bell beside it.

After a moment, the door was opened by a woman in her mid-thirties, with blonde hair and pale blue eyes. She stepped back to invite them to enter. She wore a white sweater made of some kind of synthetic fabric and a dark skirt that fell to the middle of her calves. Her hair was parted in the middle and fell, straight as a plumb line, to her shoulders. She had the rounded features and pale skin of an Eastern European and smiled nervously at them.

After asking permission to enter, Brunetti stepped aside to allow Griffoni to go in first.

The entrance was an enormously long, low-ceilinged room made even lower by dark beams running from side to side. Even the light that came from the windows at the back, windows that must overlook the garden, did little to brighten the room; the dark wooden floor managed to trap even more light. 'The Signora is in her room,' the woman said, turning towards the back of the house.

They passed two long tapestries that hung facing one another: Brunetti saw dark stags being speared by faded human figures in one, boars in the other, and was glad of the lack of light. Farther on, there were portraits of men on one wall, women facing them, staring across at the other sex, both sides in need of restoration and better spirits.

The young woman stopped in front of a door on the right and said, 'The Signora is in here. You won't say anything that will upset her, will you?' Voice growing confidential while pleading for their understanding, she added, 'She's not the same as she was.'

Her sadness was real, Brunetti thought. 'We'll certainly try not to, Signorina.'

She tried to smile and dipped low in something that resembled a curtsey but might have been a genuflection, then she opened the door and stepped into a room as dim as the corridor. 'Some friends of Signor Tullio are here, Signora,' she announced in a falsely bright voice. She took two steps into the room and turned to wave them in behind her. As soon as they were inside, she repeated the curtsey and left, closing the door behind her.

A tiny woman with flame-red curly hair, cut into a youthful cap suitable for a far younger person, was seated in a low chair in front of the windows, her feet raised and resting on a brocade-covered footstool. What light there was came in from her right side. Her blue silk jacket was patterned with interwoven red dragons, and her skirt, striped grey and green in some shiny fabric that might have been satin, fell to her ankles. On her feet, she had the sort of open-backed, high-heeled bedroom slippers

Brunetti had seen only in opera or in Longhi's portraits: they even had the fuzzy ruff over the instep. She could have been waiting to host a dinner party or preparing to perform in a Christmas pantomime.

The immobility of her face might have been the result of surgery badly performed, although, Brunetti reflected, it might as easily reflect a lack or loss of interest in what lay beyond this room. Her eyes were cloudy, not only with the faint smokiness that often comes with advanced age, but with a vague uncertainty about the reality they perceived. Her mouth was as red as her hair and just as thin.

The only animation – and Brunetti flinched from the word – came from the occasional jerks and tremors of her head, which snapped to the left with no predictable rhythm. Brunetti tried to time the motions, but they came when they wanted, after three seconds, or five, or one.

She sat in the chair as though that were her occupation. There was no cup or glass on the table near her, no fruit, no chocolates, no book or magazine. She looked at them and gave a regal wave to a row of chairs that faced her, as if part of her time were spent in giving audiences. They sat.

Around them stood large, dark, awkward pieces of furniture. The chairs seemed too padded, or too high, or too low; some were merely too ugly. One wardrobe tilted to the right and seemed in imminent danger of collapse. A table had legs that appeared to be suffering from elephantiasis, and a mirror had grown mouldy with age. The pieces looked like family heirlooms from a family with no taste.

'You're friends of my nephew?' she asked in place of greeting.

'*Sì*, Signora,' Brunetti said. Griffoni nodded and gave a small, affirmative smile. The woman barely looked at her. Every so often, her head shot quickly to the left and then back. Brunetti made himself ignore it.

'Why hasn't he been to see me?' Her voice sought anger but found only petulance.

'He's very busy, Signora. You know he has to travel for his work,' Brunetti answered, blocking out the image of the man in the hospital bed.

'But he comes to see me before he leaves,' she said uncertainly, as though in search of confirmation from Brunetti. Her voice was weak and tended to drop off in the final words of a sentence.

'Unfortunately, this trip was very sudden, so he asked us to come and tell you,' Brunetti risked saying.

'When will . . .' she began, but then seemed to forget what it was she wanted to ask, or perhaps the future tense was difficult for her.

'He asked us,' Brunetti began, as though he had not noticed that she had failed to finish the sentence, 'to bring his greetings and to ask you to help him understand something.'

'Understand what?' she asked.

'He's been trying to help with the coupons you gave him . . .' Brunetti left the sentence open, half-question, half-statement, suggesting she confirm or deny.

She shifted her feet so quickly that one of the slippers fell to the floor. As with the jerking motion of her head, Brunetti pretended not to notice it; in fact, everyone in the room pretended not to notice it.

'Coupons?' she asked in a voice that now had a quaver, as though the question had pushed her over the edge into advanced, befuddled old age.

'Yes, the ones from the Farmacia della Fontana. It seems the pharmacist is willing now to redeem them in cash.'

The prospect of cash seemed to rejuvenate her. The hesitant manner of an old woman vanished, replaced by a younger woman's ardent curiosity. Brunetti suddenly found himself thinking of something his mother had told him when he was a boy, one of her attempts to suggest to him what the world was like, without, of course, revealing that this was what she was doing. He had said – he must have been fourteen or fifteen – that he thought Venetians were different from other people, but he wasn't sure how.

They'd been in the kitchen, and she was wiping her hands on the apron that was as much a part of her as was her wedding ring. 'We're greedy, Guido. It's in our marrow,' she'd said, and that was the only answer he got.

'He said that?' Signora Gasparini asked. 'In cash?'

Brunetti said 'Yes', and Griffoni nodded.

The old woman moved her head, this time voluntarily and up and down, and glanced towards something they couldn't see; her face went slack in thought. Silence expanded; Brunetti could think of nothing to say or ask.

'When will Tullio be back?' the old woman asked.

'Ah, I don't know, Signora. He said he'd be gone at least until the end of next week. That's why he asked us to stop by and see how you are and ask if you need anything.'

She gave him a long look, and Brunetti could all but see her trying to gaze into his soul to discover what sort of man he was. 'It's hard for Elisa and the kids,' he said with easy familiarity, 'with him away for so long.' Brunetti turned to Griffoni, as though he'd just remembered she was sitting there with him. 'Did he tell you when he'd be back, Claudia?'

'No, he didn't. But we have a date for dinner with them on the twentieth, haven't we?'

Brunetti nodded and turned back to Signora Gasparini. 'He'll be back then, by the end of next week,' Brunetti assured her, smiling to show his pleasure at that fact.

'That's a long time,' the old woman pointed out.

'Oh, it will pass quickly,' Brunetti said airily and shifted forward as though about to get to his feet.

The old woman held up a hand. 'You didn't tell me your names.'

'I'm Guido Brunetti, and this is Claudia Griffoni.'

'Is she your wife?' Signora Gasparini asked.

It was Griffoni who interrupted to say, 'As good as, Signora,' and give a breathy laugh.

If Brunetti had expected the old woman to be surprised by this, he was mistaken. She turned her attention to Griffoni, looking at her for the first time. For as long as she kept her eyes on Griffoni – Brunetti counted out nine beats – her head did not move. But when she said, 'So you do things together?' the small tremors began again.

Given Griffoni's last remark, Brunetti wasn't quite certain what she had in mind.

Griffoni apparently felt no confusion, for she answered, 'Yes, we do, Signora. We shop together and share household expenses. Guido still pays for dinner, though, if we go out.'

This seemed to satisfy the woman, for she said, 'So you'll go together to get the money?'

'Of course,' Griffoni assured her. 'We're used to working as a team.' She smiled at the other woman to acknowledge the ambiguity of what she'd just said. Then, as though suddenly recalling a missing detail, Griffoni added, 'But we need to know what to tell the pharmacist.'

Suddenly alert, Signora Gasparini said, 'Are you Venetian?' It was a request for information, entirely neutral.

'No, I'm not, Signora, but I live here now,' Griffoni said and gave Brunetti a long look.

'Ah, that's good,' the old woman said and actually rubbed her hands together, a gesture Brunetti had read about in the novels of Balzac.

He turned to Griffoni, as though his role as leader was finished, and now it was time to turn things over to the person who would deal with the details. 'All right, Claudia. I'll leave you here with Signora Gasparini and ask the *badante* if there's anything else we can do.'

He got to his feet in an energetic, masculine way, went to the door, and let himself out. At the back of the house, he stopped and called, 'Signorina? Signorina Beata?' He took a few more steps to the door at the end of the corridor. He raised his voice and called again: 'Signorina Beata. Are you here?'

The door opened, and the young woman emerged into the hallway, wiping her hands on a kitchen towel. 'How can I help you, Signore?' she asked. Her Italian, Brunetti noticed, was excellent, with only a vowel here and there to show that it was an imported product.

'Signor Tullio told his wife that he's seen changes in his aunt in the last months,' Brunetti began, putting as much concern into his voice as he could. He waited for her response, which was a quick nod that could as easily be confirmation of the fact as acknowledgement that she had understood his statement.

Her silence left him with no choice but to be more direct. 'Have you noticed changes in her, too, Signorina?'

She wiped her hands again, although they must by now have been dry. 'She doesn't remember things like she used to,' she said and looked at him to assure herself that he understood. When Brunetti nodded, she continued. 'It didn't happen when the shaking disease began.' She dismissed this idea with a swift unfurling of the towel. 'She remembered to take her pills, and the shaking wasn't so bad.' Brunetti nodded again.

'Then she started having trouble sleeping. Sometimes I found her asleep on the sofa in the morning with the television on, and she didn't remember how she got there.' The young woman seemed more troubled by this than by 'the shaking disease'.

'Then that stopped and she started sleeping later in the morning. Until one time I couldn't wake her up and called 118.' She folded the towel into a rectangle, shook it out, and folded it again.

'When was that, Signorina?' Brunetti asked, wanting to confirm what Professoressa Crosera had told him.

'In the middle of October,' she said. 'I remember because she came home on the last day of October and it had been two weeks.' She closed her eyes for a moment, perhaps remembering that day, and then said, 'She's not getting better, so I think I won't be able to go home for Christmas.'

'Is that when you noticed the changes in her?'

'I didn't notice for a long time because the changes were so small. But when she came home from the hospital, there was a big change. It used to be that we went out every day to do the errands. We'd go to the supermarket in Santa Margherita together and decide what to get for dinner, or have a coffee and a pastry.' She gave him a long look, as though deciding whether she could tell him more. Apparently she could, for she said, 'It was like we were friends. One day she'd pay, and the next day she'd let me pay. And for that time, while we had a coffee and ate the pastry, we really were friends.'

Brunetti was busy doing the maths: fifteen times a month, times five or six Euros: seventy-five Euros. He thought of his mother's admonition about the Venetians and greed, to which he added cunning.

'And then, at the end of the month, she'd give me all the money back, saying it was so I could buy a pair of shoes or send something to my mother.' Beata smiled at the memory.

After he digested this, Brunetti asked, 'What other errands did you do together?'

'Sometimes we'd go to Rialto, too. Or we'd look in shop windows and talk about the things we saw. Or I'd go with her to her doctor or to the pharmacy, and once to get her eyes checked.'

'When she began to change, did you worry?' Brunetti asked.

The young woman busied herself folding the towel again while she thought about this. 'Not really, because it was so slow. Just sometimes, or with some things.'

'Could you give me an example, Signorina?'

'She didn't want me to come in with her when she went to the doctor any more, or go to the pharmacy with her, even though it's in Cannaregio. She began to ask me to leave the room when she wanted to make a phone call, and she wouldn't let me help her keep track of when she should take her medicines.' She gave Brunetti time to comment, but he did not. 'I think she was embarrassed because the shaking was getting worse, and sometimes she'd mix things up. I pretended not to notice, but she knew that I did.' Beata gave him a quick glance and tried to shrug away what she had just said.

'We still went for coffee together, but it wasn't the same as before. And she always paid. I kept offering, but she said no, so I didn't enjoy it as much because we weren't like friends any more. She was always the *padrona*, and that's not nice, not once you've been friends.' She left that in the air a long time, then added, in a voice that failed to disguise her sadness, 'I think she forgot that we'd become friends.'

Brunetti was afraid she was going to cry and so he asked abruptly, 'Do you know anything about the coupons?'

'What coupons?' she asked.

'From the pharmacy. For cosmetics.'

Her surprise was palpable, and as he watched, she glanced away from him and down the corridor, as if she could see the past there, though in better focus.

'So that's where they came from,' she said.

'The coupons?' Brunetti asked.

'No. The things she gave me. This summer, just after my birthday, she came home with a bag of lipsticks and face creams and a bottle of bath oil, and gave it all to me.' The smile had come back to her face.

'She'd already given me a birthday present; a gold chain with a cross. I'm going to give it to my mother when I go home in the summer to visit.'

'So the cosmetics were an extra present?'

'Yes. She said she'd been given them. I want to take them when I go home.' Her smile dimmed a little. 'There's no reason to use them here, anyway.'

'Could I see them?' Brunetti asked.

'What?'

'Would you show them to me?'

'But they're in my room,' she said, as though Brunetti had made an improper suggestion.

'Perhaps you could go and get them, then, Beata? I'd like to see them.' She gave him such a troubled look that Brunetti was forced to say, 'It might help the Signora.'

Beata nodded and crossed the hall to go into a room on the other side.

She was quickly back with an orange Hermès shopping bag in her hand, and Brunetti thought for a moment that the cosmetics had come from there. Seeing his face, Beata said, 'No, Signore. The Signora put them in this bag because she knew I liked it.'

She placed the bag on one of the large chests in the hall and removed, one by one, all the items in it. There were four lipsticks, a bottle of bath oil, another one, a small box that held a tub of face cream, and three tubes of something called *fondo tinta*.

'She gave them to you this summer, and you haven't used them yet?' Brunetti asked.

'No, Signore. I want to take it all home with me next summer and give it to my mother and sister. They've never had things this good.' She gave the tubes and boxes a glance filled with longing and near-reverence, as though concentrated in them were all the wealth and luxury of the West.

'Thank you, Signorina Beata,' Brunetti said. 'Do you know if the Signora brought home more things like this?'

'I think she did, but earlier in the summer. And then she didn't any more.'

'Was this after she stopped asking you to go out with her every day?'

'How did you know that?'

'Oh, it was just a guess,' Brunetti said easily.

The door to the Signora's room opened, and Griffoni came into the hallway, turned and blew a kiss into the room, and then came towards them. To Beata, she said, 'The Signora would like you to bring her a cup of tea.'

Brunetti watched the young woman stop herself from dropping another curtsey. 'Of course,' she said and walked towards the kitchen.

'How do you do it?' Brunetti asked, not having to mention the kiss she tossed towards the old woman.

'By listening. And asking questions. And then wanting to know more.' She glanced at the cosmetics set out on top of the chest, lined up like the row of objects from Gasparini's drawer. She picked up the box and opened the lid, careful not to bend the cardboard flap. Carefully, she pulled out the pale blue plastic tub and read the label.

'I looked at this two weeks ago. There are 150 grams in here, and it costs ninety-seven Euros.' She slipped the tub into the box and reinserted the tab. She opened all of the lipsticks one by one and showed Brunetti that they were unused.

'I should tell my nephews in Naples not to get mixed up in selling drugs, not when they could sell this stuff,' she said.

Brunetti let the remark pass. Griffoni had seldom spoken of her family, and he did not want to sound intrusive. But, he had to admit, she had a natural sense of the realities of the marketplace.

'Well?' he asked.

'She told me a bit about her youth.' That said, Griffoni started to replace the tubes and boxes in the bag, careful to place them neatly beside one another on the bottom, setting the tubes and lipsticks upright. She held up one of the tubes and said, 'I asked her what her secret was, for looking so young.' She stopped then and looked at Brunetti, giving him a visual prod.

'And she told you what?'

'To "stay away from doctors, and use the best cosmetics",' she said, waving the tube back and forth.

'So she paid for all of this?' Brunetti asked.

'Yes. She started to tell me she'd found a way to do it that saved her money, but then she clapped her hand over her mouth and said it was a secret and she couldn't tell anyone.'

'What did you do?' Brunetti asked.

A door opened and Beata emerged, carrying a tray with a single cup of tea and three sweet biscuits on a plate. Brunetti went ahead and opened the door for her, then followed her into the room.

When the old woman looked up at him, he said, 'Thank you, Signora, for your help. I hope we haven't tired you with our questions.'

'Not at all,' Signora Gasparini said, smiling vaguely towards him. 'Please say hello to my nephew when you see him. And perhaps you could ask him to call me?' Then she reached to take the cup of tea Beata handed her. She looked up and said, smiling, 'That young woman is charming.'

'Yes, she is, isn't she?' Brunetti said and left the room, closing the door behind him.

Griffoni waited for him in the hallway, all of the items back in the bag, which now stood in the centre of the chest. They left the apartment, and Griffoni did not start to speak until they reached the bridge in front of the building. She stopped at the top and leaned back against the railing, arms stiff and palms braced on the top.

Before he could ask, Griffoni said, 'I told her I admired her for being so clever and for knowing how to keep a secret. Then I said that I envied her for having found a way to save money because I had the same passion for cosmetics and loved to use the best. I put on my unhappy face and said how hard it was, with what I earned, to afford them.'

Brunetti listened, as fascinated as a python by the snake charmer's flute.

'Then I smiled and gave her some more compliments, and she looked at me for a long time and then asked me if I took medicine. For a minute I didn't know what she was talking about, but I said yes, tried to look modest, and said I did take something for a feminine problem.' Smiling at her own cleverness, she added, 'Even women are reluctant to ask you anything, once you say that.'

Brunetti smiled and shook his head at the same time.

'She said she might be able to help me, but she had to think about it.'

'If she chooses to remember,' Brunetti said before he thought.

'Don't be unpleasant, Guido.'

'Sorry. What did you say?'

'That there's nothing I'd enjoy more. Then she invited me to come for tea,' Griffoni explained, smiling. 'And she suggested that perhaps I could bring some pastries for her and Beata.'

Ah, how much his mother would have admired both of these women, he thought. 'And when?'

'Next Monday at three.' Griffoni pushed herself away from the railing and started down the steps.

21

As they passed in front of the church, Griffoni said, 'I wonder why she dislikes her so much.'

'Could you untangle the pronouns?' Brunetti asked.

'Why Professoressa Crosera dislikes Signora Gasparini so much. She's a helpless old woman who's putting up a good fight against bad health and declining powers and not being in control of her life any more.'

'Those are reasons to pity a person, Claudia, not to make you like them,' Brunetti said, knowing even as he spoke how sententious he sounded.

'Ever heard of jealousy?' Griffoni asked, laughing. 'Or possessiveness?'

'Her husband spends his work week in Verona,' Brunetti shot back, 'and when he comes back to Venice, she hears that his aunt is nagging at him to come and visit her and to help her with this or that.' Before she could interrupt, Brunetti went on, 'It makes sense that his wife would think the old woman was repetitive, insistent, and forgetful.'

At this, Griffoni stopped walking, swung around, and all but blocked his way. 'All right: she's all these things. But she's his *aunt*, for God's sake.' Her voice had grown louder with the last words, and Brunetti noticed a young woman turning to look at them.

Just as Brunetti was thinking how much she sounded like a southerner, with talk of the Sacred Family, Griffoni added, her voice suddenly low and almost icy, 'Besides, you've seen the apartment: top floor facing the church of the Carmini, at least 250 square metres, view of the canal, view of the garden behind.' To Brunetti, she sounded exactly like every shifty estate agent he'd ever known. 'And who do you think is going to inherit that, Guido?'

Now she sounded like every shifty Venetian estate agent he'd ever known, seeing all human affairs through the lens of location and size, but he decided it would be unwise to remark on this. Instead, recalling the way the older woman had ignored Griffoni when they met, he asked, 'You've certainly warmed towards her. Why the change?'

'Because she's tough,' Griffoni said without hesitation. 'And because, when I suggested you and I were a couple, but not married, she didn't mind at all, the way many people her age still pretend to. She also liked it that I'm not Venetian.'

'Why is that important?'

'Because I don't have preconceptions about the people here, and that means I'll listen to her opinions without adding something about the way that person's great-grandfather's brother cheated the cousin of my great-grandfather out of twenty acres of land in Dolo in 1937.'

Brunetti laughed, defusing the situation, and said, 'You've been paying attention to us, haven't you?'

Returning his smile, Griffoni said, 'You're not so different from us, although Neapolitans usually go back more than five or six generations to find the reasons we give for having a strong opinion, even a positive one, about someone.' After a moment's thought, she added, 'Strangely enough, most of what she said was in favour of people, about how she liked or trusted them.'

'Did she mention anyone in particular?'

'Oh, she had a list: her sainted uncle Marco, her doctor, her friend Anna Marcolin, two cheese-sellers at Rialto, and Signora Lamon, who lives on the floor below her.' Griffoni paused in thought until the memory came ... 'the man with the moustache who sells fish in Campo Santa Margherita.' In response to Brunetti's glance, she explained. 'She's heard talk that he sometimes sells fish left over from the day before, but she said she could guarantee that this is not true. Her family's bought fish from his family for sixty years.'

Laughing again, Brunetti said, 'That's certain proof she's one of us.'

Griffoni responded, 'It would make her one of us, too.' Peace restored, they continued on their way.

'The person at the top of the list is the pharmacist: Dottor Donato.' In response to Brunetti's blank look, she said, 'He's the owner of the Farmacia della Fontana, the one that issued the coupons. His name's printed at the bottom of the coupon, along with the tax number, address, and phone number.'

'What did she tell you?'

'That he's a descendant of a Doge who ruled in the seventeenth century for thirty-five days, and she's proud to be his client.' Griffoni let out a puff of disbelief. 'I know we're title-crazy in Naples, but it's nothing like the way people here carry on.'

'Maybe it's the little hats the Doges wore,' Brunetti suggested, straight-faced.

She stopped, looked at him, and laughed. 'This is the first time I've had a Venetian not go all buggy-eyed and fall on the ground in fits at the mention of the Doges. Are you sure you're really Venetian?'

Switching to the most impenetrable pronunciation and using the dialect he remembered from his grandparents, Brunetti said, '*Noi altri semo zente che no se lassemo strucar le segole in te i oci.*'

'What's that mean?' she asked.

'Roughly, it means that we don't let ourselves be fooled by anyone.'

He watched as she tried to repeat it in her memory and translate it into Italian. And fail. 'It could mean anything, as far as I'm concerned,' she said.

He was pleased she hadn't understood: some parts of the city still hadn't been given away. His own children spoke Italian more easily than Veneziano, probably because he and Paola spoke Italian with them. That hadn't stopped them, however, from learning Veneziano from their classmates.

Brunetti pulled his attention back to Signora Gasparini and asked, 'Did she say anything else about the pharmacist?'

'She's been going to him for a few years, so he's probably diagnosed her as many times as her doctor has.'

With no warning, the clouds parted and Campo Santa Margherita was flooded with sun; the temperature soared. 'Let's sit for a minute,' Griffoni said, moving towards one of the long benches in the *campo*.

Griffoni sat, folded her arms, and stretched out her legs. Brunetti joined her, half turned towards her; two friends, stopping for a chat. 'I have two aunts,' she said, looking at her feet and not at Brunetti. 'With Alzheimer's: well, the beginnings of. And they both jump from subject to subject with no preparation and no logic. First it's fish and then it's the rail system, or their children and then the chewing gum on the streets. If I want to talk to them about something, I have to keep herding them back to – for example – the chewing gum. They concentrate for half a minute, and we can talk, but then they're on to Mexico or Lourdes, so I have to ask them again about the chewing gum, and then they can talk about it some more. But then they start asking if I've decided what I want to study in university or where I bought my sweater. By the time I mention chewing gum again, they've forgotten we'd talked about it.'

'And?' Brunetti inquired.

'Signora Gasparini is hardly as far gone as my aunts, but she used their technique, and it might have been to avoid talking about him. I asked about Dottor Donato, and she asked where I got my shoes. I told her I got them at San Leonardo, right opposite the pharmacy, and that made her tell me that the *ex-cinema* Italia in San Leonardo is now a supermarket, and we had to talk about that for a while. That's how it went, like billiards, things always going off at crazy angles and sometimes returning to where we started, but only if I found a way to drag her back. She spoke of him with admiration and gratitude, but there was something else in her tone.' Griffoni pulled her legs in and crossed her knees, then started to wave her right foot up and down in the air.

'I got the impression,' she said, her foot continuing to move, 'that she was suspicious of him but afraid to confess it, even to herself.' She unfolded her arms and placed her palms to either side of her on the bench. After a moment, she pushed herself to her feet and said, 'That's enough for today. I'll go back now. We can talk later.' She turned in the direction of Campo San Barnaba and the closest vaporetto stop and was quickly absorbed by the crowd of people – once unusual at this time of year – moving in that direction.

Instead of starting for home, Brunetti went into a bar and ordered a coffee. While he waited for it to come, he called Signorina Elettra, gave her Dottor Donato's name, and asked her to see what she could find out about him. She asked if there was anything else he'd like, and hung up when he said that was all.

He went to the cash register and asked to pay for his coffee and was surprised when he was told it was one Euro, twenty. He paid without questioning the price, but out in the *calle*, he found himself wondering if he had been cheated or if the price had been allowed to rise since yesterday, when he'd paid one Euro, ten.

Are we really that venal? Brunetti asked himself and started walking in the direction of Campo San Barnaba.

His family, it seemed to him in retrospect, had combined poverty with generosity, but perhaps memory was adorning his parents' behaviour. He remembered a succession of men described as friends of his father who had often eaten with them and recalled that his own clothing, after he'd worn it for two or three years, often disappeared from his wardrobe after a visit from a cousin of his mother who lived in Castello with her six children and perpetually unemployed husband. Brunetti's had been a family that had nothing but could always find something amidst that nothing to give to someone who had more nothing.

'And who's more Venetian than we are?' he asked the air in a soft voice, much to the surprise of a woman who was walking past him in the *campo.*

He turned right after the Accademia and then left and into the pharmacy on the first corner. Standing behind the counter was his former classmate and first *fidanzata,* Beatrice Rossi. She saw him come in and smiled at the sight of him, as she had each time they'd met over the years. 'Well, look who's here,' she exclaimed, apparently addressing the same air he had spoken to in the *campo.*

She came from behind the counter and they embraced, two happily married people who had thought, years ago, decades ago, that this might be their common destiny. He looked at her face and, behind the wrinkles at the sides of her mouth and eyes, saw the sweet-smelling girl who had come, the first day of *liceo,* to sit next to him in history class.

'Still chasing bad guys?' It was, by now, her formulaic question.

'Still selling drugs?' was his.

'Do you have time for a coffee?' Brunetti asked, knowing that, after so many years in the pharmacy, she pretty much came and went as she pleased.

'No, I can't, Guido. Lucilla's sick, so the only one here with me is the girl, and she can't make up prescriptions.' She looked around. 'No one's here: we can talk.' Over the years, Beatrice had occasionally provided information to Brunetti about the people in her area, sometimes those she knew as clients. She never discussed their medical information nor anything they might have told her in confidence, but once or twice she had repeated gossip when Brunetti assured her that the information was necessary to him.

'Who is it this time?' she asked with easy familiarity. When she saw his surprise at her directness, she smiled and said, 'I see that hunter's gleam in your eyes, Guido.'

Rather than protest, Brunetti smiled in return and said, 'Dottor Donato, your colleague.'

Beatrice's mouth opened involuntarily 'Oh, my,' she said. 'Why ever would you bother with someone like him?'

'His name came up in another matter, and I'd like to know more about him before we bother to spend any more time taking a careful look.' This might not have been the whole truth, but it was true.

'How did it come up?' she asked.

'Oh, someone mentioned him,' Brunetti answered.

Beatrice burst into laughter. 'Next thing, you'll be refusing to tell me Paola's name,' she said and laughed again, this time at her own remark.

Brunetti pressed his lips together and raised his eyebrows in something close to embarrassment. 'All right, all right, Beatrice. The truth is I'd rather not say. I just want to have a feel of the man.'

'Give me a hint,' she said. At first, he thought she was joking, but then he realized what good sense she had: she had no business talking about Donato's sexual preferences if his children were involved in stealing cars on the mainland, nor should she reveal that he beat his wife, nor that his wife beat him.

It took Brunetti some time to find a way to explain what he wanted to know. 'Would he bend rules to increase his profits?'

A woman about Brunetti's age came in and walked to the counter; Beatrice retreated behind it and asked if she could help her. The woman turned to look at Brunetti, but he directed his attention to the contents of a bottle of shampoo and was amazed by the number of substances inside and curious about why so many were needed.

The women conversed in low voices and Beatrice went into the back of the pharmacy to emerge after a few minutes with four boxes of medicine. She took the boxes, peeled off stamps from the backs, and pasted them on to the prescriptions the woman gave her. Then she ran the prescriptions over the sensor plate next to the cash register, put the boxes in a plastic bag, and accepted a twenty-Euro note in payment. She rang up the sale and returned the woman's change, added the receipt, thanked her, and wished her a pleasant evening.

When the woman was gone, Beatrice came over to stand opposite Brunetti. 'Dottor Donato is one of the most respected pharmacists in the city, Guido. He was once the President of the Ordine dei Farmacisti.'

Brunetti waited. When she said no more, he insisted, 'Now tell me what you don't want to tell me.' Silence. 'Please, Beatrice. It might be important.' Still not a lie, but Brunetti nevertheless felt uncomfortable saying it.

'Well,' she began and turned to straighten a display of cough drops. 'There are some people who'd probably say yes to your question. It doesn't matter who they are.'

She seemed to have concluded, but then she smiled at Brunetti and leaned close, as if about to tell a secret, and said, 'There's no need to bend the rules: we earn more than enough as it is.'

'May I write that out and ask you to sign it?' Brunetti asked.

'Good God, no,' she exclaimed and raised her hands in mock horror. 'They'd expel me from the Order of Pharmacists if that got back to them.'

'It's good to hear one of you, at least, admit it,' Brunetti said with sudden seriousness.

'We all have too much, Guido; not just pharmacists. All of us. Too much money and too much stuff, and never happy with what we have.'

Brunetti looked across at this new person, wondering if he had heard her correctly. 'Do you really mean that, Beatrice?'

'With all my heart,' she said seriously. 'I'd give it all away if I could.' She smiled suddenly, 'Well, half of it. Or part of it.' Her smile grew. 'I'm such a hypocrite: don't pay any attention to me.'

'But you meant it, didn't you?' Brunetti asked. 'At least while you were saying it?'

'Probably,' she said hesitantly, and then more forcefully, 'Yes. The only trouble is that I can't keep meaning it. It comes over me once in a while when I see all the things we have, Rolando and I, and all the things the kids have. But then I forget about it.' She shook her head. 'Pretend I didn't say that, all right?'

Brunetti shook his head. 'No, I want to remember it. It's one of the best things I've ever heard you say.'

He leaned forward and kissed her on both cheeks and left the pharmacy, not looking back from the door because he didn't want to meet her glance.

22

As Brunetti walked towards home, he thought about what Beatrice had said: 'Probably.' How interpret that? She'd heard talk, but that was hardly material on which to build a case against a man. 'Some people' believed Dottor Donato would bend the rules to increase his profit. The legal profession called this 'hearsay evidence', a kind of linguistic alchemy that tried to transmute gossip into something more credible.

He recalled that Beatrice had spent two years at university studying to be a notary and then had surprised her friends and family – her father was a notary – by abandoning it and switching to *farmacia*. At the time, the best explanation she could give was that she wanted to do something that would help people, an answer which failed to satisfy her family.

Thinking of notaries, he recalled the farcical scene when he and Paola had bought their apartment, more than twenty years before. The notary, just at the moment when the bank cheque was to change hands, remembered something he had to do in some other room and left the buyer to pass it to the sellers. No sooner had the door closed behind him than Brunetti opened his briefcase and pulled from it packs of *lire* – ah, who thought of the *lira* now, dear little *lira*? He'd passed the stacks to the sellers, a young couple who had decided to move to Vicenza, and they'd started to count their way through the stacks of notes.

At one point, the notary had knocked on the door and called from outside to ask if they were finished. They'd all joined in, calling out, 'No', the seller even shouting, 'Don't come in', an order the notary obeyed.

When the hundred million *lire* was all counted and resting in a different briefcase, Brunetti pulled out a bank cheque for a hundred million *lire* less than the real price of the apartment, put it on the table, and called to summon the notary back to his own office.

Ah, where were the *lire* of yesteryear? Now there were bank transfers and a general atmosphere of distrust between buyers and sellers, for the state was no longer willing to tolerate a system that would prevent it from collecting the full tax revenue due on every sale. Unfortunately, it had not yet devised a system that would prevent that money from disappearing into the black hole of government malfeasance.

This memory forced Brunetti to consider how contradictory were his own ideas of fiscal rectitude, at least when dealing with the state. He paused at the top of the bridge leading to San Polo to consider the possibility that the coupons might be part of a system designed to cheat the state and not the customer. Were that the case, there would certainly be less – perhaps no – desire to report it, should signs of it be noticed. People cared if the state cheated them, not if someone cheated the state.

It was no subject to discuss at dinner, so instead he listened to Chiara praise her history teacher and the way she managed to interest her students in the events they read about, currently those of the first centuries of the Roman Republic. For the first time, Chiara had begun to think about how vastly different people in the past were from her. 'They could kill their children if they wanted to,' she said, horrified at the right of a Roman father to destroy a child he did not acknowledge or want. 'From what she said, it sounds as if you could just go to the nearest garbage pile and pick up a baby if it was still living and take it home.'

'And do what with it?' Raffi looked up from his plate to ask.

'Raise it as your child,' Chiara answered.

Raffi, showing that he had learned a thing or two about timing from his mother, added, 'or your slave.'

Ignoring him, Chiara looked across at her father, who was helping himself to more *gnocchetti di zucca*. With an easy smile, she pounced on him. 'I'm afraid you would have been out of a job, *Papà*.'

'Really? Why?' asked Brunetti, although he knew.

'There were no police,' Chiara declared. 'Think of it: a million people in the city and no cops.' She left it to everyone at the table to consider this and then asked, 'What did people do if something bad happened to them?'

'Your teacher hasn't talked about that yet?' Brunetti asked.

Chiara, who was taking a sip of water, shook her head.

'I think she'll tell you that your only recourse was to hire a lawyer – someone like Cicero – to make an accusation or, if someone accused you of something, to hire a lawyer to defend you.'

'But what if you couldn't afford to hire a lawyer?' she asked. '*Papà*, you read about this stuff all the time: what happened, what did people *do*?'

Hoping to remind her of what she'd begun by saying, that people back then were very different, he said, 'Most people didn't think that way, Angel. Either you put up with what happened to you, or you took matters into your own hands.'

'What does that mean?' Chiara asked, making no attempt to disguise her incomprehension.

'The same thing it does today,' Paola interrupted. 'You punished the person who caused you the trouble – whatever it was – or you hired someone to do it for you.'

'But that's crazy,' Chiara said. 'People can't live like that.'

Brunetti longed to say that many people in her own country still did, but kindness moved him to silence, and he gave her no reply. He shot a glance at Paola, who stopped herself from saying whatever it was she was preparing to say and, instead, said, 'Chiara, I made that *ciambella* you like so much.'

The reality of dessert could still haul Chiara back from the thought of social justice, and she asked, 'The one with raisins and pumpkins?'

Paola nodded. 'It's on the windowsill. Should be cooled down by now. If you bring it, I'll get the plates.' That said, Paola got to her feet and started collecting their empty dishes. As she reached across to pick up Brunetti's, she gave him a nod and a broad, fake, tooth-filled smile and then followed her daughter into the kitchen.

Later, as they lay side by side, reading in bed, Paola turned to ask him, 'Is that the right number Chiara had?'

'Of people in Rome?'

'Yes.'

'It's the number I've read,' Brunetti said, turning *Antigone* face down on his stomach, even though he was impatient to continue reading. It seemed the only time he had for serious reading was before he went to sleep. It was a bad idea, of course, because he was usually so tired he fell asleep quickly, but it was the only time in the day when claim was not made on his attention and he could at least try to concentrate on what he read.

Paola did the same with her book – he didn't know what she was reading – and folded her hands on top of it. 'A million people living without law,' she said and closed her eyes, as if better to imagine it.

'It's almost impossible to believe,' Brunetti said.

She turned to him and smiled. 'I'm glad you stopped me.' She reached across and put her hand on his arm.

'From getting up on your soapbox?'

'Yes, and saying something incendiary like, "and now sixty million of us do".'

'More polemical than incendiary,' Brunetti observed drily. 'Chiara wouldn't have listened, anyway. No one cares about it any more, especially young people.'

'It?'

'Politics.'

She turned her head and studied his face. 'We have two children, Guido.'

'Are you expecting me to say something solemn, like, "Someone has to try"?'

She closed her book and set it on the table beside her. After enough time to give his question serious thought, she said, 'The man I married would say it.'

'Antigone said it, and she ended up hanging herself in a cave,' Brunetti replied.

'The man I married would say it,' she repeated.

Brunetti turned his book back over but left it flat on his stomach. He looked in the direction of a painting on the wall between the two windows, hard to see clearly in the penumbra of light that reached it. It was a small seventeenth-century portrait of a Venetian man, quite possibly a merchant, that Paola had found in a junk shop; she'd had it restored and given it to him for their twentieth wedding anniversary.

The man, sober in dress and expression, looked directly at the viewer, as if assessing his worth. On a table to his right stood a dark green vase of what looked like gladioli, which Paola had explained were the symbol of honour and constancy. Brunetti looked at the man and imagined that the man could look at him; the light beside the bed would give him a better view.

'Yes, he would have,' Brunetti finally agreed. He picked up his book and continued reading, eager again, after a gap of twenty years, to listen to what Antigone had to say about the obligation to follow the law. How refreshing that would be to a man who had spent the last twenty years dealing with people whose only interest was to outwit the law.

Paola turned to the other side and switched off her light.

The next afternoon, when Brunetti went to Signorina Elettra's office, he sensed the tension the instant he walked in, even before he saw Lieutenant Scarpa standing in front of her. His weight supported by his hands propped on the desk, he was leaning forward, his neck seeming strangely elongated to bring his face closer to hers.

'Or am I mistaken, Signorina?' Brunetti heard him ask.

Signorina Elettra turned towards Brunetti, but not before he'd seen the emotions on her face: scorn, anger, and perhaps even fear.

Her face changed when she saw Brunetti, and she said, too brightly, 'Why don't we ask the Commissario, Lieutenant? He's certainly more likely to know something about this than I am.'

'What is it, Signorina?' Brunetti asked, acknowledging Scarpa's presence with a nod that managed to seem polite.

Scarpa pushed himself upright, waving one hand upwards in a balletic acknowledgement of Brunetti's superior rank.

'Signorina Elettra and I were trying to think of a way that certain privileged information might have escaped the boundaries of the Questura,' the Lieutenant answered. He smiled at Signorina Elettra, as though asking her approval of the explanation he had just given.

'I see,' Brunetti said, making himself sound completely uninterested in the matter. He saw Signorina Elettra's face relax minimally at his tone, and so he continued, 'And the pharmacist?'

'There's nothing that's very interesting, Signore, I'm sorry to say.' Brunetti's family had had a nondescript dog when he was a kid, and because it was his duty to take it for walks, he had learned what each backward glance, each tug of the leash, meant. So he knew, from her voice, that she was tugging at the leash and wanted very much to move along from where they were.

Thinking he'd give her the chance, Brunetti said, in the voice a superior used with a junior, 'Thank you, Signorina. I found a few things yesterday and made some notes. Perhaps you could come up and get them and add them to your report.' It was weak, and it was obvious, but it was ostensibly a request from a superior to an inferior, so she had no choice but to push herself up from her chair, saying, 'Ah, good. Then I can finish it, Commissario, and ask the Vice-Questore to take a look.'

As if Patta cared about reading reports, Brunetti said to himself while holding the door of her office open for her. He did not feel comfortable leaving Scarpa alone in her office, so he waited, looking across at Scarpa, making it obvious that he was expecting the Lieutenant to leave with them.

Scarpa must have realized he had no choice and joined them at the door, taking Brunetti's nod as permission to pass in front of him, which he did. Brunetti closed the door after them. He and Signorina Elettra started up towards his office; behind them, Lieutenant Scarpa walked to the end of the corridor and turned left.

In his office, Brunetti went to his desk and leaned back against it. 'Do you want to tell me what he's talking about?' he asked mildly.

He watched her consider, and then discard, the idea of asking what he meant. 'He's talked about it before, Commissario. You've probably heard him.'

'These leaks?'

She nodded.

'Do you know what they are?' Brunetti asked.

'He says that the name of someone who was called in for questioning has been divulged.'

'Divulged to whom?'

'He didn't say, just that the name of a suspect's been released.'

'How?'

'He didn't say,' she repeated.

'Is that all?' he asked.

'The Lieutenant seems to think it's more than enough.'

'To do what?'

'Accuse someone, I suppose. He likes to do that.'

'I've noticed,' Brunetti said. 'Do you know anything about it?'

She raised her chin and pressed her lips together. All she needed to do was put her hands behind her back and rock back and forward to look like a nervous child caught at something she'd been forbidden to do.

'Yes,' she finally said.

'Is it something I should know about?' Brunetti asked.

After what seemed a long time, she said, 'Not yet.'

Brunetti chose not to comment on her answer and said, instead, 'Is it possible to get a list of the patients registered at Dottor Donato's pharmacy?'

'I should think so. Well, at least a list of the people whose prescriptions have been filled there.'

'Have a look, then, if you would,' Brunetti said. 'And what they're being prescribed.'

'Are you looking for any particular kind of medicine? Or disease?' she asked, giving Brunetti an idea of the categories of information she might be able to open up to him.

'Anything expensive that's prescribed for older people.' He saw curiosity flash across her face and added, 'Especially if they're being treated for something that might affect their memory or their mental powers.'

She nodded.

'Can you do this?' he asked.

She looked at him but quickly lowered her eyes in modesty, as though unwilling to engage in something as unseemly as boasting. 'I have access to a wide variety of information, Signore,' she finally said.

Brunetti was about to ask about this, but caution stopped him: it would be better if he didn't know the full extent of her powers. He put his hand to his mouth and turned the question into a cough. When that stopped he put on a serious face and, turning to her, said, 'I hoped you might.'

23

Soon after Signorina Elettra left, Vianello tapped lightly at Brunetti's door and entered without waiting to be told to do so. Brunetti waved him to his usual seat and asked, 'Did you see Signorina Elettra on your way up?'

'No,' Vianello answered, then surprised him by adding, 'That's what I came to talk about.'

'Signorina Elettra?'

'Yes,' the Inspector replied, then added, 'And what's bothering her.'

'From what I've seen, it looks like Lieutenant Scarpa is.'

Vianello raised his hands and stared at his palms for a moment, then said, 'Yes, it does seem that way, I know.'

'Does that mean it's really something else?'

'Sort of,' Vianello answered.

Brunetti took a long breath and released it slowly. 'Can you tell me what's going on without talking in secret code?'

'It's confusing, Guido,' Vianello said. Brunetti remained silent, so the Inspector went on. 'One of my informants told me weeks ago he'd heard there was someone here who named a suspect we let go for lack of evidence, even though we knew he was guilty.' Vianello raised his hand and pressed gently in Brunetti's direction to indicate that he wasn't finished.

'When I asked him about it – what man, what crime – he didn't know anything and said he'd heard someone talk about it in a bar.' Vianello pursed his mouth and shot up his eyebrows to express his scepticism.

'I told him I wasn't interested and to forget about it. But then, a week ago,' the Inspector continued, his voice suddenly more serious, 'he told me he'd heard the same story again, though this time the name of the man we let go had been mentioned.'

Brunetti reached across his desk and put his fingers on a mechanical pencil; he picked it up and clicked the eraser a few times until the thin lead emerged. He studied it for a moment, then pressed the eraser down and held it while he pressed the lead back into the pencil with the tip of his finger. He glanced up from this and across at Vianello. 'Who?' he asked.

'Costantino Belli.'

Brunetti's eyes widened; he set the pencil down. 'Where is he?'

'The last I heard – about two weeks ago – he was out of the hospital and at home. Well, at his mother's home.'

'Ah, the mother,' Brunetti said.

Vianello crossed his legs and swung his foot back and forth. 'I don't know if I should say this, but we have no sure proof that he did anything.'

'No sure proof,' Brunetti repeated. 'But we can infer the truth.'

Vianello hesitated just an instant before he said, 'Judges don't convict people because of inferences, Guido. They prefer facts.'

Brunetti smiled. 'Haven't I warned you about using sarcasm, Lorenzo? All it does is make people angry.'

'Sorry,' Vianello said. 'I lost my head for a moment.'

'Lucia Arditi was in the hospital for three days after she was attacked,' Brunetti said, voice tight. 'The doctors said she'd been raped and burned with a cigarette. This happened in her own apartment. In her own bed.' He heard his tone lurching towards outrage, and paused until he felt able to continue. 'Lorenzo, you read what the ambulance crew said when they went there: she told them she'd been raped.'

'She changed that later and said that it was consensual,' Vianello said immediately, sounding not unlike a defence attorney.

'Whose side are you on?' Brunetti asked him.

Vianello folded his arms across his chest and stared across at him.

Eventually Brunetti said, 'I'm sorry, Lorenzo.'

Vianello shrugged. 'He's a vicious little shit, Guido. You know that and I know that. We know it because of what he did to Lucia Arditi. And we know there's no doubt that he did it.' Vianello waited until Brunetti nodded in agreement and then continued. 'But a magistrate would say it's only what we *believe* he did to Lucia Arditi, who has said he did not attack her.' Vianello gave Brunetti the opportunity to protest, and when he did not, the Inspector continued. 'And then the magistrate would say that, in the face of her repeated testimony and the absence of any real evidence, there is no way he could even think of making a case against Belli.' When Brunetti didn't contest this, either,

Vianello went on. 'She said they'd had sex that evening, and that's what she told her Facebook friends. Remember?' Vianello's voice changed subtly as he quoted, '"For old times' sake".'

His glance met Brunetti's. 'You read it, Guido. She told them all – after telling them that Costantino was in the shower – how right she had been to break it off with him.'

Vianello paused after that, almost as though he wanted to give himself and Brunetti, people of a different generation, time to try to understand that a person could write such a thing and want it to be public information.

'When she got to the hospital ...' Brunetti began.

'It doesn't matter what the doctor thought or what she said when she was admitted, Guido. In her statement to us, she said it was consensual.'

Brunetti opened his mouth to speak, but Vianello cut him short. 'All that matters is what she said and continues to say. He left, she went to sleep, and when she woke up she noticed blood on the sheets, so she called 118, and they sent an ambulance.'

'The cigarette burn?' Brunetti demanded.

'She insisted it was an accident,' Vianello said in a tight voice.

'His mother's message?' Brunetti asked, but there was no real curiosity in his voice; this question had been resolved some time ago.

'You read that, too, Guido. She sent the girl an SMS to wish her a quick recovery and tell her Costantino's friends were eager to see the videos he'd made.' Vianello held up a monitory hand and added, 'Signorina Elettra had no authorization to look into her telephone server. We are in possession of that information illegally.'

'It's useless, anyway,' Brunetti conceded, although reluctantly. 'The old cow didn't say what kind of videos they were. If we asked her, she'd probably say they were videos of Costantino's first communion.' He got to his feet and walked over to the window, looked across the canal to the far side, saw nothing there that helped calm him down, and went back to his chair. 'Is it because we have daughters?' he asked Vianello.

'It's because we're human,' the Inspector said.

Brunetti pulled himself away from speculation and asked, 'Did the second man who was talking actually use Belli's name?'

Vianello nodded again. 'Yes. They were talking about what happened to him; a few of them laughed and said a good beating was probably what he deserved, and then one said he'd heard that someone at the Questura had said he was the man brought in for questioning about what happened to Lucia Arditi.'

He paused to let Brunetti comment or ask questions. When he did not, the Inspector went on. 'He's looking for me to pay him something before he remembers who told him.'

'What are you going to do?'

'That's what I came up to ask you about.'

'What do you think?' Brunetti asked him.

Vianello quickly uncrossed his arms. 'I think it would be better to let it drop, tell him I don't believe him and that we're not interested.'

'Before, it sounded as though you were interested,' Brunetti remarked neutrally.

'Think about it, Guido,' Vianello said in a mild voice.

'I have been,' Brunetti said.

Their eyes met. Brunetti pulled his lips together and took two deep breaths but said nothing. They both knew that Signorina Elettra had read the report of the ambulance crew and what Lucia Arditi had originally told them, a story she had later retracted, just as they both knew that Elettra had been the one to find Belli's mother's SMS to Lucia Arditi. No wonder Vianello wanted to tell his informant that they didn't believe the story about a leak from the Questura.

'Oh my, oh my, oh my,' Brunetti whispered to himself. He addressed his attention to the wall and thought about what he did – and did not – know about Signorina Elettra. He stared at nothing for a long time and knew he and Vianello were right.

Breaking what he believed a taboo about a parent's interest in his child's sexuality, Brunetti offered a silent prayer to the protector of young people and begged that Chiara's first lover be a good boy who loved her. He didn't have to be intelligent or rich or handsome or possessed of prince-like qualities: it would be enough for him to be a good boy who loved Chiara.

Brunetti leaned forward and keyed Belli's name into his computer, searching for the report from the hospital he had never bothered to read. The young man, who had been found on the street, had been admitted to the Emergency Ward at one-thirty in the morning, more than three months before. His face had been repeatedly struck, his nose broken and the cartilage badly torn. He had apparently been kicked in the groin; one testicle was severely bruised. His left shoulder had been dislocated, though there was no sign of a bruise that would suggest it had resulted from a fall.

Brunetti glanced away from the computer and recalled the police involvement in the attack. They had not been informed until the morning after, when a call came from the hospital. Belli, who had regained consciousness, said that he had been walking home when suddenly he heard footsteps behind him, and then he remembered nothing until he woke in the hospital. The presence of his wallet in his back pocket argued against a mugging, but it was not until Brunetti saw Belli's name that he began to suspect that the attack was linked to the rape of Lucia Arditi, more than half a year earlier.

A discreet check on her family revealed that her parents, who owned a shoe factory outside Treviso, had been in Milan for an industrial fair on the evening that Belli was attacked, while the girl and her brother were visiting an uncle who lived in Spain.

The policeman who interviewed him had asked Belli if there were any people who might have wanted to do him harm, and he replied that he had no enemies. The case rested there, neither forgotten nor pursued. Brunetti remembered thinking that a lot of time had passed since the rape of Lucia Arditi. Vengeance, the adage said, was a dish best served cold, but it didn't happen that way in the real world. Vengeance lacked patience and was usually quick, impulsive, and stupidly obvious. The person or persons who had attacked Belli – and Brunetti reminded himself that he was assuming vengeance was the cause – would probably have had a more recent reason to attack him. His own experience with people whose business was violence told him that professionals would have done a far better job of it: Belli would have become familiar with pain and with the walls of his hospital room: his legs would have been in casts, and he would not have gone home to Mummy after only two days.

For some reason, he recalled the way Signorina Elettra had kept her distance from any mention of the possible leaks from the Questura, when she ordinarily would have fallen upon such a rumour with hungry curiosity. He recalled her awkwardness – one might even say nervousness – in front of Lieutenant Scarpa.

Finally accepting what he had tried to ignore, the expression on Signorina Elettra's face, and admitting that it had in fact been fear, Brunetti got to his feet and went to do what he did not want to do.

Signorina Elettra smiled at his arrival. 'Is there something I can do for you, Commissario?' she asked, and he heard, for the first time in all these years – or forced himself to hear – timidity hiding in her question.

He smiled in response and consciously relaxed his shoulders as he approached her desk. Then, realizing he was too close, he turned aside and went over to her window to admire the flowers, the ones with the heads that seemed to be made out of hundreds of narrow petals: he couldn't remember their name. He moved to the next window and leaned back against the sill.

'And the pharmacist?' he asked, another delaying tactic.

She seemed relieved by his question. Her face came alive and she turned to her computer. 'Yes,' she said, sounding pleased but not at all relaxed. She reached forward and tapped a few keys, then invited him to take a look.

'It's the geography that's confusing,' she said.

'What does that mean?' Brunetti asked, all thought of Belli, Scarpa, and Lucia Arditi pushed to the back of his mind. He moved to stand beside her and looked where her finger was pointing to a vertical list of names, arranged in alphabetical order.

'These are Dottor Donato's clients who are more than seventy years old.' Before he could count them, she said, 'There are a hundred and twenty-seven.'

She hit another key and the same list appeared again with two new columns to the right of the names. 'This shows the medicines they're each taking and the disease the medicine is usually prescribed for.'

Brunetti saw that many of them were taking the same two medicines, and most of these were prescribed for the same two diseases: Parkinson's and Alzheimer's.

Before he could ask what she saw in the lists that he did not, she said, 'Let me show you the geography.'

A shorter list appeared: Brunetti estimated fifty names. A second column was headed, 'Kilometres,' and a third, 'Vaporetto Stops'. Brunetti studied the page for some time and noticed that more than half of the names had a rating – or so he construed it to be – of at least four kilometres, and all of those listed at least seven vaporetto stops.

Signorina Elettra looked up at him and smiled. 'Let me add this, Signore,' she said and struck a single key. The same shorter list appeared, but this time a fourth column – 'Address' – had been added. Roughly half of the people on the list, one of whom was Signora Gasparini, lived in Dorsoduro, while most of the others lived in Castello.

Brunetti stared at the list, looked down at Signorina Elettra, and said, 'Even though Dottor Donato's pharmacy is in Cannaregio.'

'And all of these people are older than seventy, some of them more than eighty, and most have to travel or send someone halfway across the city to pick up their prescriptions.'

'That doesn't make any sense, does it?' Brunetti asked.

'Not unless they're getting something special at Dottor Donato's pharmacy,' she said.

'Or he's getting something special from them,' Brunetti suggested. In response to her smile, he asked, 'How did you see this?'

'My family lived in Canareggio when I was growing up, near San Leonardo, and I remember we lived at number 1400, so when I saw his address, I knew it had to be up there, almost at Ponte delle Guglie and nowhere near Rialto. People from Dorsoduro wouldn't go there, much less people from Castello. Not to go to a pharmacy, at any rate.'

'Now look at this, Signore.' She raised her right hand, fingers suspended above the keyboard, and held it there for a second, like a pianist pausing until all noise in the audience stopped. She lowered it slowly and tapped out three notes – click click click – then sat back to allow Brunetti to see the screen.

This time, only two lists: the patients, again in alphabetical order, and the name of their doctor. This list, however, had no need of alphabetical order, for there was only one name: Dottoressa Carla Ruberti, with two offices, one in Dorsoduro and one in Castello.

She allowed Brunetti time to absorb the significance of what he had just seen. 'Don't worry, Commissario: I've printed it all out for you.' When she saw that his expression didn't change, Signorina Elettra said, 'What is it, Signore?'

He took a step away from her and, pointing in the direction of the computer, said, 'I didn't come to talk to you about this, Signorina.'

She froze. It lasted only a second, and she was instantly back to normal, but he had seen it.

He shifted his weight to the other foot, uncertain how to handle this. Trust in her prompted him to say – blurt out, actually – 'What happened?'

'Excuse me?' she asked.

'With Belli? How did his name get out?' He'd used the passive voice, suggesting that the name might well have flown from the Questura on angel wings, thus allowing her the chance to lie to him if she chose.

She looked at him, away, back at him, then touched the keyboard. He could see only a sliver of the screen, but it sufficed for him to see it grow black. She straightened herself in her chair and folded her hands in her lap.

'Friends of mine have a daughter,' she said, then stopped to give a small cough and looked down at her hands. 'She's nineteen, and I've known her since she was a baby. She's a sweet girl, very clever, has always called me Zia Elettra.' She might as well have been speaking to her folded hands.

'I went to dinner with her parents a few months ago. They both seemed different, tense, so I asked them what was wrong, and they said they were worried about Livia, that she had a new boyfriend, and what she said about him made them nervous.'

'What did they say?'

'That she was completely under his control, waited around for him to call, didn't see her other friends any more because he didn't want her to.' She shot a glance towards him, adding, 'First love. It happens.'

Brunetti nodded but said nothing.

'She'd talked to me about boyfriends in the past, but that was the first I'd heard about him.

'Then Lino referred to him as "Costantino", and I told myself to stay calm: there had to be a lot of them in the city.' She opened her hands and stretched her fingers, then joined them together again.

'But?' Brunetti ventured.

'I asked, and they told me his name.' He watched her press her lips together, as though she were back in that restaurant with her friends and wished she had done that then.

'They saw my reaction and asked me what was wrong.' She looked at Brunetti then, and he saw defiance writ large on her face.

Brunetti took the familiar two steps backwards and leaned against the windowsill. He folded his arms across his chest and waited.

'I've known her since she was a baby.' He noticed that her fingers were interlocked and tightly held.

Brunetti thought – and half hoped – she'd said this to prepare a defence, to explain her obligation to the girl, to say it just slipped out before she thought about it, that she was so surprised that she had no idea what she was saying, didn't think at all about her professional responsibility.

'So I told them. About Lucia Arditi and what he did to her, and what his mother did to help him, and that this was the kind of people they were.'

Brunetti thought about this for a while and then asked, 'And when he was attacked?'

'It was three weeks later,' she said. 'I was shocked.' Then, as if Truth had reminded her to whom she was speaking, she added, 'But I wasn't surprised.'

'Have you seen her parents since you had dinner with them?'

'No.'

'Do you think her family had it done?'

She looked up and, seeing Brunetti's expression, asked, 'Would you have expected them to call me and tell me?'

Ignoring her question, he asked, 'And the girl?'

'I told you: I haven't seen any of them or heard from them since we had dinner.' She untied her fingers and waved a hand in the air. 'Maybe I never will.'

'Don't be melodramatic, Elettra,' Brunetti said before he thought.

She grimaced, embarrassed. 'I am, aren't I?'

'Yes.'

'What will you do?'

Brunetti shrugged. He turned to the window, set at the opposite end of the building from his own. It looked across the same canal but from a different floor and a different angle. The view changed: he saw the same thing, but, standing here, it looked entirely different. Creon had told Antigone that orders were orders and had to be obeyed, whether they were large or small, right or wrong.

'I don't know,' he told her, and then, 'Send those charts up to me, would you?' He left her office and went back to his own.

24

By the time he reached his office, he and his conscience had come to an agreement. Signorina Elettra had acted instinctively to save someone she loved from harm. It was different from pushing someone out of the way of a speeding car, more like pushing the loved one clear and in so doing causing the car to crash. Although he saw the difference, he told himself it was over. He had made his choice: the one she had made would remain between the two of them and, over time, would gradually disappear from the common memory of the Questura.

Almost persuaded, he decided to return to the matter at hand: he needed to talk to Griffoni about the coupons, just as he needed to get a better sense of the pharmacy and the pharmacist.

As he climbed the stairs to Griffoni's office, Brunetti reflected on the fact that few of his colleagues were as sly as Claudia, fewer still as inventive. Her ability to mould herself into the person who would be most able to understand a witness or suspect was remarkable, as was the ease with which she adapted her speech – pronunciation, intonation, range of reference – to resemble theirs in almost undetectable ways. That once established, she went on to approving of their ideas and prejudices by almost imperceptible nods and smiles. Brunetti could never recognize the exact moment she became their second selves, although he had often seen the moment the second skin dropped from her and she returned to her caustic, relentless self.

He found her in her office, leaning back in her chair, listening to someone talk to her on her phone. She was sitting sideways at her desk, so she saw Brunetti arrive. She smiled and held up two fingers, and within seconds the rhythm of her responses began to signal impatience. The other speaker did not resist for long, and the conversation ended. She stood and stretched her arms above her head. 'Does the outside world still exist?' she inquired.

Brunetti nodded and stepped back, holding up his arms in the manner of the men who direct aeroplanes to their parking places on an airfield. Repeatedly taking small steps backwards through the doorway, he waved her towards him and out of the office. She followed him gladly.

'Let's visit the pharmacy,' he suggested, handing her the coupons that had been in Tullio Gasparini's drawer.

'Oh, good,' she said with feigned delight. 'I've been wanting some new lipsticks for weeks; maybe I can buy them with Aunt Matilde's coupons.'

The day was friendly, so they decided to walk to Vallaresso and take the Number Two to San Marcuola and walk from there. Riva degli Schiavoni was crowded, even this late in November, reminding Brunetti of how empty it had been only a few years ago. Having vowed to himself not to grumble about the awful changes to the city, he contented himself with telling Claudia about some of the places they passed. There was the vaporetto that had been tipped upside down, years ago, during a storm. He could no longer remember how many people had died, trapped inside. As they progressed towards San Marco, he told her about the Sette Martiri, men shot by the Germans during the war in reprisal for a missing German soldier who, it turned out, had fallen into the water drunk, and drowned.

She gave a shrug that could be made only by someone whose grandparents had lived through the war. 'That happened to a great-uncle of mine. He was eleven,' she said. 'Nothing was named after him, though.'

They came down the bridge and decided to pass through the Piazza before getting the vaporetto. They walked out into the middle of the open glory, and Griffoni turned back to look at the façade of the Basilica. When Brunetti stopped beside her, she said. 'The first time I came to Venice, I must have been seventeen, eighteen – it was a school trip – I spent an hour standing here and turning around in a circle to see it all. Again and again: the library, the pillars, the Basilica, the bell tower. And now some days I walk across it without paying much attention.'

'It happens to us all,' Brunetti said, turning away from the Basilica and starting towards the *calle* that would take them down to the Vallaresso stop.

'My landlady: she's retired, must be in her late sixties,' Griffoni began. 'She taught little kids all her life. But now she has no work to go to, so she spends her days walking around the city with her husband.'

'Is she Venetian?' he asked.

'As much as you are.'

'She's just looking?'

'Yes. She said she finds something new every day, or they go back to places they remember from their youth.'

'Does she have a guidebook?'

'No. I asked her that. She said she just keeps her eyes open. And she said she always keeps looking up. So when there are too many tourists, she goes down into Castello or over to Santa Marta, or some place where there won't be a lot of them. And she looks at things and always manages to find something new.'

'And then?'

'From what I can understand, then she goes home, cooks dinner, and watches television with her husband.'

'Well, praise the Lord that she walks and sees the city all day.'

Griffoni stopped in her tracks and stared at him. '"Praise the Lord?"' she asked.

'Don't panic, Claudia. It's something my mother said.'

'Ah,' she said and resumed walking. They got on to the Number Two that was just leaving. There was a sharp breeze, so they went inside and walked towards the back. After they sat down, Brunetti asked, 'How do we proceed?'

Griffoni gazed at the passing buildings and finally said, 'I could be her niece, you know, the one from Naples, with the strong Neapolitan accent,' she began, and as she continued, her accent weaved away from the elegant Italian she normally spoke towards some southern variant of the same language, one in which the vowels would have to be written differently. Looking out the window, she planned her niecehood. 'I come to visit two or three times a year, and this time Zia Matilde gave me these coupons and told me to go shopping with them and get something to make myself beautiful.'

It was on the tip of Brunetti's tongue to tell her she hardly needed help to be that, but he chose, instead, to say, 'I'll go in when you do and find something to buy. I'd prefer to see and hear whatever I can of your attempt to use the coupons.'

Griffoni nodded in approval of his plan, then said, 'It might be better if I told them it's all for her.' She gave him a broad smile and added, 'Pity I didn't think of making a shopping list in wavy, uncertain handwriting: that would make things look even more authentic.'

'You'll manage,' Brunetti said just as the vaporetto pulled up at the stop: three people got off with them. They went around the back of the church and out to San Leonardo and turned left. As they approached the pharmacy, Brunetti fell behind and let Griffoni proceed and enter alone. He paused to study the masks in the window of the shop next door and gave each one the same glance he gave to tourists: distant, uninterested, and faintly displeased.

He allowed a few minutes to pass before he went into the pharmacy. His eyes passed over Griffoni, alone at the counter, talking to a salesgirl. She had had time to do her shopping: before her on the counter, Brunetti saw three boxes of lipstick and a few other small items he couldn't recognize. She was just handing the coupon to the younger woman.

The salesgirl took it and examined it, then looked at Griffoni. 'But you're not Signora Gasparini,' she said with no special inflection.

'No, I'm her niece,' Griffoni said, dulling her consonants so that her Neapolitan accent all but fell on to the counter with a heavy thud.

'Ah,' the young woman said. Then, quite pleasantly, she asked, 'Could you wait a moment? I'll get Dottor Donato.'

'Certainly,' Claudia answered. 'I'll go and have a look at the face creams.'

Brunetti busied himself looking at dental floss and toothbrushes, even took one down and studied the bristles through the plastic container.

An older man came to the counter, tall and robust, with dark hair and a moustache. Brunetti saw his name on the plastic card on his lapel: 'Dott. Donato.'

Griffoni had returned to the counter, a pale blue box in her hand. The man asked her, 'May I help you, Signora?'

Brunetti replaced the toothbrush and picked up a bottle of mouthwash.

'Yes, if you'd be so kind, Dottore,' Griffoni said. 'My aunt asked me to come and pick up some things for her. She gave me some coupons and told me I should pay with them.' Her voice was filled with the warmth and friendliness of the South, and Brunetti, who was looking at the bottle and not at Griffoni, was sure her smile was equally warm.

He took a glance and saw that the coupon was still on the counter; Griffoni picked it up and handed it to the pharmacist. He nodded his thanks and examined it carefully, his eyebrows raised. He had a face on which suspicion would look out of place: round and rosy-cheeked, he had large brown eyes that looked on a world they had judged to be a friendly and interesting place. Smiling, he set the paper back on the counter and asked, 'And you're Signora Gasparini's niece, you say?'

'Yes, I am,' Griffoni answered, just as if she had not heard his last two words. 'I come up to visit her every few months.' She shifted the tenor of her voice to semi-guilt and added, 'I don't come as often as I should, I know.' Then lightness played forth again as she said, 'But she's my aunt, and I'm always glad to come here to visit her and try to help her while I'm here.'

Dottor Donato braced his hands against the counter and leaned closer to her. In a voice so low that Brunetti could barely make out the words, he said, 'I can understand how someone would want to help her.' His voice was filled with affection and regard. 'She's been my client for some time.' Brunetti, who knew the date on which he'd filled Signora Gasparini's first prescription, looked down to continue reading the label on the bottle in his hands.

He moved to the left, farther away from them, and began to study the tubes of sunblock. A moment later, a young male pharmacist was at his side, asking, 'May I help you, Signore?'

'Yes,' Brunetti said. 'My wife and I are going on a cruise, and she asked me to get some sunblock because she read somewhere that we should wear it even in the winter, especially if we're going to be at sea.' He smiled at him and added, 'The reflection, I think.'

'That's certainly true,' the pharmacist, whose plastic tag also read 'Dott. Donato', answered and asked what level of protection his wife had told him to get.

Brunetti first looked startled and then said he didn't know anything about that and asked what the doctor would recommend. As the young man explained the difference between the various creams, Brunetti shot a glance at Griffoni and the older pharmacist, with whom she seemed to be in the midst of a discussion. He heard the pharmacist say, 'any such person', but the rest of the phrase was blotted out by the voice of the young man, who held out a yellow tube, saying, '... fifty. It should be good for even the brightest sun.'

Brunetti smiled, thanked him, and said, 'My wife asked me to get some aspirin, too.'

'Pills or effervescent, sir?'

'Pills, please,' he answered, hoping they would be behind the counter or in the back room, somewhere that would take him away and allow Brunetti to hear the continuing conversation between Griffoni and the pharmacist, who was still behind the counter but now looking stiffer and decidedly less amiable than before.

'If you have no objection, Signora,' Brunetti heard when he tuned back into their conversation, 'I'll keep the coupon until your aunt comes in.' The tone was pleasant and light; his face was not. 'If you'd like to pay for those items you've chosen ...' he began but left the sentence unfinished and lingering in the space between them.

'No,' she said amiably, 'I think it would be better to let my aunt decide what to do.'

'Then I'll keep them, shall I, until she comes in?' Saying this, Dottor Donato swept the items towards him.

Brunetti's pharmacist stepped out from the back room, and he went to the counter to pay for the sunblock and the aspirin. Two other people had come in while the younger man was getting the aspirin and they stood between Brunetti and the owner, whose full attention was still on Griffoni.

'I look forward to seeing your aunt,' the pharmacist said, opened a drawer, and placed the items into it. Griffoni thanked him for his help and started towards the door. The pharmacist stared after her, cold-eyed, the intensity of his expression at odds with his rosy cheeks. Then he turned to the next client, a robust woman with tightly permed white hair who gave him a warm smile. 'Ah,' he said in a voice grown suddenly friendly, 'Cara Signora Marini, how can I help you?'

Brunetti waited until Signora Marini began to speak, took his change, turned and walked slowly to the door.

Outside, Griffoni stood a few metres away, looking into the window at a panorama of masks. The Chinese proprietor sat at a counter at the back of the shop. When Brunetti stopped beside her, Griffoni said, 'I was at the hairdresser's last week, and the girl who was washing the hair of the old woman beside me asked her if she wanted the "anti-yellow treatment".' She pointed to one particularly horrid mask and continued, 'I interrupted and told her I thought that was an unkind thing to say in a city with so many Chinese residents.' After a moment, she turned away from the window, and added, 'But now I think I shouldn't have reproached her.'

'I've noticed how your sense of humour wins you friends everywhere you go, Claudia,' Brunetti said and then asked, 'What did Dottor Donato tell you?'

'First, that my aunt has often told him that she has only one nephew, so he wondered how it was that I could be her niece. I laughed and told him that I was actually the daughter of a cousin of hers and that in Naples, that fell into the category of niece.'

'And he . . .?'

'He was very apologetic but insisted that he couldn't allow it because her name was on the coupon, and only her signature was valid.' She pulled the coupons out of her bag and handed him one, pointing to Signora Gasparini's surname written at the top. 'There's no place for a signature.'

'What do you make of it?' Brunetti asked.

'It could be that he's a scrupulously honest man and won't permit it because he thinks it's wrong,' she said, then grew silent as she considered other interpretations.

Impatient, Brunetti asked, 'Then why lie about needing a signature?'

'Exactly,' she said in full agreement. 'There was no need. He could simply have refused.'

They had been idly walking back towards the *imbarcadero* when Brunetti said, 'I think we should talk to your Aunt Matilde again.'

'So do I,' Griffoni agreed. Like characters in a cartoon, they wheeled around and turned into the *calle* that would take them back to the home of the old woman.

As they passed in front of the church of the Carmini, Brunetti said, 'Since you're best friends now, perhaps you should do the talking.'

'But you're the man.'

He turned his head slowly towards her, not breaking step, and said nothing.

'She's in her eighties, Guido, so however much she might find me amusing and good for a talk about this and that, the man is still the one who decides.'

'You sound pretty accepting of that,' Brunetti remarked.

'It's her age,' Griffoni said. 'Besides, she didn't spend all that money on cosmetics to make herself more attractive to women.'

That remark brought them to the front door. Brunetti rang and explained to Beata that they'd like to speak to the Signora again. With no hesitation, she snapped open the door that let them into the entrance hall.

Upstairs, the young woman welcomed them with a smile. 'The *padrona* was very happy about your visit, signori. She's talked about it ever since. I'm happy you came again.' She stepped back to let them enter and turned to lead them down the corridor.

At the door of the living room, she paused. 'Let me tell her you're here.'

'Of course,' answered Brunetti, to whom she had spoken, ignoring Griffoni.

They heard indistinct voices from inside, then Beata came back and opened the door fully to allow them to enter. She left, closing the door behind her.

Signora Gasparini sat where she had been the previous day, looking as if she had not moved from her chair. The dragons were still upon her, and the stripes still led from her waist to just above her feet. Nor had the tremor abated. The motion, still minimal, was each time made more obvious by her red cloud of hair as it jerked to the side and back.

'How nice of you to come to see me again,' she said, speaking in the singular, smiling at Brunetti with real delight and raising her hands in a welcoming gesture.

'We're delighted to come back, Signora,' Brunetti said, stepping aside to give the old woman a clearer view of Griffoni. 'It's a pleasure to come into such an imposing room. And even more pleasant for both of us to be so warmly greeted.' Signora Gasparini looked at Griffoni then and gave the cool nod courtesy demanded a stranger be given.

'Yes,' Signora Gasparini said, looking away and around the room as though seeing it for the first time. 'It is lovely, isn't it? It was my grandfather's study, and I use it to receive visitors.' She smiled and waved to include everything in the room. 'I think it gives them a sense of who we are.' Brunetti had no way of telling whether the rhythm with which the tremors came and went was the same as the last time.

'Indeed it does, Signora,' gushed Griffoni, looking around as though she could not have enough of it. 'It's all so beautiful.'

Signora Gasparini, who still apparently did not recognize Griffoni, smiled, unable to contain her pleasure at such heartfelt compliments. She invited them to sit, and they did. 'Could you tell me again what you've come for?' she asked, trying to sound forceful but unable to disguise her confusion at their return. Brunetti was pierced with pity for her. Griffoni was right: she was tough and asked no quarter of life.

'We came because of your nephew,' Brunetti began and then added, 'Tullio,' just to be sure. 'He wanted us to try to sort out the confusion with the pharmacy. But I'm afraid I still don't understand what happened, so I've come back to ask for your help. I think that will make it possible to have the cash returned,' he said, including the talismanic word to maintain her interest.

'Help?' she asked, as if she could not understand the word.

'Could you explain to me how you were given the coupons, Signora? I don't think I can try to persuade Dottor Donato to give you your money until I understand just how this came about.'

Brunetti saw her grasp her hands together.

'It's because of the prescriptions,' she said.

'Which prescriptions are those, Signora?'

'The ones I have filled every month. I go to the pharmacy and give in my prescriptions, and I get the medicines.'

'I see, Signora. And are you exempt from paying the full price for this medicine?'

'Of course. It's the least I can get for the taxes I've been paying all my life.' And why should the rich not get something for what they contribute to the health system? Brunetti asked himself.

From beside him, he heard a whispered, *'Brava'* from Griffoni. He saw that her praise had captured the older woman's attention, as well.

She looked at Griffoni. 'Mark my words, my dear: by the time you're my age, there will be nothing left. They'll have stolen it all, the swine.'

'Could you tell us the name of the medicine, Signora?' Brunetti interrupted, not wanting to open those particular floodgates.

'Oh, don't ask me about things like that. They're what my doctor prescribes, and I take them.'

Brunetti understood her reluctance to name her diseases, although their signs were evident in every tremor, twitch, and failure of memory. 'I see, Signora. And the coupons?'

'Sometimes, when I'm very busy or I have too many things on my mind, I forget to take my prescription with me.' She spoke as though her days were a succession of meetings and boardroom decisions instead of time spent in this room, without books, without television, without company.

'And then what happens, if I might ask?'

'Oh, Dottor Donato knows how important my medicines are for my health, but without the prescriptions, he can't submit the forms to the health system.'

'Of course,' Griffoni muttered, as if involuntarily.

'So what does he do to help you, Signora?' Brunetti inquired.

'He asks me to pay for it, the full price, instead of the two Euros I'm supposed to pay, and then he gives me a coupon.' She looked at them, and they smiled. Encouraged by their approval, she waved them closer to her with her bent fingers and pointed to the door so that they would understand that Beata was not to hear this. Lowering her voice, she went on. 'Dottor Donato told me that, if we did it this way, he'd be able to add twenty per cent to the value of the coupons.'

Both of them smiled, and Griffoni could not resist exclaiming, 'Oh, that's very kind of him, Signora,' as though to suggest the pharmacist should be given an award for exemplary citizenship.

'He doesn't have to, I know. But he's a kind man,' Signora Gasparini said with a smile that showed the perfection of her teeth. She sat up, wiped away her smile, and said, 'And it doesn't hurt anyone, does it?'

'Not at all,' Griffoni assured her.

They had obviously won her confidence because she continued. 'Dottor Donato said it's an offer he makes only to faithful clients; people he can trust.' She stopped abruptly, as if she'd heard an echo of what she had just said. 'He asked me not to talk about it, so please don't say anything.' She studied them closely, as though suddenly noticing them there, listening to her, and said, 'I know I can rely on you.'

'Of course you can, Signora,' Griffoni said with just the right note of piety in her voice.

'I understand him completely,' Brunetti began, voice rich with admiration, 'And what with the cost of medicine today, twenty per cent would ...'

He was cut off by Griffoni, who waved a hand in the direction of the Signora's face, as though she were a magician and Signora Gasparini the rabbit, saying, 'And your complexion is certainly proof that a woman should buy only the best.'

Signora Gasparini's face grew thoughtful when she heard that, and she started speaking again. 'He's apologized to me, more than once, that the regulations of the health system are so complicated that he really can't return the money to me without them finding out he gave me the drug without a prescription. If that happened, he told me they'd take his licence away. He's been such a good friend to me that I can't risk that.'

Griffoni and Brunetti nodded in agreement, which created a grotesque scene of three nodding heads in the same limited space.

Using his most concerned voice, Brunetti asked, 'Do you recall how many times this has happened over the years, that you've forgotten to bring your prescriptions with you?'

Friendly and solicitous, he paid close attention to her face; he saw her eyes close slowly and, when they opened again, seem faintly out of focus, as though a different person had been called upon to play the next part of the scene.

'Over the years, it's been ... oh,' she said, her surprise conspicuously audible, 'I don't really remember.' She looked from one to the other, as though the missing number might be written on their foreheads, and if only she looked hard enough, she'd find it. But apparently this was not to be.

Ordinarily, Brunetti would have repeated the question, but it was evident that Signora Gasparini had decided not to remember. Consequently, he changed the topic and said, with great earnestness, 'How lucky you are to find a pharmacist who cares enough about his clients to take that risk.'

She smiled, hearing her sudden loss of memory dismissed by this man as both convincing and unimportant. Her confidence in them and their discretion restored, she leaned forward again and, in a lowered voice, said, 'That's exactly what Signora Lamon told me. She was at the counter ahead of me one day, and I couldn't help hearing their conversation. She'd forgotten her prescription, and Dottor Donato took out one of the coupons for her. When I saw her in Tonolo a few days ago – I go there for the mini *bignés*, especially the dark chocolate ones – and when I saw her, I told her that he'd done it for me, too.' She paused here, as one does in a long conversation, trying to remember if one has already said something. Perhaps assured by her memory that she had not, she continued, 'She told me she has two friends he also does it for.'

She clasped her hands in front of her bosom in an old-fashioned gesture and said, 'He's so kind, that he does it for us.'

Seamlessly, as though one person's virtue led to another's, Brunetti said, 'He's lucky to be able to work so closely with Dottoressa Ruberti, who surely must be another extremely kind person.' He continued without pause, hoping to divert her from asking how he knew who her doctor was, and added, 'My mother-in-law's gone to her for years and never ceases to sing her praises.'

Griffoni put on a smile and nodded a few times at the truth of this. The old woman saw the smile but had apparently forgotten the face on which it appeared.

'Yes, she is,' Signora Gasparini concurred. 'And she's brave, like Dottor Donato, ready to take chances to see that her patients are well taken care of.'

'Oh,' Griffoni said with the enthusiastic curiosity of a younger person, 'what has she done for you, Signora?'

Signora Gasparini opened her mouth to answer but paused, as if struck by sudden difficulty in recalling just what the doctor had done for her.

Brunetti saw the same panic in her eyes that he had seen in his mother's when, in the early stages, she had failed to remember something, so he asked, 'How long has she been your doctor, Signora?' as if Griffoni had not asked the other question.

Perhaps this was less complicated, for she said, 'For the last ten years. My family doctor retired, and Dottoressa Ruberti took over the practice.' At the sight of these two young people, nodding encouragingly, she went on. 'She's Venetian. My father went to school with her grandfather.' She smiled, perhaps at having been able to remember this. 'We discovered this a few months after I started to go to her, and I suppose it was a sort of bond for us.'

'Of course,' Brunetti muttered. 'That way, you could be sure she'd take a personal interest in your health.'

'Exactly,' she said. Then, almost proudly, she went on, 'I didn't go to her often at the beginning, you understand. Not like many of the old women around here. Not until about a year ago, when ... when I had a few tests at the hospital, and Dottoressa Ruberti prescribed me some medicine.' She stopped, and Brunetti wondered if she was willing herself to forget about her illness and to ignore the continual snap, snap, snap of her head. He certainly could not.

She pulled her hands from the arms of her chair and interlocked her fingers, forcing her joined hands down on her lap. 'I went to my old pharmacist, the one I used to go to, and he told me that there was another medicine identical to the one Dottoressa Ruberti prescribed that was ... what do you call it?' She brought one hand to her forehead. 'What is it? Something with "G".'

Brunetti saw her fear, the tightness of her mouth, and asked, 'Do you mean "generic", Signora?'

'Yes. Yes. That's it. Of course. I was just about to say it.' She smiled and made no attempt to hide her relief.

'I told him I had to speak to my doctor about this, and when I did, she told me that the medicines weren't the same, that the one she'd prescribed for me cost more because it had been proven to be better.' She closed her eyes in the frustration of age and powerlessness. 'It's what they do to us, try to save money in any way they can, no matter if it kills us.'

Brunetti made a comforting noise but said nothing.

'I went back the next day and told the pharmacist I wouldn't take the generic,' she began, evidently proud of having remembered the word, 'and when he refused to listen to me, I walked out. When I told Dottoressa Ruberti what had happened, she said she'd wanted to warn me about the pharmacist, but she couldn't do that because of professional ethics. She said she was glad I'd seen for myself, and she knew a pharmacist who would give me the right medicine.'

'Thank God,' Griffoni whispered.

'Yes. Thank God, indeed. They saved my life.' Instead of thankful, the old woman sounded anguished, as if the struggle had exhausted her and haunted her still.

'So that's how you came to be a client of Dottor Donato?' Brunetti asked in childlike innocence, as though he were eager to hear the end of a fairy tale.

'Yes, it's the best thing that could have happened. To have a wonderful doctor and a pharmacist who have the same concern for the well-being of their patients.'

25

Outside, the day was drawing down, bringing with it a taste of the deeper chill that would soon be upon them. Griffoni turned up the collar of her jacket and kept her arms across her chest while they walked towards Rialto. When they arrived at Rizzardini, Brunetti asked if she'd like something to drink and she said she needed a coffee. Inside the tiny *pasticceria*, they both asked for a coffee, and she asked for a *cannolo*, saying, 'It's the only place here where I might be at home. At least for the pastries.' The pastry and the coffees came, and they moved to the end of the bar, close to the door.

She took a sip and made a face.

'What's wrong?' Brunetti asked.

'I'm not in Naples is what's wrong,' she said seriously but then remembered to smile to suggest she was only joking. She picked up the cylindrical pastry and took a bite; crumbs rained down the front of her coat. 'It's not that the coffee's bad; it's more that people up here simply don't know what good coffee is or don't know how to make it.' She pushed the cup farther away with a stiff finger and took another bite, then finished the cream-filled pastry and wiped her mouth with a paper napkin, the front of her coat with her hand. 'The pastry's very good, though.'

Brunetti finished his coffee, having thought it was fine and trying to remember the coffee he had drunk, ages ago, when he was stationed temporarily in Naples. He remembered the pasta and the fish but not the coffee, save that it was half the size of the one he had just drunk, and two were enough to energize him for hours.

The bar was warm, and they were alone at the counter. 'What do you think?'

'My best friend's grandmother suffered from Alzheimer's, and Signora Gasparini ...' she began, then corrected herself with a smile, 'and my Aunt Matilde reminds me of her. Sometimes her memory works; other times it doesn't. When she lets down her guard, she's a feeble old woman who's showing signs of Parkinson's, losing her memory, and trying to hide those facts for as long as she can.'

She reached into the pocket of her jacket and put a five-Euro note on the counter. The barman brought her change and took the cups and saucers away.

'And so?' Brunetti asked.

Griffoni didn't answer but turned to the door and opened it. She walked out into the main *calle*, turned into the first on the left, and stopped, looking at the pastries in the window. 'Gasparini had the coupons. He got them from his aunt,' she said, speaking slowly as she ordered things in her mind. 'She knew the same was being done for other people, and she may have told her nephew that, as well.

Perhaps he confronted Donato and told him he knew what he was doing. Or threatened to come to us.' She paused but did not look at him.

'Why would Gasparini bother to tell him?' Brunetti asked. 'Why not simply *do* it, come to us with the coupons and whatever information his aunt had given him? About Signora Lamon, for example.'

Griffoni put her hands into the pockets of her jacket and rolled up and down, up and down, on the balls of her feet. Brunetti could all but hear the gears in her mind shifting higher, then back again to a low steady beat, then up again to high.

When she still failed to answer, Brunetti said, 'You're right that he might have known about the others. It took less than half an hour for your aunt to tell us about them.'

Griffoni said only, 'Signora Lamon.'

'Why would Donato limit himself to medicines for Parkinson's and Alzheimer's?' Brunetti asked. He thought for a while and continued, 'The ones for psychological problems are expensive, especially when they're first put on the market.' He thought, but did not say, that the people who were prescribed this kind of drug were also the people most likely to forget to take their prescriptions with them to the pharmacy and the least likely to pay close attention to the price of their medicines or how or what they paid for them.

People trusted their pharmacists as much as they did their doctors, he knew; perhaps even more – and trusted them with their secrets. 'Donato would know if the families were rich or whether someone in the family would become suspicious at the disappearance of a hundred Euros every once in a while,' he said.

Griffoni took her eyes from the pastries and turned to look at him. 'A pharmacist would probably be able to judge how serious their disease had become from reading the prescription: he could probably estimate how forgetful they were likely to be. Especially people with the beginnings of Alzheimer's.'

Brunetti nodded, asking himself how many of the coupons would be forgotten about or lost by the people who paid for them. If, months later, they found a few stuffed in a drawer, how many of them would remember what they were?

'It could be a gold mine, couldn't it?' Griffoni said.

'But what about the other people working there?' he asked. In response to her glance, he said, 'I don't know if they'd all suggest a client pay the full price in return for a coupon.' He drew to a sudden halt. 'Are we agreed that they'd all have to be complicit in what's going on?'

'They'd have to know,' Griffoni said. 'I don't know if that's complicity.'

'What else would it be?' Brunetti asked in a voice he intentionally kept calm.

'Avoiding trouble, keeping your job, minding your own business.' She paused to see that he'd heard and understood her and then said, 'Remember the Bible, Guido.'

'What?' he asked, unable to disguise his astonishment. 'You? Saying that?'

She smiled at the intensity of his response. She patted his arm and said, 'Don't worry, Guido. I'm talking only about the seven fat years and the seven lean years. We had lots of fat years; now the lean years have begun. So people, even pharmacists, are far less brave than they were in the past, far less able to risk losing their jobs.'

'Able or willing?' Brunetti asked with northern rigour.

'Willing,' conceded Griffoni, the Neapolitan.

'They take an oath. Like doctors.' Brunetti insisted.

'Certainly,' she said amiably. 'But I'm not sure that means much any more. Not to most people. They want to survive, keep their heads down and survive. So that's what they do.'

'Keep their heads down?' he asked.

'Yes.'

Brunetti didn't like knowing that she was right.

He looked at his watch and saw that it was after six. Idiotic to go back to work when he was so close to home. 'You going to get a boat?' he asked Griffoni.

'Yes. But I'm not going back to the Questura. If Lieutenant Scarpa asks me where I was, I'll say I was following a suspect all the way down to San Pietro in Castello.'

He laughed at the idea of anyone who was not Venetian trying to do that, and they turned back towards Rialto, Brunetti having decided to accompany her to San Silvestro.

'Last weekend,' she began, 'I went over to Angelo Raffaele and spent two hours walking around.'

'Were you lost?' Brunetti asked.

'I don't know. I wasn't going anywhere or looking for anything. I simply walked around in circles – well, rectangular circles – until I began to recognize shops I'd passed or restaurants that were on corners where I'd turned before. I always turned at the bottom of the second bridge I came to.'

'And?' he asked.

'I think I have a vague sense of where things are.'

'It's not easy.'

'I know. I know. You have to have been born here.'

'It helps,' Brunetti said, just as they turned into the *calle* that led to the *embarcadero*. He looked at his watch. 'There's a boat going towards the Lido in two minutes.'

She turned and stared at him. 'Do you have them programmed into your memory?'

'This is my stop, so I know the times.'

'Ah,' she said. She pulled her wallet from her bag and extracted her imob.

Brunetti heard the motor of the approaching boat; after a few seconds, so did she. 'And tomorrow?' she asked. 'What do we do?'

'I'll think about it,' Brunetti answered and turned back toward the underpass.

After dinner, Brunetti went into Paola's study and extended himself on her sofa, hands clasped behind his head. He had left the door ajar, allowing light to come into the room from the hallway. Outside, it was dark. Dimness was the proper setting.

He stared at the ceiling and thought about his own pharmacy, in Campo San Bortolo, just to the statue's left. He went there because, well, because he had always gone there.

He closed his eyes and imagined walking in, going up to the counter with a prescription.

From the front room of the apartment, he heard voices: Chiara and Raffi. One of them laughed. It was such a normal sound that Brunetti barely noticed it.

Barely noticed it. Of course, no one paid any attention to what a pharmacist did. He took your prescription, brought you the medicine and told you what to pay. Had his pharmacist told Brunetti that a medicine cost twenty-two Euros, instead of two, he would not have questioned the price. If the pharmacist told a person taking medicine against mental confusion, but who had forgotten to bring the necessary prescription, that the only way they could have their medicine was to pay full price for it and receive, as a guarantee of future repayment, a coupon from the pharmacy, who would question him?

If the client refused, then the pharmacist had only to apologize for having suggested an alternative procedure in hopes of saving his client another trip to the pharmacy, and tell them they simply had to return with the prescription to have the medicine they needed at the usual price. And never try it with that client again.

Would someone actually *do* this, risk his profession for so little? He remembered a well-known and very successful lawyer who had been caught last year shoplifting three ties from Hermès. Vice-Questore Patta had put a lock-down on that one: no charges had been brought, nor had information been slipped to *Il Gazzettino*, which would certainly have smacked its lips over the story. Brunetti had understood Patta's decision: a moment's folly should not incinerate a career and a reputation.

Twenty years ago, he knew, his response would have been different, more punitive, more fierce. 'How Italian you're becoming,' he said out loud.

'That's a good thing. I'd hate to think I'd married an Australian and never noticed,' Paola said, pushing the door open with her foot. She carried a tray with two cups of coffee, two small glasses, and a tall, thin bottle that looked as if it might contain grappa.

26

Brunetti was awakened from deep sleep at about four by the sound of rushing wind. He sat up, alarmed at the noise and uncertain for a moment where he was. He extended his right hand and found Paola's shoulder, searched for and saw the familiar pattern thrown on the far wall by the light that managed to filter in from the street lights five floors below. He waited for the noise to come again; it did not. He lay back on his pillow, but the sound did not return. The night lay silent on his ears.

Had he been dreaming of something? Where had the wind come from? Where had his sleeping self been? He had nothing more than a vague memory of having been in a dimly lit room. He studied the light, uncertain whether he would be able to return to sleep.

He thought of Dottor Donato and the many things they did not know about him: family, habits, friends, business history. From nowhere came the realization that he had the same absence of information about Gasparini. He was a man with a problematic son and was now a figure attached to machines and lying inert in a hospital bed. Like Donato, he surely must have a past that might help explain his present.

The same could easily be said of Dottoressa Ruberti.

He started to make a list of what he would ask Signorina Elettra to examine but soon gave up at the awareness that she had become so adept at the hunt that she was now the person who best knew what to look for, and where. He began, nevertheless, to list the things he wanted to know: family, possible previous contact with the police, financial status, other ... the ideas loosened in his mind, and Brunetti soon drifted off, carried on far more gentle winds than those imagined ones that had torn him from sleep.

He went directly to Signorina Elettra's office when he arrived at the Questura, not at all sure what the mood would be after their last, awkward, meeting. That was left unsettled because she was on the phone when he entered. The first thing he noted was a vase of flowers on her desk: he had no idea what they were – surely not tulips or roses – dark, almost purple; he could not remember seeing flowers so sombre, as if they believed that brightening a room was not part of their mission.

She sat behind them, partially obscured. Seeing him, she raised a hand in greeting, then used it to point repeatedly to the door to Patta's office, and said into the receiver, 'He's just come in, Dottore. Do you have time to see him now?' During the brief pause while she waited for Vice-Questore Patta's answer, she raised one hand and gave a shrug, to suggest she had no idea what her superior wanted from Brunetti.

'Good, I'll ask him to go in.' She replaced the receiver and pointed to the door.

He took two steps, paused and turned back to her. 'I know you've already had a look at Dottor Donato, but could you take another look at his private life: same with Gasparini and Dottoressa Ruberti?' Before she could answer, Brunetti went to the door and entered without knocking.

The Vice-Questore was bent over behind his desk; visible only were his shoulders and part of his back. As Brunetti watched, his back moved up and down, each time just a few centimetres. 'Is something wrong, Vice-Questore?' Brunetti asked, moving quickly towards his superior's desk.

Suddenly, like a marionette popping from a box, the rest of Patta appeared, facing Brunetti, who had stopped just short of his desk. 'Just tying my shoe,' Patta explained, his face flushed by having risen up so quickly.

When Brunetti failed to answer, Patta said, 'Have a seat, Commissario. There's something I'd like to inform you about.'

Brunetti did as he was told, crossed his legs, and placed his hands on the arms of the chair. He set his face in what he tried to make an easy, interested smile and waited.

'It's about the baggage handlers at the airport,' Patta said.

Brunetti applied psychic botox to his smile and nodded while turning his attention to Sant'Antonio, patron saint of lost things and lost causes. *Dear Sant'Antonio, lift this weight from my shoulders, and I shall give you my gratitude and thanks for ever and ever, amen*. His mother had taught him, when he was still a boy, that it was vulgar and offensive to try to bargain with the saints, to offer them prayers or good works in exchange for favours. 'Just tell them you will thank them and be grateful to them,' she had told him, and then explained, 'After all, they're in Heaven. Could they want anything more?'

This, even to a child, had seemed eminently sensible, and he had never wavered from her teaching. Brunetti thus had a number of saints he more or less kept on call, invoking their aid when in need of it, always grateful to them for their help and vociferous in giving them his thanks.

'Ah, yes, the baggage handlers,' Brunetti said, as though he found the topic mildly interesting.

'It's been years that we've been playing cat and mouse with them,' Patta began. Brunetti nodded. He'd spent days, weeks, months investigating them, overseeing the planting of micro-cameras in various parts of the airport, arresting them, taking them in for questioning, confronting them with the videos of their pilfering of the suitcases entrusted to their care. And was one of them in prison? Had one of them ever been fired?

'And I'm tired of it,' Patta, who had occasionally had to approve the attempts to gather conclusive evidence against them, said wearily.

As were they all, Brunetti longed to say. Instead, he adjusted his face to display curiosity. Patta either did not register or chose to ignore his expression, so Brunetti asked, 'And so, Vice-Questore?'

'We've wasted enough time on this and I've decided to put an end to it,' Patta said in his most authoritarian voice. Brunetti was curious about how the Vice-Questore planned to accomplish this. Forbid them entry to the airport? Arrest them all? Build a wall?

'The airport is not in Venice,' Patta declared. 'It is in Tessera,' he added. Then, making it evident that he was irritated by incompetence but not such a bad sport that he would make an issue of it, he added, 'No one seems to have noticed that before I did.' He paused to allow Brunetti to become aware of his own partial responsibility for this legal oversight and then continued. 'I spoke with the city's lawyers today and told them that, because Tessera is a part of Mestre and not of Venice, it is therefore within their jurisdiction, not ours, and thus the police of Mestre are responsible for law enforcement at the airport, and we are not.'

'What answer did they give you, Signore?'

'They will look into the legal background of the matter, but until then . . .' Patta said and, deliberately teasing, let his voice drift off and made an airily dismissive gesture with his hand.

'Until then, sir?' Brunetti, who could not bear the suspense, inquired.

'Until then, there will be no police interference with or surveillance of the baggage handlers,' Patta said, as if he'd arranged the arrest of the entire leadership of the Sacra Corona Unita and farther attention was redundant.

'None at all?' Brunetti asked.

'None. I've ordered our patrols there stopped and informed my colleague in Mestre of this fact.' He aimed a smile at Brunetti and said, 'I wanted you to know this so that you will not question the new schedules.'

'And your colleague in Mestre, Vice-Questore?'

Another smile radiated out from Patta's face. 'He's refused to assume any responsibility and will not order his men to patrol.'

Brunetti, thinking of his conversation with Griffoni about the complicity of the pharmacists who remained silent, said, 'That was a very wise decision, Dottore.' He smiled and asked, 'Will that be all, Signore?'

At Patta's nod, he got to his feet and left the office.

Signorina Elettra glanced at him as he emerged into her office. Brunetti studied her face and saw in it traces of its usual warmth, noticed as well that the dark flowers had been exiled to the windowsill.

'The Vice-Questore has told me that there will be no more investigations of the baggage handlers.'

'Yes,' she said, all but glowing. 'I know.'

Well, well, well, Brunetti thought. Signorina Elettra was much given to elliptical remarks, and so ordinarily he would have thought she meant that gossip had wafted this news towards her. But there was nothing in her remark but granite-hard fact: she had heard because of the listening device she had planted in Patta's office.

'You seem pleased,' Brunetti said. 'If I might observe.'

'Oh, I am pleased. Very,' she said, idly touching the top button of her blouse.

'Might I inquire why?'

'Because this path was suggested to him – very strongly suggested to him – by Lieutenant Scarpa, who was the one who told him about the separate jurisdictions of the cities. Quite authoritatively, if I might say so.' As she'd said the Lieutenant's name, Brunetti was reminded of a remark made by Creon: 'Once an enemy, never a friend, even after death.'

But then Signorina Elettra smiled, and had they been standing in a field of flowers, the bees most surely would have come to sip honey from her lips.

'May I farther inquire where he obtained his information?'

Her smile broadened, and Brunetti was forced to turn away for fear of insulin shock.

'I'd heard him discussing the subject with the Vice-Questore, and the Lieutenant said he'd take it upon himself to find out what the territorial division was.' She paused and leaned to the side to flick a speck of invisibility from her desk.

'He was free, of course, to find this information himself, but he told me ... he *told* me to find it. And so I did.'

'It was really made, this division of jurisdiction?' Brunetti asked.

'Of course,' she answered. 'In 1938.'

After a long pause, Brunetti asked, 'And since then?'

'I've no idea, Commissario. The Lieutenant *told* me to find any record of the administrative decision that separated the two cities, and that's what I found.'

'And so, when all police oversight ceases, with the inevitable result, the Lieutenant will be discovered to have cited a regulation from almost a hundred years ago?'

'Precisely.'

'Presumably, this will not work to the Lieutenant's advantage,' Brunetti offered.

'I'm afraid not,' she answered with a smile that hinted at, but did not reveal, the size of her teeth.

Brunetti stood for some time, so struck by her cunning as to be deprived of the power of coherent speech. Finally he freed himself from the spell and said, 'I'll be in my office.'

She nodded and returned her attention to her computer.

It was not until the afternoon that he saw Signorina Elettra again. She knocked on the door of his office about five, and when she came in, he saw that she carried some papers.

'The Three Musketeers?' he asked.

'*Sì*, Signore,' she answered.

'Anything interesting?'

'Oh, I prefer you to make that judgement yourself, Commissario.' She came across the room and laid the papers on his desk.

As she did, he said, 'Could you send copies to Commissario Griffoni and Ispettore Vianello?'

'Of course, Signore,' she said and left him to consider the documents.

There were three small piles of paper, each clipped together, the name 'Donato' at the top of one, 'Gasparini' another, 'Ruberti' on the third.

He opened the first and learned that Girolamo Donato had been born in Venice sixty-three years before. His family had owned and run the same pharmacy at San Leonardo for three generations. He had studied *farmacia* at the University of Padova and gone to work in the family business when he was twenty-five. During his career, he had once been elected the President of the Ordine dei Farmacisti della Provincia di Venezia. A son and daughter, both pharmacists, worked with him, as did two young women who helped with sales and the general upkeep of the shop and stock.

The family lived in three separate apartments in a large building on the Fondamenta della Misericordia. His son and daughter-in-law had two sons, five and three; his daughter, in her early thirties, was unmarried.

Brunetti glanced up from the page, amazed that a family could be so apparently normal. They studied, worked, got married, had children, and worked. He glanced at the next page, which showed that Donato had given both his son and his daughter their apartments. After salaries, expenses, insurance, and taxes, the pharmacy earned approximately 150,000 Euros a year. Brunetti was surprised at the sum, had thought it would be much greater. After all, a pharmacist worked far more than eight hours a day, had to stay open on weekends and holidays according to a strict rota, which also demanded frequent all-night openings.

He set the first report aside and looked at the papers about Gasparini. He, too, had been born in Venice, a bit more than a decade after Donato. He had studied Economy and Commerce at Ca' Foscari and started working in Treviso immediately after graduation. He had, in the course of eighteen years of work, changed jobs four times; he had been at his current job in Verona for three years and was now the assistant to the chief accountant. Brunetti went back and looked at the names of the companies for which he had worked and tried to understand what they might reveal about the possible nature of his job. 'Textiles', 'Leather'. All well and good. 'Holdings', 'Enterprises'. Anything at all.

Brunetti made a list of the cities where Gasparini had worked over the years and saw that he had never remained in the same city for two successive jobs. He had moved from Treviso to Conegliano, to Padova and then to Pordenone, and was now in Verona. Brunetti tried to imagine what it must have been like for them, both for the children and for the marriage, to uproot themselves and move to a new city or to become one of the families in which the father makes his ghostly appearance after the children are in bed, only to leave before they are awake.

As if Signorina Elettra had read his mind, farther information from the Ufficio Anagrafe followed in the next paragraph: during the previous twenty years, both Gasparini and his wife had maintained the same legal address, and the children had been in regular attendance at the Albertini for the last four years.

Brunetti paged back and took a more careful look at the financial details of Gasparini's life. The salaries listed for each position he'd had were no more than average. If his wife were making the same salary as Paola, they could probably not afford to send their children to the Albertini.

An explanation sprang unsummoned to Brunetti's mind: fiscal misconduct of some sort, followed by dismissal. No sooner thought than discarded: Gasparini was unlikely to have managed that repeatedly without having been caught at it. Brunetti tried to think of some other reason for such a strange work history, common perhaps in other countries but not here, where many men stayed at the same job for decades, if not for their entire careers. What about blackmail? Who better than the accountant would know what the real finances of a company were? If officers of the Guardia di Finanza could be arrested for not reporting fiscal illegalities in return for money, how much easier for an accountant to plan, and then profit from, the same irregularities.

The next page revealed that his third company had, two months after Gasparini left his employ, been raided by the Guardia di Finanza, and its computers and records sequestered. It had taken the investigators very little time to discover parallel systems of bookkeeping that recorded the true, not only the purported, profits and losses of the company.

Brunetti looked up from the page and all but saw it written: work in a company long enough to discover if they were keeping a second set of books, or even devise the system that created them; then help keep those same books long enough to understand how the system worked; and then demand payment not to reveal it. If they paid, then take the money and change jobs; if they did not pay, find a new job and, once there, call the Guardia di Finanza.

Of course there could be some other explanation, but this one made sense, at least to someone with the professional inclination to treat all human behaviour with suspicion and the presumption of guilt.

He pulled the third pile towards him and started to read through it. Average student, medical diploma from the University of Padova in 1987, where Dottoressa Ruberti remained as an intern for four years, after which she joined two other doctors in a joint practice in Abano Terme. She left the practice after six years and returned to Venice to open her own private practice with offices in Dorsoduro and Castello.

Married, divorced, one son with severe physical disabilities who lived in a facility for the handicapped. Never arrested, no driving infractions, owner of both her apartment and the ground-floor space in Dorsoduro where her office was located. She rented the one in Castello.

The report, sparse as it was, ended there.

27

Though it was late in the afternoon, he phoned both Griffoni and Vianello and asked them to come to his office because he wanted to talk to them about the information they'd all received from Signorina Elettra.

He leaned back in his chair and folded his arms and studied the sky visible from his window, sombre and sad and grey with the approach of bad weather. Life would retreat inside for months, the lack of sun would lead to grumpiness, and people would long to flee to the sun to go swimming or to the mountains to ski. He loathed skiing because, like polo, it required an enormous amount of equipment. Truth to tell, Brunetti loathed most sports, save for football, which his father had adored and taught him to love and which had the redeeming virtue of requiring only a ball to kick around. Although he believed the sport was corrupt to its very core, millions made or lost by betting on games whose outcomes were preordained, he could not stop himself from being thrilled by those same preordained moves. He recalled a day when his father had taken him to see a game between Inter and …

His brief reverie was broken by the arrival of Vianello, who came in without bothering to knock, and quickly after that, Griffoni, who walked in through the door Vianello had left open. They sat in front of him, each with a folder and pen, both obviously eager to hear what he had to say.

'I'd like to take a look at what Signorina Elettra found about the number of times Signor Gasparini changed jobs.' The other two pulled out their copies, and when they stopped turning pages, Brunetti asked, 'What do you make of the fact that he's changed jobs so often?'

Griffoni looked up, confused by the question, but Vianello said, 'It's unusual, isn't it, to move around like that?'

Brunetti nodded. 'I think it is. Yes.'

Griffoni glanced at Vianello but said nothing.

With a vague gesture towards the folder, the Inspector said, 'It could be that he's not a very good accountant.' It was audible to Brunetti that this was merely an introduction to what Vianello really wanted to say, which was, 'Or that he's indeed very good at it.'

'Meaning?' Griffoni asked.

'Meaning that people don't change jobs so often, especially not in these times, and especially not a man who's married and has children.'

Vianello paused to look at her. 'Not unless they have some reason to do so,' he concluded, confirming Brunetti's belief that Vianello, too, was aware of the dark corners of human possibility.

Neither of them said anything, so Vianello asked, 'What about the visit of the Guardia di Finanza three months after he left the third place?' He ruffled through the papers and gave the name of the company: 'Poseidon Leather.'

'Two,' Brunetti said.

'Excuse me?' he asked.

'It was two months.'

Griffoni turned in her chair and asked Brunetti, 'Are you and Lorenzo jumping to a conclusion about this man that I don't see?'

Though the question was addressed to them both, Vianello chose to answer it. 'He didn't change only his job: he changed city each time. Do you have an explanation for why he'd be willing to disrupt his family's life so frequently?' Vianello asked her in a voice that struck Brunetti as being more insistent than necessary.

'What needs explanation?' Griffoni asked sharply. 'Why can't he simply have changed jobs a number of times?' Then, glancing at Brunetti in order to include him, she added, 'You both seem to assume – with what I think is very little evidence – that he's up to something.'

Brunetti and Vianello exchanged a look, which provoked Griffoni to say, 'Oh, stop it, both of you. Am I the goose girl of the village who can't see what the clever, experienced men can see with one glance?'

'Claudia,' Brunetti said, 'We aren't plotting anything. We're all looking at the same information.'

'What does that mean?' she asked.

'That we all read this,' he began, holding up the folder, 'and it seems we read it differently.'

Griffoni gave him a cool look. 'And because two of you see it one way, that means you have to be right? If suspicion has company, it's suddenly the truth?'

'It might explain Gasparini's interest in the coupons. He might have seen them as an opportunity,' Brunetti said, glancing at Vianello, who nodded in agreement. 'If it happened that, as an accountant, he had to prepare the real books a company keeps, as well as the ones they show to the Guardia di Finanza, then he'd be in a position to make use of that information for his own purposes.' Brunetti looked at both of them; neither had bothered to question his use of the phrase, 'real books'.

Griffoni was busy examining the papers in her hands, as though trying to translate them into some other language.

'It would explain why he changed jobs,' Brunetti continued. 'And cities. Either he found that they were doing nothing illegal and left, or he found that they were and used his information to blackmail them, and then left.'

'Then why would the Guardia di Finanza raid the leather company?' Griffoni asked.

Vianello suggested, 'Because they refused to pay him and fired him. What better proof could he offer of what he could do to an employer if they refused to pay him?'

'Claudia,' Brunetti began patiently, 'I'm not trying to ram this down your throat; I'm merely asking you to consider it as a possible explanation for the way he kept changing jobs.'

'How would he find another job?' she asked. 'Especially if he's a blackmailer.'

'They'd be eager to get rid of him, wouldn't they?' Vianello asked. 'What better way to do that than by writing him a letter of recommendation praising him so highly they could slough him off to some other company?'

'I think you're both crazy,' Griffoni said abruptly.

Both men stared at her, but Brunetti decided to attempt sweet reason. 'Oh, come on, Claudia,' he said. 'Just because we disagree with you?' Leaving her no time to protest, he continued, 'The pharmacist is just another person for him to blackmail, like his former employers.'

'I'm still waiting for evidence that it happened like that,' she said.

Vianello interrupted to say, 'Let's talk about Dottor Donato for a moment.' He held up the sheaf of papers. 'He seems like a decent, honest man who's worked hard all his life.' Both of them heard the sharp emphasis he put on the word 'seems'.

'He worked out this scam with the coupons,' he went on. 'Signorina Elettra found the rules for pharmacists. They can add thirty-three per cent to the cost of medicines: no more. But with cosmetics, they can ask whatever they want. She found one pharmacy with a seventy per cent markup.'

Brunetti looked at Griffoni and said, 'Think about what it does to his profits to sell cosmetics, instead of medicine.' After a pause, he added, 'Gasparini's an accountant. No matter how confused his aunt's story was, he'd see the advantage of the coupons in an instant.'

Vianello, in a far less combative tone, and careful to speak equally to Brunetti and Griffoni, added, 'Signora Gasparini had almost a thousand Euros in coupons. She's been accepting them for a long time and so has her friend, Signora Lamon. The person who profits from that is Donato.'

This time, Griffoni did not protest about what they said. Brunetti saw her abstracted gaze; he wondered whether she were trying to calculate Donato's added monthly earnings.

Brunetti and Vianello shared a glance and lapsed into mutually agreed silence.

Speaking slowly, as if begrudging every word, Griffoni said, 'All right: Donato would be better off if Gasparini didn't talk about this.' It was a long way from agreeing with them, but at least Griffoni was willing to accept the possibility. She went quiet again, and only after some time had elapsed, asked, 'Has either of you thought what would happen if you had Matilde Gasparini speak to a magistrate or try to give a statement about what happened? Or what a good defence attorney would do to your parade of old women with Alzheimer's and Parkinson's?' She held up her thumb and then her other fingers as she counted out her objections. 'You'll have only the testimony – if you can call it that – of these addled old women. Or men. You have the coupons with Signora Gasparini's name on them and her confused account of a twenty per cent increase. You have no evidence of any connection between Gasparini and Donato. You have a colleague of Donato's who has repeated gossip about him. If you think this is enough to take to a magistrate, then good luck to you,' she said.

Vianello looked sobered by what she said. 'We've found no one else with a motive to attack him.'

'No robbery,' Brunetti reminded them.

Silence returned. Brunetti saw that the sky had darkened, and night was fast upon them. He heard a sudden gust of wind, and across the canal, leaves tumbled from the trees in the garden of the house with the fence. The wind banged the shutter of the last window on the right of the top floor back and forth, noisy witness to the increasing dilapidation of the building.

'So?' Vianello finally asked.

'His wife would know,' Griffoni said.

'You sound sure of that,' Vianello said.

'Would your wife know?' she shot right back.

Vianello laughed, and the situation deflated.

*

'How *dare* you suggest that about Tullio?' Professoressa Crosera shouted at them.

She'd agreed to let them come to her home the following morning, had welcomed him and Griffoni with cool politeness. Brunetti had decided a third person would be too much, and Vianello had made no objection when asked not to go with them. The Professoressa led them into the sitting room.

Her husband, she explained, in response to Brunetti's question, was a quiet, serious man whose life centred on his family and his – here she had paused and looked across at them nervously – passion for cycling. He'd competed in the *Giro d'Italia* when he was still a student but realized that he lacked the stamina to be a professional. But still he rode, kept three bicycles in a garage in Mestre and spent at least one of the days he was home at the weekend, in all weathers, riding long distances and returning home exhausted and tranquil.

The thought of how normal this sounded made it difficult for Brunetti to go on to his next topic, his chequered work history. Nevertheless he had, with some trepidation, asked why her husband had changed jobs so often, and she'd said, showing the first overt signs of irritation, that it sounded as though they suspected he'd been fired for some incompetence or irregularity at his work.

'That's what we'd like to exclude, Signora,' Brunetti said seriously. 'Not incompetence, Signora. Irregularity.'

Brunetti had read, and often, that a person's mouth fell open in surprise. This is exactly what happened, and then Professoressa Crosera sat immobile for some seconds before she demanded, 'How *dare* you suggest that about Tullio?' She seemed about to ask something else, but choked on her rage and had to stop, her hand to her mouth to stop her coughing, face red with fury.

Griffoni, who had sat quietly through Brunetti's questioning, had winced with shame when he made his final suggestion. She sat immobile, face forward, not looking at either of them.

Professoressa Crosera closed her eyes and, in what in other circumstances would have been an act of conscious melodrama, placed a hand on her heart. Brunetti heard, for the first time, the ticking of a clock somewhere in the room.

It ticked more than a hundred times before Professoressa Crosera opened her eyes and looked at him. 'I will tell you this once, and then I want you to get out of my house, both of you. You will not speak to me again, and I will not speak to you, not unless I am ordered to do so by an officer of the court.' She hadn't bothered to look at Griffoni.

She asked Brunetti, 'Do you understand?'

'Yes.'

'My husband's parents died of cancer, six years apart; their deaths were very ugly and very long. In each case,' and here she paused and spoke with a tight, closed voice, 'his employers were so pleased with him that they gave him leave of absence and allowed him to work from Venice. And in both cases, he realized he could no longer do his work well enough, and so he resigned from the positions to take care of his parents, and we lived on my salary.'

She looked at them to see that they were following her story. 'He did this because that's what seemed right for him to do, as did I. In the third case, he quit because the son of the owner asked him to do something illegal, and in the last, the company relocated to Shanghai, and he did not accept their offer to go and work there.' She looked back and forth between them. Brunetti met her glance, but Griffoni did not.

'And the Albertini? Who pays for that?' Brunetti asked, playing his last card, but playing it, he knew, badly.

'His aunt,' she answered, this time her contempt palpable. 'So you can put to rest your idea that he was embezzling from his employers, or whatever it is you think him capable of doing.'

She got to her feet and moved towards the door. Brunetti and Griffoni, each avoiding the other's glance, followed her. Professoressa Crosera closed the door after them.

Brunetti explained all of this to Paola after dinner; she listened silently, sipping at the tisane they had decided to have instead of coffee and grappa. She sat on the sofa, her feet side by side on the floor in front of her, cup and saucer on her lap. Brunetti had chosen to sit in the chair opposite her and to drink from a mug.

'You didn't check with his employers first?' she asked.

Refusing to answer, Brunetti shook his head.

After a time, Paola said, 'I'm sorry for Elisa.'

'I wanted to tell you,' Brunetti said. 'She might be ...'

'Yes, she might,' Paola agreed. 'I would.' Then, after a moment, she asked, 'What did you do?'

'When?'

'After she threw you out.'

'I called Signorina Elettra and asked her to check on the dates of death of his parents and then call the places where he was employed at the time to confirm what she said.'

Paola's chin snapped up and she stared at him. 'You did this after not bothering to check it all before?' Paola asked.

'Yes,' Brunetti said.

Paola thought about this for a long time but made no comment. Finally she asked, 'And?'

'She was telling the truth.'

'Elisa usually does,' Paola permitted herself to say. And then, 'Now what?'

'I want to speak to Dottor Donato.'

'What do you want from him?'

'I want to see how he reacts when I tell him Gasparini knew about the coupons.'

'Why tell him you know?'

'Because he'll realize we'd see the connection with the attack on Gasparini.'

'Have you considered that you might be as wrong about Donato as you were about Gasparini?'

'He's given the coupons to a number of people, so we're at least not wrong about that,' he said, hearing how relieved he was to be able to say it.

'That's considered small change in our world, Guido,' she said and waved it away with her hand. 'How much could he manage to make from them in a year?'

'Would it be easier to believe he did it if he'd made more? Would it be worse?'

'No, it wouldn't, Guido, though the law certainly has degrees of culpability.'

'You don't approve?'

'What he's doing is dishonest, tricking these old people into spending a hundred Euros a month on cosmetics,' she said, allowing no compromise. 'Stealing and cheating have become so normal that we're ready to dismiss anything that seems to be a small crime, as if it weren't wrong. Isn't there a law which says that if you're sentenced to three years or less, you don't have to bother to go to prison?'

Brunetti nodded. 'More or less.'

She paused, but when he started to speak, she stopped him by saying, 'Think of the *Antigone* you're reading. Who's right? Antigone? Creon? No one's hurt by what she does, so should she be allowed to break the law? She says she's obeying the law of the gods, doing what humanity knows is right, so can she break the law?'

Brunetti didn't answer. He didn't have an answer, nor did the play. The play asked questions and asked the reader to consider them, answer them if they dared. Paola went on: 'If she insisted on burying two brothers, three, would she be braver or more noble? Or, for Creon, would her crime be two or three times worse?'

Brunetti put his hands up to signify that he didn't know.

'That's why people like novels,' Paola surprised him by saying. 'In most novels, things get *explained* to them by a narrator. They get *told* why people did what they did. We're accustomed to that voice, telling us what to think.'

'You sound as though you don't like it,' Brunetti said.

'I don't. It's too easy. And in the end, it's so unlike life, so fake.'

'Because?'

'Life doesn't have a narrator – it's full of lies and half-truths – so we never know anything for sure, not really. I like that.'

'So fiction really is fiction?' Brunetti asked.

Paola looked across at him, open-mouthed in surprise. Then she put her head back and laughed until the tears came.

28

When he entered the Questura the following morning, the young officer at the door saluted him crisply and said, 'Dottore, Signorina Elettra said she'd like to see you as soon as you came in.'

He thanked her and started up towards Signorina Elettra's office, wondering what fresh information she'd managed to unearth since yesterday afternoon. He had slept badly, asking himself over and over how his suspicion about Gasparini – which he saw now had been based on nothing more than desperation to find a reason he had been attacked – had so easily spiralled out of control. Had Vianello's agreement spurred him on to behave so rashly? He'd read how much more aggressive men became when they were part of a group. Had he and Vianello become a group? Reluctantly, he conceded that their thoughts had formed a gang.

The first thing he noticed was that the sober flowers in Signorina Elettra's office had been replaced by an immense bouquet of bold yellow ones. Zinnias? He never knew. They seemed pleased to be sitting in the light and looked as though they were planning to create some sort of commotion in the room.

Signorina Elettra, he noticed as he approached her desk, gave off the same energy as did the colour of the flowers. Her expression made it clear that trouble was brewing, but trouble for someone else.

'And what have you discovered, Signorina?' The tone in which Brunetti asked the question was as good as a signature on a peace treaty.

'I saw Barbara last night,' she answered.

'I hope she's well,' Brunetti said. He knew Signorina Elettra's sister and liked her.

'Very, thank you,' she answered politely. 'I thought I'd ask her because she's a doctor and might know something.'

'About Dottoressa Ruberti?' Brunetti asked.

'Proust,' Signorina Elettra said and smiled. 'Barbara told me that's her nickname among the other doctors.'

In the face of Brunetti's evident incomprehension, she added, 'Because she writes so much.' When she saw that he still did not understand, Signorina Elettra said, 'So many prescriptions.'

Of course, of course. 'For old people?' he asked.

'So long as they have Parkinson's or Alzheimer's, it seems,' she specified. 'She has a number of other, sometimes younger, patients who are depressed or bipolar. In both cases, she is said to have a predilection for prescribing new medicines and generally avoids the generics.'

'Did your sister tell you this?'

'Of course not,' Signorina Elettra said. 'All she told me was the nickname. I started having a look when I came in this morning.' Her face hardened and she said, 'The health system never stops surprising me with the extent of its inattention: its data bank is protected by a system that is an invitation to steal.'

'"Having a look?"' Brunetti asked, choosing to ignore her indignation.

She gave the side of the keyboard an affectionate pat and said, 'I did the same as I did for Dottor Donato, Commissario. I found her patient list and saw what she's prescribing.' She shook her head in feigned disapproval. 'Much of the medicine is new.'

'"New" as in "expensive?"' Brunetti asked.

'Yes, and in some cases, very.'

'How does she get away with it?' he asked. 'I thought the health service would at least keep an eye on what doctors prescribe.'

'They do,' she answered. 'But her patient list is enormous, more than a thousand, so what she prescribes for other patients probably makes it balance out to some average cost per patient that the calculations of the health service will accept.' Her voice veered towards indignation again. 'They're very careless. It would take no time at all to flag something as conspicuous as what she's doing.'

Before she went on to explain the details of this perfect system to him, Brunetti asked, 'Could you make me charts like the ones you made for the pharmacy?'

'Of course, Dottore,' she answered. 'I've got a program that . . .' she began but, anticipating his lack of interest, let it drop. She reached for a piece of paper and asked, 'What would you like me to list?'

'I'd like one with the people who are taking medicine for psychological problems and one with the people with any form of dementia. Names, addresses, ages, what she's prescribed for them and its cost. In the cases where she's prescribed an expensive new drug, give the cost of the generic or the standard medicine she chose not to prescribe.'

She looked up for long enough to smile. 'Of course, Commissario.' She bent her head to continue writing.

'Could you find out, as well, where the prescriptions were filled?'

She nodded quickly to show the ease of this.

The faintest memory of something he had read in the *Gazzettino* some time – perhaps years – ago flitted through his mind. 'Could you check to see if she's ever written prescriptions for people who were already dead?'

She pulled her hand back so quickly that her pen left a black trail across the sheet of paper. 'What?'

'It happens,' he said calmly. 'At least the *Gazzettino* told me it happens. If people don't die in a hospital, the Ufficio Anagrafe sometimes isn't informed. Or the health service. It can take months, even longer, before they're officially declared dead.'

Signorina Elettra stared off into space, her face rapt in the consideration of possibilities. 'So they go to Limbo and stay there, getting their pensions and having prescriptions written for them?' She shook her head a few times in a gesture that could as easily be admiration as astonishment. 'Very tempting,' she whispered.

'I'm particularly interested in which pharmacy fills their prescriptions,' Brunetti said.

She gave a smile utterly deprived of mirth. 'So am I.' She turned to face her computer, and it was evident that her attention had pulled up stakes and was moving off in the direction he had indicated.

Realizing there was no further need for him to stay, Brunetti went back to his office.

He had bought a copy of that day's *Gazzettino* on the way to the Questura, and he could think of no better way to while away the time waiting for Signorina Elettra to call: he knew she would think of nothing else until she had let herself into the information bank of the health system and helped herself to whatever she pleased. He set the newspaper on his desk and looked at the front page, which held a photo of the mayor, smiling broadly, posed in front of a map of the Canale Vittorio Emanuele, the city's latest attempt to keep the cruise ships coming at whatever cost to the citizens. Brunetti looked upon his works and despaired.

At the bottom right was a small headline about the Carabinieri's dismantling of a drug ring in the city. See page 27. Page 27 told him that the Carabinieri, after a year-long investigation, yesterday had arrested six suspected dealers in an operation called 'Iron Fist'.

The sellers, it was revealed, had worked virtually unobserved near three of the city's schools, even in the face of complaints from nearby residents and the parents of the students in these schools. Finally, however, 'the dealers' time ran out', and an early morning raid by the Carabinieri led to the sequestration of thirteen kilos of hashish, marijuana, and synthetic drugs and pills. All of the men arrested were in the country illegally; all were taken to the Carabinieri station, questioned, and released with an order to leave the country within 48 hours.

Questions of jurisdiction neither concerned nor much interested Brunetti. Nor did he understand why people took drugs; it might be nothing more complex than that they were there for the having. Brunetti was pragmatic enough to approve of anything that interrupted the flow of drugs into young bodies; beyond that, he took the short view. Maybe the pause in supply would help Sandro Gasparini; maybe his father's situation would function as a slap on the back of the head and turn his mind to more serious things. Maybe not.

Brunetti saw that there was a pile of new files in his in-tray but ignored them and returned to the front page of the *Gazzettino*. As usual, he skipped over every article dealing with national politics, sighed at the international news, and ignored sports. That left him precious little, and he was quickly done with it. The options open to him seemed either to hurl himself from the window of his office or accept his responsibilities and read the files.

He slid the newspaper to his left, then turned it over to hide the photo of the mayor and pulled the stack of files towards him. Noon was ringing from the bells of San Giorgio dei Greci when Signorina Elettra appeared at his door and knocked lightly on the jamb. 'May I come in, Commissario?'

Looking up from the file he was reading, Brunetti observed, 'Either I hear your news, Signorina, or I continue to read the discussion of how – in the absence of a city law regarding bicycles – to classify riding a bicycle in the city, whether as a crime or an infraction.'

'I've read those directives carefully, Signore,' she said with every semblance of seriousness. 'I think it's better to consider it an infraction.'

Brunetti closed the file and placed it on top of the others that had already migrated to the left. 'Thank you, Signorina,' he said. 'And what do you bring me?'

'The charts, Signore.'

'Ah, good,' he said. 'Is there anything I should pay special attention to?'

'No, Commissario. I think the numbers make it clear enough what's going on.' That said, she came across and set the papers in front of him then left his office.

Signorina Elettra had commented on how many patients Dottoressa Ruberti had, yet when he looked at the list headed 'Dementia', he was still surprised to see that it consisted of four pages of patient names listed single-spaced, each name followed by the name and price of the medicines Dottoressa Ruberti had prescribed. There followed the name and price of similar, often generic, medicines that were also available. In some cases the difference in price was triple, though it was usually a bit less than double. More than half of the prescriptions had been filled by the Farmacia della Fontana.

In the second chart, Dottoressa Ruberti's patients with 'Diseases of the Psyche' – also running to four pages – the same pattern was repeated, as was the name of the pharmacy. The medicines she prescribed for her patients were always much more expensive than the generic products listed beside them.

The third chart – *I Morti* – introduced a bit of variety. The name of the patient was followed by the date of death registered in the Ufficio Anagrafe and then by dates when each prescription had been filled posthumously. In some cases, there were more than two years between the first date and the last. All but six of these prescriptions were still being filled by the Farmacia della Fontana.

Brunetti found himself thinking of the chicken and the egg. Which would have come first, the suggestion from the doctor that the pharmacist pass on to the health service the cost of the prescription for the more expensive medicine and thus claim the higher refund? Or was it the pharmacist who went in search of accommodating doctors who would write the prescriptions the pharmacist could most profitably process? And which of them would offer, and which of them accept, whatever financial inducement was made?

Brunetti realized he would have to speak to both of them to see what their truths were, but he had better begin with the temptee and not the tempter, if only because this weaker person would be more likely to tell the truth. It seemed to him more likely that the pharmacist would be the tempter.

He turned on his computer and searched for Dottoressa Ruberti's address and office hours. She would be there today, he learned, in Campo Santa Margherita, not far from Signora Gasparini's home, until one-thirty, which meant he could easily make his way there, take a seat in her waiting room, and then allow himself to become the last patient of the morning.

For a moment, he considered asking either Vianello or Griffoni to go with him, but he still felt sufficiently embarrassed about his complete misjudgement of Gasparini that he preferred to go alone.

He got off the Number One at Ca' Rezzonico and walked through Campo San Barnaba, past the fruit vendor's two boats, covered during lunchtime with green tarpaulins, over the bridge and down towards the Campo. It was already after one when he got there; it took him a few minutes to find the address, just next to the estate agent. The sign gave her name and the hours of opening and asked that the patient ring and enter. He did the first, heard the door click open, and did the second.

He climbed to the first floor and saw another sign, with her name and an arrow pointing to the back of the building. At the end of the corridor was a door with her name on a brass plaque. He went in.

Three people sat in the room, two women and a man. Four chairs were empty. Six eyes observed him as he entered and chose the chair farthest from them. Before he sat, he nodded at them and, at their failure to respond, reached forward and took the magazine on the top of the pile on the table.

The women, he had noted, were both very fat, and the man very thin. He had remarked nothing else about them, nor did he glance up to study them. Instead, he read six reasons to become a vegan and waited. A door opened to the left of the three waiting people, and a woman's voice said, 'Signora Tassetto'.

One of the women pushed herself to her feet and, not without difficulty, walked to the door and inside. Brunetti observed the pale-skinned woman standing at the door: she was easily as tall as he was, wore a white lab coat; she turned away to follow the woman before Brunetti had time to study her. Fifteen minutes later, the woman emerged and made for the door, and the doctor called for 'Signor Catucci'. This time, Brunetti noticed that the doctor wore no makeup and had light brown hair pinned back on both sides of her face. His eye caught hers; it was evident that she was surprised by the presence of an unknown man in her waiting room. She followed the patient into her office.

Only five minutes passed before she came to the door again and allowed the man to leave: he walked slowly, as though he had just heard news he didn't like. There was no need to summon the woman, who had got to her feet as the door opened and passed in front of the doctor. Again, her eyes went to Brunetti before she turned away from the room.

It seemed a long time before the woman emerged, although it couldn't have been more than ten minutes. When she had left, the woman in the white coat walked over to Brunetti and asked, 'May I help you, Signore?' Her voice was tentative, as though she were the person seeking help. She was in her forties, he'd guess.

Brunetti stood and set the magazine back on the pile. 'I'd like to talk to you, Dottoressa,' he said.

'And you are?'

'Guido Brunetti,' he said and paused. But then, still penitent over his treatment of Professoressa Crosera, he added, 'I'm a Commissario of Police.

She relaxed but did not smile. 'Ah, yes,' she said, stepping back from him. 'Come into my office. We can talk there.' She started to turn towards the other room but stopped and said, 'I've been expecting you,' then continued towards the door.

Brunetti followed her inside. She closed the door and went to sit behind her desk, moving with an easy grace often seen in tall women.

Her office was vastly different from that of Dottor Stampini at the hospital: neat, orderly, with a comfortable chair for the patient at the end of the doctor's desk and an examining bed, covered with the usual sheet of paper, against the far wall, in which there were two windows with a view to the building on the other side of the *calle*. A glass-fronted cabinet was filled with packages of medicine. Her desk had a computer on the right side; on the surface were two piles of what must be patient files and nothing else.

The usual medical diplomas were interspersed with photos of single flowers enlarged to unrecognizability as anything other than exercises in construction. Brunetti sat in the single chair and looked at Dottoressa Ruberti. Her face was long, as was her body; her thinness made her seem taller. Her glance was level and did not shy away from his, her eyes light brown, the sort of colour that admirers would call 'amber' and detractors 'muddy'.

Brunetti had often felt uncomfortable in social situations with doctors: he wondered if they were always assessing a person's health when they looked them in the eye or took their hand or asked them if they'd like more wine. She, instead, looked at him as though wondering if there were anything she could do to help him.

'You said you'd like to talk to me, Commissario. Could you tell me about what?'

'Tullio Gasparini,' Brunetti said.

'Ah, yes,' she said neutrally. 'Signora Gasparini's nephew.'

'How is it that you know him, Dottoressa? He's not a patient of yours, is he?'

Her glance was suddenly disapproving. 'Commissario Brunetti,' she said with what seemed an exercise of patience, 'may I suggest some courtesies we might observe during this conversation?'

'Of course,' Brunetti said.

She returned his glance without smiling. 'Good.' She nodded a few times, as though finishing a conversation with herself, then said, 'I'll tell you the truth: you don't have to trick me into saying something I should not.' Before he could feign innocence, she went on. 'Is this acceptable to you?'

'Yes,' Brunetti said. 'But all the people I talk to say that they're telling the truth.'

'So do my patients,' she said tiredly. 'That they drink only so much or smoke only so much or never eat more than six grains of rice a day.' She looked at him directly. 'It's one of the reasons why I can't stand dishonesty any more. Do you understand?'

'Yes,' Brunetti answered, then was forced to remark, 'But I'm not sure I should believe you.'

He had hoped to provoke her with the remark, but he failed. 'I don't lie, Commissario, even though I'd like to. It would be so convenient at times.'

'If that's true,' Brunetti said, already following the new rules and telling her what he thought, 'it's very rare.'

Her face softened as she said, 'Unfortunately, Tullio Gasparini is another person who cannot lie or be dishonest. He came to me and told me what he knew and what he was going to do.'

It was too early for Brunetti to ask about that, so he asked, 'How did you know he wasn't lying?'

'Experience. Many people, especially those who are going to die and know it, stop lying or lose the taste for it, or the necessity for it. So, over the years, I've come to recognize the symptoms of truth, as well as of disease.'

'And Signor Gasparini?' he asked.

'Unfortunately, he never learned to recognize other people who are like him, so he refused to believe me when I tried to talk to him.' She rubbed at her right cheek as though it were a habit that helped her think. 'Or perhaps it's because he's worked all his life with numbers and so doesn't know how to read people.'

'What did he tell you, Dottoressa?' Brunetti asked.

'Before answering, Commissario,' she said, 'could I ask you how you found me?'

Brunetti saw no reason to play games with her by saying he'd googled her and found the address. Instead, he said, 'I learned of your connection with Dottor Donato and decided I should talk to you.'

'Connection?' she repeated, face softening at his word. 'What a delicate way you have with language, Commissario.' She smiled for the first time, and he saw that she must once have been lovely before life thinned her down with trouble she'd not had the skill to lie her way out of.

'Could you tell me how it happened that you met him?' Brunetti asked.

'I met him years ago because I'd occasionally go into his pharmacy to speak to him about some of my patients. I wanted to be sure he'd give them a written explanation of when and in what sequence to take their medicines and remind them to consult it every day.'

'Isn't that on the prescription?' Brunetti asked.

Her look was level and cooler than it had been. 'Please, Commissario,' she said. 'If a patient is taking six, or ten, medicines a day, it becomes difficult to remember when to take them. I asked him to write out a schedule for each of them. That's all.'

'Did he agree to do it?'

She thought about how to answer this for some time and finally said, 'I persuaded him. I told him I had many patients who were so old and confused that they needed this help.'

'And he did it?'

'Yes.'

'And your connection?' Brunetti asked, giving no special emphasis to this final word.

'That came some years later.' She paused like a driver at a fork in the road, considering which way to turn.

'You're from Castello, Commissario?' she asked, calling attention to the fact that they had not been speaking in Veneziano. Seeing his surprise, she said, 'Your accent, I mean.'

'I lived there when I was a boy,' he said. 'I don't hear it any more, but I'm sure I'll never lose it.'

'We never do. Not completely.' As if he'd asked for an explanation, she said, 'My father was a voice coach at the Goldoni, so he raised us to listen to people's voices carefully.' Her eyes wandered over to one of the windows, and she remained silent for some time, until she said, 'I never thought about it, but that's probably one of the reasons I know when people tell the truth. It's in their voices, as well.'

Brunetti had known this for most of his professional life but said nothing.

'We were talking about Dottor Donato, Dottoressa,' he reminded her.

'Of course. Excuse me. I suppose I'm delaying things.' She sat up straighter. 'Because you're Venetian, you know how small the city is.'

Brunetti nodded.

'It means that you could easily find out whatever I tell you. Little remains private in a small town.' After a long pause, she continued, 'I was married for some years and am now divorced. I have a son who has severe mental and physical disabilities. I'm a doctor, so I know how seriously he's impaired and the physical path his life will follow, but I also have an idea of what his ... social future will be.'

'I'm sorry to hear about your son, Signora,' Brunetti said.

She smiled again. 'Thank you for that, Commissario.' She studied his face, and then said, 'In this case, my telling you is not an appeal to pity: it's something you have to know.'

Brunetti nodded again.

'My son, Teodoro, is in a private facility, and that's because I'm a doctor and have seen how some of my patients and former patients are kept in public institutions.' Her voice had tightened as she said this. 'I am a family doctor, Commissario. I have more patients than I can take care of while working a normal schedule, so I work even longer hours in order to earn more. But still it is often not enough to pay for Teo's care.' She saw Brunetti begin to speak and held up a hand. 'Before you ask, no, I do not receive anything from my ex-husband. I don't care for myself, but I do care for Teo.

'My husband is also a doctor and is remarried and now working in Dubai. There is a court order against him, claiming half of the cost of Teo's care, but he refuses to pay it. So long as he remains in Dubai, there is no way to make him pay.'

To Brunetti, Dubai was a new element, but the story was certainly a common one.

'As I said, this is a small town, and I suppose my story is common knowledge in the world of medicine. Which includes Dottor Donato.

'Two years ago – when I'd already missed a few payments for Teo's care – he came to me with a proposal, asking me to write prescriptions for my patients for one medicine while he would give them a different one. I refused and asked him to leave. I'm afraid I got up on my high horse and told him I'd vowed to do no harm to my patients, but he insisted that no one would be harmed by what he had in mind.'

Brunetti, from long experience, had observed that most people, when speaking to him and knowing him to be a policeman, displayed their nervousness in many ways: they fidgeted in their chairs, brushed their hair this way and that, touched their faces, folded and unfolded their hands. Dottoressa Ruberti, instead, looked him in the eye and remained motionless.

'What did he propose?' Brunetti asked.

'He told me that, if I'd write prescriptions for the most expensive medicines, he in his turn would select the best of the current generics of that medicine and promised that my patients would get that. Farther, it would be packaged like the more expensive medicine and look exactly like it.'

'How could he do that?' Brunetti asked, although he had a suspicion.

'He refused to tell me in detail. All he said was that he had built up friendships with the salesmen from some of the pharmaceutical companies, and he promised me they would take care of supply.' She let Brunetti think about this for a while and then said, 'When I still refused, he assured me – though in a very oblique way – that the boxes would be from the same company that produced the expensive medicine, and the bar codes would be the real ones.'

Brunetti nodded. The stratagem was not unknown. 'What did he offer you?'

'Thirty per cent of the difference between what he actually paid for the generic and what the health service repaid him for the more expensive medicine. I made it clear that the patient had to receive a medicine identical to the one I prescribed.'

'And the risk?' Brunetti asked.

'None. He would be giving them a medicine that was in the same boxes and had the same effect as the medicine I'd prescribed.'

'And?'

'I asked for a day to think about it and went home and became – though I didn't know him then – a kind of Tullio Gasparini.'

'Meaning?'

'Meaning that I spent the night looking at numbers: what Teo's care would cost in five years, ten years, and how much I'd be making then and whether I could afford it.' She gave him a direct look. 'And the numbers told me that I could not, which meant Teo, sooner or later, would have to be put in a state institution.' She looked at him. She did not ask if he had children. She did not say that, as a mother, she could not … She did not ask him to understand her situation.

'The next day, I stopped in his pharmacy and told him I'd do it, and he gave me a list of medicines he suggested I prescribe for a number of diseases and told me that he would leave it to me how to convince my patients to go to his pharmacy to get their medication.'

'In the far reaches of Canareggio,' Brunetti said.

The look she gave him was steady, followed by a small nod of resignation: so the policeman knew where Dottor Donato's pharmacy was. 'Indeed. In the far reaches of Canareggio.'

'When did the escalation start?' Brunetti asked.

Surprised, she asked, 'Do you know him?'

'I know the type,' Brunetti allowed himself to say.

'Yes. As do we all,' she answered and remained in silent thought until she finally said, 'Some months later, he asked me to write some other, expensive prescriptions and simply give them to him and not to the patient for whom they were written. He'd obviously seen which of my patients were least able to pay attention or remember what was prescribed for them, or perhaps he'd found out which of them lived alone. All I had to do was write prescriptions and he'd process them: they'd pass through the system effortlessly and he'd be paid for medicine he never sold.'

'It would surely be less trouble for your patients,' Brunetti said, thinking of the trip these old people would no longer have to make to Canareggio.

She leaned forward slightly, as if waiting for him to add some ironic coda to what he had said. When he did not, she said, 'And more profit for me.'

Brunetti resisted the urge to comment. He suddenly recalled his classes in logic in *liceo* and his old favourite logical error, the *reductio ad absurdum,* and thought he'd give it a try by making a ridiculous comparison. 'Is this why people wait six months for a hip replacement?'

She looked up, startled and, it seemed, prepared to be angry. But when she saw that his question was deliberately provocative and not serious, she did not answer him, so he asked, 'What if someone found out what you were doing?'

'That was impossible,' she said with every sign of certainty. 'The only people who knew about the prescriptions were Dottor Donato and I.'

'It's very clever,' Brunetti said, as though 'clever' were a dirty word.

'And very common,' she added.

'But Gasparini found out,' Brunetti finally said.

She smiled; it was a small, pathetic thing. 'It had nothing to do with the prescriptions,' she said and instantly amended her remark, as if for the sake of precision, 'at least as far as I was involved.'

Brunetti made a small noise but said nothing.

She braced her hands against the front of her desk to push herself back in her chair. 'It was greed,' she said. 'Donato is a greedy man, and I'd allowed myself to ignore that.'

'The coupons?' Brunetti suggested, if only to give her an idea of what he might know.

'Yes,' she said and shook her head in what appeared to Brunetti to be honest confusion. 'He wanted more. I knew nothing about them and thought he was cheating only the state. But now it turned out that he was also cheating these old people.' It was clear from the way she spoke that she saw a vast difference between the two.

'Cheating them how?' Brunetti asked, not because he didn't know what Donato was doing so much as to see how she'd define 'cheating'.

'He'd make them pay cash if they forgot their prescriptions and give them a coupon equal to the value of the medicine. Eighty Euros, sixty. One hundred and sixty. It didn't matter to him, so long as they gave it to him. Her voice tightened even more, and she said, 'And then he'd give them a coupon, pay the two Euros to process the prescription, and keep the entire sum they'd paid.

'By the time they came back for the money – a day, two, a week, a month – they'd have forgotten what he'd told them, and then he'd explain in his comforting manner that he'd only tried to help them, that he'd made it clear at the time that the coupons couldn't be redeemed for money or used for medicine, but that they had to redeem them for other products.'

She held both hands to the corners of her mouth and pulled the skin tight. 'Oh, he's very clever. He knew they'd never admit not remembering what he claimed he'd told them. To confirm the fact that they'd forgotten was to confirm my diagnosis, and many of my patients can't or won't do that.'

She pulled her hands away, and the lines fell back in place on either side of her mouth. 'To keep them from feeling cheated and perhaps to stop them from talking about it to someone who might understand what he was doing, he invented the ruse of the extra twenty per cent. So instead of thinking they'd been cheated by having to pay eighty Euros or fifty-nine Euros for medicine that should have cost them two Euros, they could feel good about having been given twenty per cent extra in what he must have made sound like a bonus, when it was merely a way to force them to buy products that make him a much higher profit. That is, if they remembered what the coupons were.' He watched her consider whether to add something here, and he went quiet as a stone, waiting.

She looked across at Brunetti, and he saw her eyes grow cold. 'One of my patients told me how generous Dottor Donato always was to her.'

'Is that how you learned about it?'

'No. I knew nothing about it until Gasparini asked me. After his aunt told him about it, he spoke to one of her friends, and she told him the same story.'

'And the dead people?' Brunetti asked, curious as to how Donato would have justified it.

She looked away, then down at her desk to study her hands, which she had folded after she heard the question. 'That was ...' she started and gave a small cough '... his idea. He told me the husband of one of my patients had come in to tell him his wife had died and to ask him to come to the funeral: I saw him there. He waited two days after the funeral before he came and asked me to write some prescriptions for her.'

Her eyes flashed up to his. 'I tried to resist.'

Brunetti did no more than meet her gaze, and she lowered her eyes again.

'He offered me half,' she said, speaking very quickly, as if eager to get this over with. 'So I agreed.'

Brunetti waited for her to explain or offer some excuse about special costs for her son at that time, or some immediate need for the money, but she said no more.

She raised a hand to stop him from speaking, and said, 'There's a bank account in my son's name. All of the money that I've got from Dottor Donato – he always paid me in cash – is in that account, as well as any money I've managed to save since I accepted what Teo's future will be.'

'Is your son legally able to ...?' Brunetti began but failed to find the right words for the question.

'No, he's not. But a friend of mine is the signatory on the account and will see that it's used for Teodoro while it lasts.'

'You're prepared for what will happen?' Brunetti asked.

'Ever since I agreed to write the prescriptions for him, I've been prepared, Commissario. I'll never be able to practise medicine after this.' Her expression grew distant in thought, and she said, 'How strange, that I went ahead with this, when I knew where it might lead.'

Brunetti disagreed: he knew of cases where doctors had performed unnecessary surgery with no damage to their careers. 'But ...' he began, only to have her cut him off.

'It seems strange for me to have to remind you, Commissario, but aren't you forgetting about Signor Gasparini?'

He had not forgotten; he had merely delayed. Following the Ariadne's thread of her involvement in the prescriptions and having been moved to sympathy by the story of her son had not led him away from the straight path that had led him here.

'Would you tell me about that, Dottoressa?'

'There's very little to tell, really. He came to me a few weeks ago, asking if I knew Dottor Donato, his aunt's pharmacist. I said that I did. He asked if many of my patients went to that pharmacy, and I said that it might well be the case because I had great confidence in the professional competence of Dottor Donato, which is certainly true. Then he asked me if I knew about the coupons that Dottor Donato was giving his clients, and I was relieved to be able to say that I had no idea what he was talking about. He thanked me and left, but I knew I'd see him again.'

'Why did you know that, Dottoressa?'

'Because I saw what kind of man he was. And because I know what kind of man Dottor Donato is: he'd manage to turn Gasparini's suspicions towards me.' She paused long enough to draw another breath and added, 'Which is exactly what he did.'

Brunetti thought it best to say nothing.

'He was back a week later. Angry. Donato had told him, it seemed, that I had suggested the idea of the coupons to him. I tried to explain that I had nothing to do with it, but Signor Gasparini didn't want to listen to me. He had been persuaded by Donato that I was the guilty party: divorced woman, living alone, son put in a private institution, instead of a public facility, where most people have to send their children.' She shrugged. 'He'd bought it all: man-to-man talk. When I asked him how I could possibly profit from the coupons, he refused to listen.'

'What happened?'

'He called me one day – I suppose his sense of justice made him do that – and said he was going to go to the police. Once they started investigating the coupons, I'd have no choice but to tell them what else was going on. And that would be the end of my career, wouldn't it?'

When Brunetti remained silent, she demanded, 'Wouldn't it?'

'What did you do?' he asked, rather than answer.

'I forced myself to calm down and asked if I could see him before he went. I said it was only correct to grant me at least that.' She shook her head, as if amazed that she should have sunk to something like that.

'He said he'd meet me near his home late the next evening, after he got home from work. It could not be in a public place because people knew him in the neighbourhood, and it would look strange for him to meet a woman in a bar that late in the evening.' She looked at Brunetti again and opened her eyes wide in disbelief.

'We agreed on the bridge, at quarter to twelve. I was there early. I'd planned to bring him Teo's clinical records, but I decided not to bother because that wouldn't have made any difference to him. I was just another person living off the state system, living well on what I'd stolen, and I had to be punished. I think it was as simple as that to him.'

She looked at Brunetti and, in a normal conversational voice, asked, 'Do you think it's because he worked with numbers all his life?'

'It could be,' Brunetti admitted, then asked, 'What happened?'

Again, she put her face in her hands and wiped away the years, then let them return and looked at him. 'He was right on time, and no one to see us.' Her smile was a grim thing to see. 'I tried to explain that I wasn't involved with the coupons, but he wouldn't listen, didn't even let me talk. He started again about people who had no respect for the state and who spat in the common plate we were all meant to eat from and then stole from it to profit themselves.' Seeing Brunetti's expression, she paused and then said, 'Yes. That's the way he spoke. And then he told me he'd done enough by meeting me, and now he was going home.

'We'd both moved around while we were talking, and I had my back turned to the direction he had to go in and was standing in his way.'

She raised both hands to the level of her shoulders, palms turned forward, like a child in a game told to stand stock still. 'So he would have had to move around me to go down the bridge.' Startled, she looked at her hands and lowered them to her lap. 'And then, as he was trying to get around me, he said something about how shocking it was for me, a doctor, to steal from the weakest and most undefended and then to justify it all with the story of my son, who would be perfectly well off in a public institution.'

Her gaze drifted away, no doubt to the scene that had led to her being there with Brunetti. 'I must have raised a hand to try to stop him; he grabbed it and pushed it away. I braced the other against his chest, and he said I should be ashamed of using my son as an excuse for my greed.'

She was breathing heavily and spoke in a strange, erratic cadence. 'I don't remember what I did. He started to move around me and brushed me aside with his body. I grabbed for him then. Maybe I wanted to push him away or maybe I wanted to hurt him. He moved suddenly, but he was falling, not walking.'

She stopped then and, after allowing herself enough time to grow calmer, looked across at Brunetti. 'In all of this,' she said, 'I did one consciously wicked thing.'

'What is that?'

'I left him there.'

Brunetti could think of nothing to say.

'I'm a doctor, and I left him there.'

'Why?'

'I heard the boat from the station pulling up at San Stae, and then people in the *campo*. I could hear their voices, coming towards me. Us. I knew they'd find him. Or maybe I only hoped they would and decided that was enough. I don't know. I ran away. I turned back towards Rialto and ran to the first turn and then walked back towards San Stae. I went out to the *embarcadero*, and about ten minutes later, I heard an ambulance coming. I waited until it turned in at Ca' Pesaro. When it left, I went home.'

She stopped and looked across at Brunetti, then lowered her eyes.

Brunetti noticed her hands, folded properly, like a schoolgirl's, on the table. They were smooth, and as yet there were no dark spots. He thought of those amber eyes and pale skin. She'd done right to stay out of the sun. Well, she was a doctor, and doctors knew enough now to warn people to avoid the sun if possible. Pity that she had not managed to avoid the other risks life had presented to her. If only Gasparini had been a blackmailer, after all. She could have paid him from her share of the illicit gains made possible by her violation of her oath. And so much pain could have been avoided.

'Do no harm.' Well, to whom had she done harm? The health system was an open fountain from which all could drink to the degree of their thirst. Have your bunion fixed because you need to walk. Have your hip replaced for the same reason. Everyone paid; everyone was helped.

Brunetti pulled himself free from his reverie and looked across at Dottoressa Ruberti. She appeared distracted and inattentive: Brunetti wondered if she, too, was thinking of choices she'd made or not made.

She unfolded her hands and slid them back and off the table. She looked at him. 'Do you know what will happen?'

'I can't tell you, Dottoressa. It will depend on how the judges view what happened and what they believe were the causes of it.'

She tilted her head to the right and looked upwards in an attempt, he thought, to let her eyes focus on something more distant than him or his face. A long time passed, but there was no help he could give her.

Finally she asked, 'What do I do until it all starts?'

'You continue with your life, Dottoressa.'

'What does that mean?' she asked with sudden anger, as if he'd provoked her. 'Don't you want to arrest me?'

'I'd like you to come to the Questura with me and make a statement to a magistrate and sign it. The magistrate will decide whether to let you go home or not.'

'And after that?'

'I don't decide that,' Brunetti said.

She lapsed into silence again and looked out of the window at the opposite wall.

How many questions she had, Brunetti thought; so much uncertainty. How very much like Professoressa Crosera she was, their lives dependent now on what happened to Gasparini, whether he lived or died or what he could remember if he emerged from his coma. What would happen to their children? To their professions? To their lives?

They both seemed, he thought, decent, honest women, but in the case of Dottoressa Ruberti, that was now to be questioned. There was the son, who would have his father's surname. Knowing that, Signorina Elettra could find his medical records. Dottoressa Ruberti was probably ingenuous enough to have opened his bank account at the same bank where she kept her own money, and thus it could be easily found, at least by someone who knew about the existence of the account and knew enough to search for it under the father's name.

It came to him then: if she said nothing about the account while being questioned, it might well be left undiscovered and untouched and could eventually be used for her son's care after whatever money she had was gone. If she spoke of it to the magistrate, what was to stop the judges from eventually declaring that, as the profits from a series of crimes, the money was forfeit to the state? How much care would go into deciding the origin of the money deposited; what rapacious functionary of the state existed who would see a difference between the money she had stolen and the money she had earned? They'd confiscate the lot and have done with it, and tough luck to her son.

If she told the magistrate about it, she'd lose it all.

'Dottoressa,' he began, swept by the temptation to tell her what to do.

She continued to stare out of the farther of the two windows, seeming no longer to be aware of his presence.

'Dottoressa,' he repeated. This time she looked up, perhaps responding to some sudden urgency in his voice.

Brunetti paused, thinking about what he wanted to say, but then thinking of the needle stuck into the back of Signor Gasparini's hand. 'If you're ready, we can go back to the Questura.'

She got to her feet and followed him from her office. Though it took them twenty minutes to walk there, neither spoke until they reached the Questura, when Brunetti left her with the officer at the door, said goodbye, and went up to speak to the magistrate who would question her.

ALSO AVAILABLE IN ARROW

Earthly Remains

Donna Leon

Granted leave from the Questura, Commissario Guido Brunetti decides to finally take a well-earned break and visit Sant'Erasmo, one of the largest islands in the Venetian *laguna*.

The recuperative stay goes according to plan until Davide Casati, the mysterious caretaker of the villa Brunetti has been staying in, goes missing following a sudden storm. Nobody can find him – not his daughter, not his friends, and not the woman he's been secretly visiting . . .

Convinced that this was no accident, Brunetti feels compelled to set aside his holiday and discover what happened to the man who had recently become his friend.

'When she's writing about her beloved Venice, Donna Leon can do no wrong. And *Earthly Remains*, her new mystery featuring Commissario Guido Brunetti, is one of her best . . . once again earning the gratitude of her devoted readers.'
New York Times

'Donna Leon's recreation of Venice and her depiction of the series' core characters . . . is, as always in this long-running series, a triumph.'
Literary Review

ALSO AVAILABLE IN ARROW

The Waters of Eternal Youth

Donna Leon

Fifteen years ago the teenage granddaughter of the grand Contessa Lando-Continui was rescued at the last moment from drowning in the canals. But young Manuela's life was never the same again. Now aged thirty, she lives trapped in an eternal youth.

The Contessa, certain that this was no accident, implores Brunetti to find the culprit she believes ruined Manuela's life.

But once Brunetti starts to investigate, he finds a murky past and a dark story at its heart ...

'There is no one better than Donna Leon at showing the ripple effects of a single traumatic event ... Throughout this astonishingly consistent series Leon has recast the city in her own venerable image: full of surprises and hidden beauty.'
Evening Standard

arrow books

ALSO AVAILABLE IN ARROW

By Its Cover

Donna Leon

When several valuable antiquarian books go missing from a prestigious library in the heart of Venice, Commissario Brunetti is immediately called to the scene.

The staff suspect an American researcher has stolen them, but Brunetti concludes that he cannot have acted alone.

Soon Brunetti is immersed in the dark secrets of the black market of antiquarian books, as he investigates some of the library's mysterious regulars.

And when the case takes a more gruesome turn, Brunetti must delve into the pages of the past to uncover a terrible truth.

'A great mystery.'
Scotland on Sunday

'With the subtlety and elegance of her prose, and the sweet and savoury pleasures she evokes, Leon's books are an antidote to the dark, unsettling landscape of so much contemporary crime fiction.'
The Times